Angel's Sin

Vincent P. Sanchez

Outskirts Press, Inc.
Denver, Colorado

This is a work of fiction. The events and characters described herein are imaginary and are not intended to refer to specific places or living persons. The opinions expressed in this manuscript are solely the opinions of the author and do not represent the opinions or thoughts of the publisher. The author has represented and warranted full ownership and/or legal right to publish all the materials in this book.

Angel's Sin
All Rights Reserved.
Copyright © 2011 Vincent P. Sanchez
v2.0

Cover Photo © 2011 iStockphoto LP. All rights reserved - used with permission.
Cover Design by: Greg "ITIS" Davidson for DZYNiD Inc.

This book may not be reproduced, transmitted, or stored in whole or in part by any means, including graphic, electronic, or mechanical without the express written consent of the publisher except in the case of brief quotations embodied in critical articles and reviews.

Outskirts Press, Inc.
http://www.outskirtspress.com

ISBN: 978-1-4327-5774-8

Outskirts Press and the "OP" logo are trademarks belonging to Outskirts Press, Inc.

PRINTED IN THE UNITED STATES OF AMERICA

Scene One

We got lucky; the rain had stopped by the afternoon, and by nightfall the streets were dry enough to go riding. It was the last weekend of summer before school started, and I wasn't tryin' to let it go by without hitting the dirt hills. Mama don't go to sleep till after the honeymooners go off, but fate was working with us tonight 'cause it was only ten o'clock and me and Sin could already hear her snoring from her room down the hallway. The hard part wouldn't be climbing out the window and scaling down the side of the house into the backyard; we'd done that thousands of times. The hard part was tryin' to creep by Mama's room without waking her up. The hallway floors are made of wood panels and so old that every step would make a loud creaking sound; and for someone who snores so goddamn loud, Mama sure was a light sleeper. I can still hear her yelling now, "Sincere… and…and…Angel, don't make me go get the switch!!"

Sin went first since he knew the spots on the floor that made the least noise. I liked it that way anyway because if we got busted I could get back in the bed in time enough to front like I was still sleeping. Whoever went first had no chance, but Sin seemed to get off on taking the risk. Even though it was dark as hell we made it through the hallway, out the window, and into the backyard. After all, we'd been livin' there since Jesus walked on water.

It had been a week since we stole them bikes from Flushing Meadow Park so the heat was off of us; nobody ain't gonna be looking for these bikes now. The white boys we stole them from wouldn't dare come to South Jamaica looking for their bikes even though they knew that's where they were. Their pops probably bought them another one by now anyway so fuck 'em.

We usually didn't wait a week to take the bikes out because we always spray painted them once we got back to the garage. We'd always strip the pads off. White boys always had pads on their bikes...pads are for pussies. These bikes were too hot to spray paint. I had a chrome BMX with power handlebars, bent seat pole, and dirt wheels. Sin had a blue steel Piranha with hand brakes and front and back chrome pegs. I couldn't wait to test this baby out on the dirt hills. Sin told me his boy told him about this new dirt road in back of Rockaway Blvd. by Kennedy Airport, said ain't nobody even rode on it yet. We didn't usually ride over by the boulevard 'cause them want-to-be fat cat niggas always be fucking with us little dudes. They ain't got shit else to do but stand on the corner and fuck with us every chance they get. It's like the freakin' highlight of their day. It's mostly Shakim, Black, and Boogie that be always tryin' ta start some shit. Breeze be on the block hustlin' too but he's cool; he stay lookin' out for us young dudes. I guess that's why they call him "Breeze"; 'cause he's a cool ass individual. He's the only cat that keeps Shakim and them from beaten us down every time we come through the block. Last summer my boy Jeff from up the block broke rule number one and tried to ride his bike across the boulevard by himself (it was common knowledge amongst us young dudes that you never cross the spot by yourself). I guess he felt 'cause he was on a bike he'd be all right, no way Sha' and them can catch him on his ten-speed that was damn near bigger than him. That's because the ten-speed was his uncle's. Jeff didn't have the heart to vic a dirt bike from one of them white boys so he had to settle for his uncle's ten-speed even though only the last two high gears worked. It was hard as hell to get the bike movin', but once he did Jeff was floatin'. I swear to God he be hittin' like 50 mph. I guess that's why he thought he'd be all right...he was wrong....

    I never did find out where Jeff was heading, maybe because after the "violation" the question "why" outweighed the question "where." So here goes Jeff flying down 148th Street coming from Foch Blvd. heading toward Rockaway Blvd. The forces were already against him because he flew right through the red light and damn near got hit by a Hostess Cake truck. The truck screeching to a halt is what actually caught Boogie's attention. Maybe if the light had been green things would have turned out different for Jeff, but it wasn't and all it took was Boogie to see Jeff flying through the light to stir up Boogie's appetite for torture.

    First Boogie tried to call Jeff over in a cool manner, but Jeff had been their victim enough times to know not to stop. After nearly getting hit and realizing he had now become prey he developed tunnel vision, and he wouldn't allow himself to see anything else but the end of the block. Boogie saw that Jeff wasn't slowing down, so he stood in his path in the middle of the street. Knowing Jeff wouldn't have the heart to mow him down. By the time Boogie got in his way it was too late; Jeff couldn't slow down, let alone stop. The bike collided into Boogie and lifted him off his feet and onto the street. Somehow Jeff managed to stay on the ten-speed but was knocked toward the sidewalk. He crashed into the curb so hard his chain came off the crank. There was no time to try to fix it 'cause Boogie was picking himself off the pavement with the look of murder in his eyes. So Jeff hit the ground runnin' and the chase was on.

Boogie didn't earn his name from dancing. At sixteen years old Boogie was six feet, slim, and ran like a mongoose. By this time Shakim and Black were in full stride after Jeff. Jeff had no chance. He didn't make it to the end of the block before Boogie was close enough to grab the collar of Jeff's Le Tigre shirt. Shakim was right behind Boogie, and Black didn't make it the first ten yards of the chase before he got winded. At 5'7" and 200 pounds, Black wasn't built for running. Boogie grabbed little Jeff in a sleeper hold and dragged him into a vacant lot in back of the store. Shakim said in a sarcastic tone, "If you be quiet you might make it out of this alive." Jeff was well aware of their reputation and what they were capable of so he took heed to Sha's advice. By this time Black caught up and was instigating the "violation." "Give 'em the pole, Sha', give 'em the pole!" Black insisted. Shakim cracked a devilish smirk at Boogie, and Boogie returned the same grin. All the while Jeff was choking and gagging from being yoked out by Boogie's long, skinny arms.

Shakim and Black grabbed Jeff, and at the same time Black grabbed a fistful of Jeff's Fruit of the Loom's. They both hoisted Jeff up on the lower peg of the telephone pole and hung him by the back of his drawers. In South Side Queens we call this the "wedgie of death," and until that point no one was hung for longer than sixty seconds. To be hung longer than that can cause serious anal damage, which may not be reversible.

So here was Jeff hanging ten feet off the ground and screaming so loud that you could've heard him in Brooklyn. Black and Boogie were literally on the ground laughing so hard that tears were streaming down their faces. Shakim standing there staring at Jeff emotionless, feeding off Jeff's pain, his fear, his suffering. Then out of nowhere Shakim pulled out a black .38 revolver and aimed directly at Jeff's suspended body. Then everything stopped. The laughter, the screaming, the crying; all stopped. Black and Boogie both looked at Sha' with amazed expressions. Jeff's expression was one of confusion; he couldn't understand how getting caught riding through a block could become a death sentence. Jeff's chin dropped to his chest and his body went limp from exhaustion. By now the blood had begun to flow from under Jeff's "nut hugger" shorts. His Fruit of the Loom's had cut into his ass from the weight of his body. Black's expression went from amazement to excitement, and a smile that was wide enough to display all twenty-seven of his teeth had spread across his face. Boogie looked uncertain but game and Sha' was ready. He readjusted his aim, tightened his grip, then squeezed off a round. He connected dead square to Jeff's chest with a pellet from the CO_2 (compressed air)-powered BB gun. The blow made Jeff cry out like a wounded animal. Boogie had a look of relief that he tried to shadow from Black. Black had a look of disappointment with a hint of anger.

They all took turns at the human target displayed on the telephone pole. Jeff absorbed shots to the body, the head, his nuts and ass. By the time Sha' and his boys were finished with Jeff, he was bruised to the bone throughout his body and had to receive twenty stitches to reseal his asshole. Sha' and his boys probably would have done a lot worse if it wasn't for Breeze.

Breeze was like the lieutenant on the block. He's King's right-hand man. (I'll tell you about King a little later.) When Breeze hit the block, the first thing he noticed was that Sha' and his boys weren't on their posts and they were missing out on customers. He knew the only other place they could be was in the back lot, probably smokin' a blunt. When Breeze got around to the lot, he saw Black squeezing off shots from the BB gun at a limp body on the telephone pole. Shakim and Boogie were a few feet away sitting on a trash bin passing a blunt. When Breeze realized what was going on, he sprinted towards Black and tackled him to the ground. Even though Black is pretty husky, Breeze lifted him off his feet. Breeze is a couple of years older than the rest of them, 5'11", big-boned and muscular for his age. The gun flew out of Black's hand from the blow. Breeze collected the gun and stepped toward Sha' and Boogie. "What the hell are you assholes doing?" Breeze said heatedly.

"Calm down man, we just teaching this little mutha fucker a lesson," Shakim said as he took another pull on the blunt and passed it to Boogie.

"Yeah, Breeze, this little nigga ran me over with his bike. He had to pay," Boogie added as he coughed from the weed smoke in his lungs.

"Man, if ya'll bitches don't get back on that block and finish sellin' them cracks I'm gonna bust a cap in all ya'll asses and it ain't gonna be from no fuckin' BB gun," Breeze barked in frustration.

Black picked himself off the ground and dusted his jeans off. Shakim and Boogie both hopped off the trash bin at the same time and started walking out the lot.

"Where ya'll assholes going?" Breeze yelled.

"You just said go back on the block," Black replied.

"First, bring Shorty down off the pole, then ya'll three stooges mutha fuckers get back to work!"

Breeze ended up taking Jeff to the hospital, where he was admitted for the next week. Since Breeze was eighteen, he told the receptionist that he was Jeff's older brother and guardian. When the receptionist asked about medical coverage, he told her he'd be paying in cash—and he did.

After they admitted Jeff, Breeze went to speak to Jeff's uncle, who was his true legal guardian. Jeff never knew his father, and his mother was strung out on drugs somewhere in Brooklyn. The state had awarded his grandmother custody. She died two years later, and on her deathbed she made his uncle promise to take care of Jeff as a condition before signing over the deed to the house to him. Jeff's uncle Bam (short for Bamboo) was an unwilling participant. When Breeze finished telling Bamboo what had happened, he seemed more interested in where his ten-speed bike was than in Jeff's condition.

Scene Two

I'm glad I didn't wear my new shell-top Adidas 'cause I landed right in a patch of mud when I hopped over the backyard fence. I had my old city wings on so I didn't care. We kept the bikes stashed down the block in this tore-down garage. We kept them under an old car cover so the rain wouldn't rust the crank and chain. We also put them under there so other niggas don't be tryin' to swipe 'em from us.

So here's me and Sin riding down the back streets of South Jamaica. The longer we riding, the hyper I'm getting. In those days it seemed like the farther away you were from your block, the more exciting things were. The rain had passed, the sky cleared, and the stars began to illuminate the streets. Looking into the sky, all I could think about was how small I felt in comparison to the rest of the world. The way I felt, I could have rode all night.

"Yo, Angel, I've been working on this new move. It's so fresh man! I'll show you when we get to the dirt hills," Sincere said.

"Where the hell are these hills anyway? By the time I get there I'm gonna be too tired to make any jumps," I said in excitement.

Dirt hills are what kids in Queens called construction sites. Back in the early eighties, there was a lot of real estate construction going on in the southern part of Queens. The workers would break the ground up and lay new dirt over the foundation. It took a couple of weeks for them to lay it flat, so they would leave the mounds of dirt hills lying around. It was perfect for dirt bike riding.

When we got there we noticed someone had already cut open a hole in the gate, which pissed me off because I thought for sure me and Sin would be the first to make tracks in these hills. It didn't matter though—I was on my new BMX and ain't nobody can tell me shit! The ride over here gave me a feel for the bike, and I already felt connected with it. Like my body and the bike were one. As soon as I got through the gate, I headed straight for the highest dirt hill. Sin went through the fence first so he was ahead of me, but we were both in full sprint. When we got to the hill we had to walk our bikes up. The incline was steep and the dirt was still muddy from this afternoon's rain. Before we got to the top of the hill we heard something. It sounded like crying but not quite. More like screaming and pleading. We both stopped midway up, bikes still in tow, and looked at each other with the same look.

"What the hell is that?!" I asked.

Sin shrugged. He didn't have the answer to my question; if he did, I would have never gone over that hill and maybe my life would've turned out different. The answer to my question was over that hill, and what I didn't know then is that what we would witness on the other side of the hill would forever change our lives.

Scene Three

The cries were high-pitched and penetrated my body to the bone. There was a pounding or thumping sound that echoed through the night air, and the combination of the two gave me goose bumps. I had a notion to turn around and get the hell out of there. Whatever…or whoever it was…was in a world of hurt, and I was too young to help it and didn't want no taste of what it was feeling. But my adolescent curiosity outweighed my common sense. I glanced over to Sin, and I could see he was just as indecisive as I was, but both of us had too much pride to say so, so we kept pushing up the hill. As we got closer to the top I could hear voices; they were muffled but threatening. I could now tell that the cries were human; it was a guy's voice, but it was hard to tell through his weeping.

The dirt was still moist and our sneakers began to sink into the hillside. Our bike wheels made tire tracks parallel to our footprints. The plateau was a few feet away, and the voices were more pronounced.

"You think you can steal from me and just walk away, you think I didn't know you were skimming off the top," the voice hollered. "See that's what happens when you let niggas get too familiar, they think they know you, they think they can get over on ya!" the voiced continued.

I reached the top of the hill first, and I had to crunch down so that them dudes at the bottom of the hill wouldn't see me. As Sin reached the top, I motioned for him to get down. Though the construction site was fenced off and lined with blue tarp, the area was illuminated by the streetlight. It was enough lighting to make out the figures at the bottom of the hill, and unfortunately it would be enough to identify us if we weren't careful. The opposite side of the hill was dangerously steep, and we couldn't get too close to the edge 'cause one wrong step and you'd be going down, and there would be no turning back. As my eyes adjusted to the light, I could see that there were three dudes down there. Two were standing and the third was on his knees. I recognized the first guy off top. It was Breeze, and he was standing a few feet away from the other two. The second guy was King; he controlled all the drug spots in South Side. He was the most feared drug kingpin in Queens. His reputation was notorious. His workers had a tendency of coming up missing if they fucked up on money or drugs. I'd see him come through the block pulling up in his GMC Blazer on the regular. I knew of him and he knew of me and my crew from seeing us jet through the block with our bikes. He would always say to us, "When ya'll lil' niggas wanna make some money let me know, but until then stay the fuck off my block."

The third dude I couldn't make out right away; he was on his knees and his head was dropped to his chest. He was covered in blood and wheezing. I recognized him by his rope chain and Mercedes medallion; it was Boogie and he looked half-dead. His shirt was ripped up and barely hanging onto his body. The lower part of his jeans was soiled in damp dirt, and his face was concealed with thick, dark red blood tainted with mud.

I couldn't believe what I was seeing. Boogie was one of King's workers; why would he beat him down like this? I whispered to Sincere, "Oh shit, Sin, you know who that is?" I knew he knew who we were looking at, and he also knew exactly what we were looking at. I also knew but I was too scared to say it. Sin didn't respond to my question; I doubt if he even heard it. His attention was frozen on the scene at the bottom of the hill. His face was full of amazement, eyes wide as flashlights and mouth cocked half open. I tried to slow down my breathing. My heart felt like African drums pounding inside of my chest.

"So you wanna test King...you wanna try to make King look like a chump!" King hollered, speaking in the third person. Boogie cried out some unrecognizable words, and before he was able to finish, King kicked him in the face and Boogie slumped to the ground.

King pulled out a nickel-plated .45 caliber from a holster inside of his jacket, shoved the barrel into Boogie's mouth, breaking his front teeth. Horror flooded Boogie's face. With a smirk King said, "See ya when I get there…"

King pulled the trigger and Boogie's head exploded like a watermelon. The sudden blast jolted both me and Sin. My heart was racing a mile a minute. The scene was unreal; instantly there was a puddle of blood. Oh my God, so much blood, and pieces of his brain were scattered yards from his body. I felt myself about to cough up Mama's dinner. I had to get out of there.

"Come on Sin, let's get the fuck out of here!" Sin didn't move his eyes, still focused on the bloody scene. His face was full of amazement. The drama seemed to excite him. "Sin, come-the-fuck-on! What are you doing?" I said frantically. Sin finally snapped into reality. When he went to pick up his bike, the dirt shifted and caved in from under his feet. "Angel," Sin yelled, reaching out for me with the last ounce of balance he had. The dirt quickly rushed down the hill toward King and Breeze. It was only a matter of seconds before they would spot us.

I caught Sin's right wrist and grasped it. Only his torso was grounded—the rest of his body dangled off the hill. "Sin, give me your other hand and pull yourself up." I strained. "I can't, if I give you my other hand I'll drop the bike," he yelled. I couldn't see from my angle, but Sincere caught the bike by the handlebars with his free hand, and it was also dangling along with the rest of his body.

"What...nigga, let the bike go!" I barked.

Sin hoisted the bike onto the hill, causing an avalanche of dirt down the hill, catching King's attention as he began to walk away.

"What the hell... Who the fuck!" King yelled. He looked up at the top of the hill the instant I pulled Sin to firm ground. We both looked down as he looked up and met each other's eyes.

"What the hell...ya'll lil' mutha fuckers," King said in shock. "Breeze, get those little niggas!" he ordered.

Scene Four

In one motion Sin jumped on his bike and began pedaling down the hill. I was right behind him, riding in the tracks his bike laid. My heart was racing a million miles per minute, and we must've been doing like eighty miles per hour down that hill—or so it felt like. I glanced over to Sin, and his face was full of excitement. I couldn't understand how we could be facing certain death and he was enjoying himself. I have to admit: to see Sin so excited calmed me down, and for a second I began to get a feel for the dirt hills. But like I said, it was for a second. I was blinded for an instant from the headlights reflecting off the metal construction sign on the fence. I glanced down on the road below and saw King's Blazer coming up on us. Every time the engine accelerated fear shot through my body.

Breeze must have been driving because I could see King hanging out of the passenger window. The dirt hill began to descend, and I could see ahead where the bottom of the hill connected with the road below—the same road that the Blazer was on, the same road we had to pass to get to the opening in the gate. By this time Sin and I were shoulder to shoulder, on the road about fifty yards from the cut-out opening in the gate. The problem was that the opening was a crawl space and only allowed one person to squeeze through at a time. It wasn't even big enough to ride the bikes through; we would have to come to a stop and get off. All I could hear was the Jeep's engine accelerating and getting closer. "We're not gonna make it," I yelled. "Just keep riding!" Sin barked. My legs were burning and I felt like I was gonna pass out. That was until I heard the gunshots coming from the Blazer, which was about twenty yards behind us. I could see the opening in the gate, but it wouldn't be enough time for both of us to get through with our bikes. We both skidded to a stop inches from the gate. Sin hopped off, slid through the hole, and pulled his bike through, seemingly in one motion. When I turned around, the truck was on us. The lights were so bright it blinded me. In a panic I hopped off my wheels and tried to slide through the hole with the bike, but like I said the hole wasn't large enough, and my pedal got caught in part of the fence that was cut. By this time Breeze and King arrived at the fence and were rushing out of the truck. I struggled to try to get the bike loose from the fence. My body was clear on the other side, but I had to get the bike. Sin was grabbing at me, screaming for me to let the bike go. I know it sounds crazy but I loved this bike, and although it was only my first time riding it, I felt a kinship toward it. Plus it was the end of the summer and if I lost this bike, it would be some time before I could steal another one. I quickly snapped back into reality when through the headlights I saw King and Breeze's silhouette with guns in tow. Just as I let go of the bike I heard a bullet ricochet off the concrete inches from my leg. The bullet kicked up gravel, stinging my leg and arm. As I rose off the ground, Sin was already mounted on his bike preparing to pedal like there was no tomorrow. "Hop on the pegs!" he motioned. Sin quickly sped off out from a clear path of our chasers. There were a few more gunshots fired and I could hear King screaming, "I know who you lil' mutha fuckers are and I know where to find you... THIS IS NOT OVER!"

The next couple of days were torture. Despite it being a beautiful weekend, Sin and I confined ourselves to the house. We watched old Clint Eastwood movies and Kung Fu flicks. I couldn't stop thinking that once I walked out the door, King would be waiting, gun cocked at the ready. The reality was that our time in hiding was running short. The first day of school is tomorrow, and Mama didn't care if the Grim Reaper himself was waiting outside; we were going to school. Tomorrow would be the first day of my senior year in junior high school and Sin, who is a year older than me, would be starting high school. This in itself was going to be bugged out because we'd never attended different schools. Together we terrorized grade school and took over junior high. For every fight, every bum rush, and every extortion deal, we did it together. His beef was mine and vice versa...'til the sun burns out! Our loyalty for each other ran deep even though we bumped heads on occasion. We both had strong personalities. Growing up in a foster home will do that to a kid. With nine other kids in the house, some who stayed and others that were here just until the agency found them permanent placement, made for a domestic war zone. Every one of these kids had their own physical, mental, and emotional scars from their prior lives. A badge of abandonment branded in their psyche from their families. If you were here, you knew no one else wanted you.

I didn't always live at Mama's house. My moms, she wanted

better for me and my sisters. So when my pops returned from the service, she took a shot at a normal family life and moved in with him. It was like jumping out of the frying pan and into the fire. He was stationed in Germany for most of his tour at an outpost outside of the city. The days were long and his nights were filled with binge drinking. I don't know when it happened, but sometime during my pops' call of duty he got himself hooked on heroin. When he got back he was a different person; nothing like my moms remembered him to be. She would later say he'd turned into a monster when he was chasing that high, but in reality he was running from a low.

I remember watching a movie about the life of Bruce Lee. And the narrator spoke about how Bruce Lee believed that he was being taunted by demons, which manifested in giant Asian warriors. For years Lee was perplexed about how to escape the torment of these demons. Ultimately when he sought counsel, a wise man told him that the warriors that haunted him were demons passed down from his late father, which in turn he inherited from his father. The wise man advised Lee that if he didn't confront these demons and break the cycle, not only would it result in his demise, but he would also pass these demons down to his young son Brandon.

Bruce Lee suffered an untimely death that many attributed to his unsettled demons, which raised much speculation after his son Brandon also met his demise under questionable circumstances. The point is that Bruce Lee's story got me to thinking about my situation. My father never knew his biological parents; they abandoned him at the hospital when he was born and he was placed in a foster home. I can imagine the self-loathing he experienced growing up, struggling with the deepest denial and rejection. His demons conquered him and he found solace in a needle that rushed heat through his veins and evil through his heart.

At first, I'm sure life was pretty normal, although to be honest I have no recollection of normal family events. No memories of eating at the dinner table or playing family games; no Cosby Show moments. I think we may have had a dog or wait, maybe not; it's hard to say. My memories of those years are so jumbled up in my mind. All I do know for sure is the day it all turned for the worst.

It was the day after Christmas and I had gotten what every seven-year-old boy wanted: a match box racetrack. It took me all night to set it up, so when I got up the next day it was the first thing I thought of. By the time I got myself together and made my way to the living room, which doubled as my parents' bedroom, I heard the high-pitched cries of my mother. It was the familiar screams that pierced my soul and shook me to the core. I stepped into the living room at the same moment my pops threw my moms across the room. She was pleading about not having any money or something. I later found out that she would hide the rent and grocery money from my pops so that he wouldn't use it for drugs. She sacrificed herself to assure we had food and shelter. But that day he wasn't taking no for an answer. I doubt either of them noticed me standing in the doorway hoping that they wouldn't go near my newly set-up racetrack. She struggled to pull herself up from behind the white-branched Christmas tree that sat atop the end table; we never had the money to get a real tree, so we stacked the gifts under this three-foot, sparsely decorated bush.

"I'm telling you the truth, Victor, there's no more money. Please, the kids are in the house!" my moms pleaded while scrambling to the other side of the room. "I know you got the fuckin money, woman. Don't fuck with me, get it now!" My father grabbed my moms by her small frame and pulled her close to him. "Don't make me have to kill you, bitch!" Through her cries, she tried to reason with Victor Sr. "The rent, Victor, what about the rent and the kids...the kids need food..." The fact that she threw the kids in his face pissed him off even more. He slapped her across the room and stormed out. He was so enraged that he didn't realize that he'd bumped me to the floor on his way out. From my bumped position, I saw my moms sprawled on the floor crying in a fetal position. My pops had smacked her into my no longer new racetrack, and they both lay in pieces.

Sleepless nights haunted me as I wrestled with nightmares of my heroin-addicted father storming the house on a rampage. His addiction fueled his violence, which my mother protected us from, but not without absorbing his wrath. I would lie in the bed as a child and try to drown out the sounds of my mother's cries, her screams and pleas.

When the money ran out, the beatings got worse. I would walk my little sister home from school and silently pray that we wouldn't walk into a war zone. And on the days that there was peace, we were assured that something would be missing from the apartment. First it was the television, then the stereo. I think it was when my father sold our Atari game system that my moms finally decided she had had enough. One would think the beatings would have sent her running, but it's something about seeing the look in your child's eye when you run out of excuses for why their toys are missing.

We moved back into Mama's house a few days later, and my

moms never looked back. My pops continued to spiral downhill, and his addiction got him into a deal he couldn't break. HIV was a relatively new disease at the time, which not many people knew much about, especially in my hood. So when my moms told us that my pops contracted the disease, I really didn't know what to make of it. I damn sure didn't know it was a death sentence. He eventually sobered up and became a devout Christian, I guess in a last attempt to save his soul. If God did forgive him, forgiveness wouldn't come as easy with us. The pain and images were too recent in our minds, so when he did come around for atonement he was met with cold hugs and disrespect.

He never did get to make amends with us, and I'm sure he didn't conquer his demons. No, those sins were passed down to me to bear. A short time thereafter, on a hot Fourth of July day, my pops died and I moved on to the next chapter of my life.

I remember there was one girl that was placed at Mama's house for temporary stay. Must'a been sixteen or seventeen and spoke little English. Her name was Sanku. She was half-black, half-Vietnamese, and the word was she was a product of a U.S. troop laid over from the war. Her mother was a prostitute and started selling little Sanku's pussy by the time she was eight. During a raid on the brothel, it was discovered that Sanku was half-American, so she was shipped to the States and taken in by social services. She'd already been placed in a few different homes by the time she got to Mama's house. But she was pulled out of those homes after a short time due to obscene circumstances. Sanku was a broken child, and her only form of communication was through sexual intimacy. Not that it was intentional. It was just the only way she knew. When she was twelve back at the brothel, she was gang-raped and forced to have sex with another woman in order to stimulate some of the men that were impotent. She was pulled from one foster home after a social worker walked into the home through a back door and found Sanku in the den sucking her foster father's dick. She would later say that she was sucking him off because he and his wife were giving her a place to stay. In her mind, this was a rational way to compensate for their hospitality. For a teenager, Sanku looked very mature for her age. Her body was very developed, she wore bright makeup that didn't agree with her complexion, and her clothes were worn and appeared to be hand-me-downs from an older woman. Despite her appearance, she was a very scared girl. She wore her hair over her face and rarely made eye contact. The reason I knew so much about Sanku and her background is because I learned very early to ease drop under the staircase when Mama was meeting with the social worker. The social worker indicated that the agency wanted to place Sanku in a safe environment until permanent placement could be found. She had no idea she was feeding the lamb to the wolves.

I learned how to take different routes home so I won't bump into King or any of his crew. This wasn't an easy task 'cause there were only so many ways you could go to reach one location. I would get off the bus two stops ahead of my stop and sometimes get off a couple of blocks past my street. Whatever way I took, I was sure not to cut through the Projects 'cause that would've been my ass. Aside from King's crew, there was a whole other breed of goons that wanted blood from me 'cause of shit I did in the past. With all this heat on me, I started to carry a shank on me daily. I stole a "Rambo knife" from my uncle Ray, who was briefly in the army. He was dishonorably discharged due to mental defects. Now he just sits on a milk crate in the kitchen watching WWF wrestling. He would have you believe he was a lifelong member of the service with his deranged stories and his army fatigue jacket that he's been wearing since he came back. And he wore this fuckin' jacket every goddamn day—winter, spring, summer, and fall. Lucky for me he wasn't playing with a full deck 'cause he never noticed that I swiped his knife. Even though I was holdin', I played this cat-and-mouse game and made Sin promise to do the same. I told him we couldn't take a chance of getting caught by King and his crew. My plan was to try to lay low and hope the beef would blow over. This went on for a few weeks before word got back to me that Breeze wanted to meet with me and Sin. The message was delivered by the neighborhood loudmouth, Chase, a.k.a. Fat Ass, or at least that's what I called him. Chase had a unique way of getting on people's nerves. Like for instance, every time you'd see this fat fuck he would be eating a bag of *hot* barbecue potato chips. He would chew the chips with his mouth wide open while he was talking to you, then suck the potato chip crumbs off his fingers. This wouldn't be so bad, but he was the type that always had to touch you when he was talking; pissed me off to no end. Despite Chase's disturbing idiosyncrasies, he was useful in the hood. Somehow he found a niche between the various gangs in the hood and often served as a messenger. So when I saw Chase through my kitchen window walking toward my side door, I knew the news couldn't be good. I met him at the door before he could knock so he wouldn't have to touch my door with his nasty potato-chip fingers.

"Oh, Angel, what's up, I was just looking for you," Chase said as he held his hand up to slap me five.

"Yeah, whatever, man, how can I help you?" I said, waving his handshake off (it was common knowledge in the hood that no one gave Chase pounds 'cause his hands were always nasty, and Chase knew it too).

"Oh, you just gonna leave me hangin…aiight whatever. Listen, I have a message for you and Sin…is he around?" As he crunched on his *hot* barbecue potato chips.

"Well, what's the message?!" I barked in frustration.

"Where's Sin?"

"He ain't here, nigga, what's the message?"

"Well, I just got back from King's store and I was talking with Breeze. Breeze sent me over here to tell ya'll niggas that he wants to meet tomorrow at King's store. He also said that he know where ya'll niggas live so if he wanted to hurt ya'll he would've did it a long time ago. I don't know what ya'll mutha fuckers did to piss him off, but you need to go handle that." Chase grinned.

I just stood there trying not to look scared out of my mind. I didn't even respond to Chase. I just let the storm door slam in his face and walked back in the house. By the time Sin got back home, I ran through the scenario in my mind a hundred times. I sat Sin down and told him Chase's message.

"Look, I've been thinking about this all day. We'll go over to King's store right after school so we know it'll be crowded with kids. I doubt they'll try anything in the middle of the day with all those people around. Plus, this message came from Breeze so hopefully King won't be there. If we have a shot of getting out of this with our heads still attached, it'll be with Breeze," I explained in a whisper.

"Angel, I'm tired of running and hiding and feeling like

somebody's pussy. We been doin' this shit fa weeks," he replied in frustration.

"So what do ya wanna do?" I asked sarcastically.

"Let's run up in there and shoot the shit up!"

"Shoot it up…shoot it up with what, we don't have no freakin' guns!"

Sin's eyes fell low as he reached into his jean pocket and slowly pulled out a nickel-plated .25-caliber pistol. I immediately recognized the gun. It was Uncle Ray's. When we were younger, we used to sneak down to the basement where my uncle stayed; we'd flip on the mattress and have karate fights when he wasn't there. One day while I was doing a Bruce Lee vs. Chuck Norris on Sin, I kicked him into Uncle Ray's sneaker boxes that were stacked along the wall. As the boxes tumbled, a shiny gun dropped out of one of the boxes—the same shiny gun that Sincere was fittin' to run up in King's spot with.

"The fuck you doin' with Uncle Ray's gun?!" I barked.

"With all these mutha fuckers after us, I ain't had no choice. Plus don't act like you a fuckin angel…Angel! I know you swiped Uncle Ray's Rambo knife."

"Yeah, his knife, not his freakin gun."

"Look, we gonna sit here like a bunch of bitches and argue, or are we gonna shoot dem niggas before they shoot us?"

I exhaled and looked up at the *Scarface* poster on the wall. "Nah………we ain't gonna argue……….and we ain't gonna go up in there blastin either…we gonna go to King's spot…and we gonna listen to what the hell they have to say," I said calmly.

Scene Five

Jeff returned home from the hospital, but he didn't come out much now. His body was fully recuperated by now, but he still bore the psychological scars of being tortured and tormented. I had seen him a few times going to the store for his uncle. His face was different; the look in his eyes was full of malice and revenge. For the three weeks Jeff was in the hospital, I went to see him twice and it was like I visited two different people. The first time I went to see him, he kept a blank expression on his face as if he was in shock. When I talked to him, he would respond but seemed distant. He wasn't the same. Jeff heard about Boogie's beaten and bludgeoned body found at the construction site. This news enraged him because all he could think about while in the hospital was how he was going to murder every one of the mutha fuckers that violated him. He decided right there, lying in the hospital bed, that he would never again be afraid of anyone or anything. Jeff thought to himself that although Boogie being dead had altered his plans, it would not change the outcome. People will die!

Jeff still had plans for Shakim and Black. He promised himself that he would unleash all of his rage and fury on these dudes until it was over, until there was no more hurt…no more pain. He was convinced that this would free his burden. Jeff knew that Shakim and Black stayed on the block to about twelve at night. He also knew that this would be the best time to ambush them. During the fall season, the streets are empty at night. There are no civilians out, only crackheads. And the "heads" are out only long enough to cop drugs and then they'd tend to fall back into the shadows of the ghetto. This meant Sha' and Black would be on the block alone.

10:58 P.M.

Jeff had been lying in bed on his back staring at the ceiling for the past hour, gripping the butcher knife that he had swiped from his grandmother's kitchen. He had been playing the scenario over and over in his mind. What he would do and how he would do it. He methodically made his way out of the house and down the street where Sha' and Black were posted against the light pole. He made sure to make his way through the Projects so that he could approach them from the rear. If they caught on to him, he would never be able to overpower them. The streets were black and empty when Jeff crept down into the shadows of the vacant lot adjacent to where they were standing. The sounds of their laughter enraged him; every breath they took mocked Jeff and he could stand it no more. Jeff shot out of the darkness like a caged animal, but with the swiftness of a cheetah. Knife cocked back at shoulder level. The running footsteps must have alerted Black but it was too late—by the time he turned around, Jeff had already boosted himself off the hood of a car and was dropping down on him. The knife thrust so deep into Black's chest it immediately pierced his heart, and he dropped to the ground gasping his last breaths. The force of the collision flung Jeff into the garbage cans. The knife was still imbedded in Black's chest when Jeff bounced up. It happened so fast, Shakim didn't realized that Black was stabbed. He thought Jeff had tackled Black to the ground. It wasn't until he stepped closer and saw Jeff pulling the knife from Black's chest that he realized he was dead. By this time Jeff had retrieved the knife and was heading toward Shakim. Jeff thought to himself that this one wouldn't be easy, being that he had lost the element of surprise. He was able to smell the fear reeking from Sha'. Sha' froze, and it wasn't until he felt his arm being sliced that he realized Jeff was on him. Sha' reacted and grabbed Jeff's hand in defense. The sight of his own blood enraged Sha' and he overpowered Jeff, tackled him into the garbage cans, and knocked the knife loose. Sha' mounted himself on Jeff, pinning him down while he pounded him. Jeff was able to grab Sha's wounded arm and dug into his cut with his thumb. He screamed out in pain and fell off of Jeff. They both scrambled up and Jeff was able to secure the knife. He lunged toward Sha', Sha' grabbed Jeff's knife-wielding arm, which nearly sliced his throat. But the momentum stumbled Sha' back and he tripped over the legs of Black's dead body. Bodies locked; they both fell back to the ground and Sha's body went limp. When Jeff looked up, he noticed that the fall had catapulted the knife into Sha's throat. With the fear and adrenaline still running through Jeff's body, he almost didn't realize that he continued to slice at Sha's throat until he was damn near decapitated. He blacked out, not realizing that he'd cut himself with his own knife from his hand sliding off the handle onto the blade. As quick as he'd appeared on the scene, Jeff stumbled back into the darkness, leaving the bodies as they lay.

By the following day the news of Shakim and Black's murder had already spread throughout the hood. Homicide detectives were scattered all over the streets looking for witnesses. Ordinarily I wouldn't be happy to see cops on the block, but in light of us having to meet with Breeze at "King's Game Room & Candy Store," I'd make an exception. I met with Sin on Jamaica Ave. so we could head to the meeting together. When we stepped off the bus, the scene was crazy. Damn near the whole boulevard was sectioned off with yellow police tape. White dudes in suits and trench coats huddled together drinking coffee. Crowds of nosy-ass people pressed up against the barricades. By now white chalk outlined where the bodies once lay, and all that was left now was blood-stained sidewalk. It was like a scene from Hill Street Blues. It wasn't that these images were new to me; homicide was always around the hood, investigating one dead body or another. They'd always try to question us; I don't know why 'cause they knew we weren't tellin' them shit. Shit! They even tried to talk to the niggas that was hustlin'. They didn't care what you were sellin'; all they wanted was a tip on who murdered who. Homicide was cool though; they weren't like them other uniform mutha fuckers that wanna drive their car all up on the sidewalk, damn near run a nigga over, hop out their whip like they're Hawaii Five-0 and shit… Sin nudged me, breaking my thought.

"Yo, Angel, let's go, man, we gotta meet up with Breeze before them niggas start looking for us," as he grabbed me by my book bag that was still attached to my back.

"Alright, alright, I'm comin'," I said as I pulled away, walking across the street toward King's store.

The store was unusually empty. No kids on the video games; no kids at the counter scraping up nickels to buy candy. Yeah it was empty, with the exception of Breeze sitting behind the counter. He motioned to us to go to the back. As we passed by the counter he followed us to the back, leaving the counter unattended. When I entered the storage room, it dawned on me that as many times as I'd been in this store, I'd never been this far back. It's funny—I always imagined a huge office with a big desk and leather chairs behind this door. The reality was that it was nothing but a small room with a bunch of boxes, one dim lightbulb that dropped from the ceiling hanging from a single wire, a back exit door, and a tiny bathroom off to the side.

"Relax, I just wanna talk to ya'll for a minute. If we wanted you dead, you would already be dead. I would have shot you dead back at that hole in the fence. You didn't really think I was that bad of a shot, did you?" Breeze said in an even-toned voice.

I guess no matter how much we tried, we couldn't hide the nervousness in our eyes.

"Listen, I don't know what ya'll little dudes thought you witnessed back at that construction site. But whatever you thought you saw, you didn't see...understood," Breeze dictated.

Sin and I nodded our heads in unison.

"Nah, we ain't seen nothin'," I said as Breeze's glance left me and focused on Sin.

"Nah, we ain't seen nothin'," Sin repeated.

"Gooood, now that we cleared that up, we can move on to the next reason why I brought you here," a familiar voice from in the shadows said.

We both looked to our left to see King's silhouette emerging out behind the shadows. He was slowly twirling a long Rambo-style knife and looking at it as if it was a new toy. My first thought was that he was much bigger than I remembered him to be, and a lot uglier.

"You know, my first instinct was to cut both your tongues out and put 'em in a jar. But in light of my recent loss of staff, I find myself in need of a few good soldiers. So I have a proposition for you two young dudes. Go to work for me on the block and keep your lives, or defy me and I will slice your throat and dump your bodies in Baisley Park pond," King said as he thrust the knife into one of the boxes.

"Yeah, and you might even come out of this making some money," Breeze cracked.

Me and Sin looked at each other with defeated expressions on our faces. The irony is that I think we both knew that we would eventually be on the block hustlin', although we didn't expect it would be under these particular terms.

"Proposition? That ain't much of a fuckin proposition!" Sincere sarcastically remarked.

King backslapped Sin damn near off the box he was sitting on, and in the same motion grabbed him by the throat.

"See that's the problem with you young mutha fuckers. You don't have any respect. You don't know when to talk and when to shut the fuck up!" King gritted as he tightened the grip around Sin's throat.

Sin clinched King's hands and struggled to pry them apart.

"King, let him go, let him loose, man!" I said frantically.

King continued to choke Sin out as he preached. "Soldiers, huh…mutha fuckin soldiers must be obedient…they must be dedicated…loyal…they must be…"

"Let him the fuck loose, King," I barked as I pointed Uncle Ray's gun five feet away from King's face.

I was pretty sure that Sin didn't listen to me when I told him not to bring the gun to the meeting. So when I saw him grabbing for his book bag as King was trying to choke the life from his body, I knew what he was reaching for. I slid the book bag toward me and immediately felt the grip of the gun when I reached in. To tell you the truth, I was surprised that I didn't hesitate to draw the gun on King. This dude was a certified killer and a cold-hearted sociopath. He would kill both of us in this storage room and wouldn't give it a second thought. On the other hand, he had my brother in a death grip and showed no signs of letting up. Unfortunately, no sooner than I finished my demand to King, Breeze had his 9mm pistol pressed against my head.

"Now, Angel, why would you wanna go do something like that?" Breeze said in his consistent, even-toned voice while still pressing the barrel of the gun to my head.

At that moment I couldn't help glancing over the room and absorbing how small it was. My eyes refocused on King as he continued to preach.

King slid his grip off of Sin's throat down to the collar of his hoodie. Still grabbing Sin with one hand, he gestured toward me with his other. "Now here you have a true soldier: obedient, loyal, and above all willing to die for his brother. Gooood, that's real good. Breeze, you see this soldier right here. This is exactly the type of recruit I need in my camp. The only problem is, is that he might get shot in the head before he gets his stripes."

King and Breeze both laughed as if my brain's being blown out was so comical; to tell you the truth, I didn't see what was so fuckin funny.

"Listen, just let 'em go," I said in a much calmer voice. A gun upside your head tends to calm a person down.

Sin was still coughing, trying to catch his breath, but was able to blurt out, "Breeze! *cough, cough* Angel! There are about fifty cops outside. If ya'll niggas start shootin up in here…*cough, cough*…we all go down."

Sin focused his eyes on me. "Angel, go ahead, put the gun down."

As King released his grip off of Sin's hoodie, I lowered my arm. Breeze snatched the gun from my hand and he holstered his gun. As he passed my gun to King, I would have bet good money we were dead.

"You got a lot of heart, shorty," King remarked as he stepped toward me.

"Sometimes having heart can save your life and then again sometimes having heart can get you killed. So you see, having heart is not enough; you must exercise discipline!"

King swiftly pistol-whipped me with the butt of Uncle Ray's gun, and I collapsed to my knees like a prostitute on the hoe stroll. The last thing I heard before I passed out was King saying, "You start tomorrow. I want you two little niggas on the block by three o'clock; Breeze will walk you through the first day."

I must have come to a few minutes later. Sin had dragged me out the back exit into the alley behind the store. The hot sun beamed on my face, making me squint my eyes to adjust to the light. The fall breeze felt good as I climbed to my feet and gathered myself against the wall. Although we got out with our lives, I still felt defeated. Indebted to one of the most notorious drug dealers in Queens, there were only two ways out of this life: prison or death. Tomorrow would be the first day of the rest of our lives. Life as we knew it would never be the same.

Scene Six

Over the years, Sin and I hustled on the block under King's régime. We moved up in rank and established ourselves as one of the more ruthless duos in the hood. The drug game makes you grow up quick; it hardens your soul and numbs your conscience. There's no room for hesitation, no room for compassion. This was a lesson Sin and I learned quickly. Fortunately or unfortunately, depending on how you look at it, growing up in a foster home prepared us for some of the cold-hearted shit we'd experience in these streets. We built up King's clientele to a level that allowed him to send soldiers out of town to set up shop. We expanded his territory in the hood, and these things weren't accomplished without bloodshed. King was famous for sending his soldiers, as he liked to call them, to other drug locations bordering his territory. If the report came back that the block was making profit, then he would move to take over his smaller, weaker competitors and expand his territory. By the spring of 1995, King had taken over the most southern part of Jamaica—from Foch Blvd. down to Rockaway Blvd. across from the Van Wyck Expressway straight through to Sutphin Blvd. He had taken out every other competitor in the hood either by force or intimidation. All but one—a very powerful and feared drug boss named Jazz, formerly known as Jeff, commonly known in the streets as the dude that stabbed two lower-level drug dealers to death when he was a kid and got off clean. There was a lot of bad blood between Jazz and King. And me and Sincere would find ourselves caught right in the middle.

Some years back, an eleven-year-old girl was leaving her building in the Projects on her way to school. It was dusk and there was an overcast, so when she saw the massacred bodies lying on the sidewalk from a distance, she didn't immediately realize what they were. As she crossed the street and got closer, she froze in shock to see that she recognized these were the two teenage boys that were always on the corner across from her building. It was a massacre. They both lay in puddles of blood, and one boy's head was nearly decapitated. The coroner determined that the bodies were there for about six to eight hours based on the blood coagulation. This was surprising being that they were left in the street in clear view.

Months later, detectives got a tip from a crackhead that was busted for snatching a gold locket from the neck of a nurse coming home from Jamaica Hospital. She was known in the hood as "Crackhead Brenda"; we called her that because there was another Brenda in the hood who we called "Big-butt Brenda" and we needed to distinguish between the two. Anyway, Crackhead Brenda claimed that she witnessed the murder of the two boys and would identify the killer if cops dropped her robbery and aggravated assault charges. Detectives agreed to reduce the charges to possession of stolen property if the information she provided led to a suspect. So she commenced to snitchin. She explained to the detectives that on the night of the murders, she was heading to the block to cop some drugs and witnessed this young skinny kid knifing the hell out of these two dealers. She indicated that she didn't immediately believe what she was seeing, being that she was so high on crack. When it dawned on her that she wasn't trippin, she admitted that she watched the scene play out and afterwards robbed the dead dealers of their money and drugs.

Crackhead Brenda explained in her slurred toothless speech, "Yeah...I didn't think any more of it...yaknowatimsayin...shit like that happens in the street. Until one day I was getting *hiiig-ggghhhh* wit my main man Bam."

"Bam?" Detective Mills questioned.

"Yeah, Bam...as in Bam-boo!" Crackhead Brenda said with pride as if Detective Mills should have already known.

"What the hell kind of name is Bamboo?" Detective Mills barked.

"Bamboo...'cause when it was time to get high, he always had that bamboo paper," she said with a toothless grin.

"Okay, okay, so you were getting cracked up with Bamboo, then what?" Mills snapped in frustration.

"So Bam was telling me yaknowatimsayin......he was sayin that on the same night of them killings yaknowatimsayin...he seen his nephew come in the house looking like somebody beat his ass with a bloody maxi pad. And I said Bam you bullshittin and he said sho enough and I said stop bullshittin and he said nah sho enough and I said........"

"Ms. Williams, Ms. Williams," Detective Mills shouted. "Please stick to the facts."

"Well...that's it!" she responded with an attitude.

"That's it?" Mills said with disappointment.

"That's it, mutha fucker, what else you want!"

There was a long pause as Mills leaned over the table and locked eyes with Brenda, searching for more.

Mills gestured to the uniform officer, "Okay, send her ass back to the cage."

As circumstantial as it was, Mills followed up on Brenda's lead and ran the alias "Bamboo" through the system. Kenneth Herns, a.k.a. "Bamboo," had a long rap sheet dating back to the seventies for burglary, drugs, and weapons possession. It also provided an address, which appeared to be the only residence he ever had: 148-10 Foch Blvd. While on the way to the location, Mills didn't really pay any mind to the horns and sirens of the fire trucks that sped past him. By the time he pulled up to Foch Blvd., he was already coughing from the smoke and was able to see the flames in the distance. He had a bad feeling in the gut of his stomach. And his fear was realized as he approached the address. The block was sectioned off; he jumped out of his unmarked car, flashed his detective badge at one of the fire chiefs, and raced toward the house. The house was an inferno. He never made eye contact with the fireman who grabbed him back. His eyes fixed on the doomed house. Because of the chaos, he didn't hear the fireman yelling that the chief ordered their men to pull back. The fire was too intense. Mills pulled away from the fireman's grip, surveying the area. His eyes settled on the EMS truck and focused through the window on the kid in the back of the cab. Mills couldn't help but notice the way the flames illuminated the night. There was an awkward beauty to it. When he opened the cab door to the EMS truck, the paramedic explained that the kid lived in the house with his uncle.

EMT Jones explained, "He claimed that when he got home, he found the house ablaze. We found him sitting on the curb; it wasn't until one of the neighbors pointed him out that we knew he lived in the house."

"Any sign of the uncle?" Mills questioned.

"We think he's still in the house..." EMT Jones responded with a blank look.

Mills' eyes drifted back to the blaze. He knew Bamboo was dead. And he knew the kid in this ambulance was most likely the same kid Crackhead Brenda described as being at the murder scene. After Jeff was medically cleared, Detective Mills transported him down to the station for questioning. It was discovered that Jeff had no next of kin, and Bamboo was his last known relative. Social services was called in to be present during the interrogation. It didn't matter; Jeff didn't say much of anything.

Mills kept Jeff for twenty-four hours until he was able to bring Brenda in to I.D. him. The I.D. was all the Queens D.A. needed to indict Jeffery Herns and remand him to the island. By the time the trial started Jeff had been able to obtain a decent lawyer, make bail, and was back on the streets. The homeowner's insurance payout was issued to Jeff. Jeff's uncle Bamboo was torched beyond recognition in the fire, so the proceeds of the insurance were surrendered to Jeff. His lawyer established a bank account and deposited the $150,000 check, but not without taking his percentage. Jeff was released on a $50,000 bond and placed in a temporary group home. The irony was that they sent Jeff to a group home right in the middle of South Side. Jeff was able to send for Chase, the neighborhood know-it-all. Chase told him that he got word that Crackhead Brenda was the one that pointed him out to police and made the I.D. at the precinct. Jeff knew what had to be done.

Jazz knew it wouldn't be hard to find Crackhead Brenda; fiends are creatures of habit. Jeff was now known as Jazz, a name he inherited during his time at the group home. One of his roommates put him on to how to sneak out of the home during the night without being detected. What had to be done, had to be done soon.

After lights out Jazz slid out the bedroom, through the kitchen, and out the back door. The boys knew that the overnight counselor always snuck his girlfriend in the house and stayed in the office throughout the night. Jazz made his way through the hood like an alley cat on the prowl. He systematically made his way through the back streets and buildings. New York winters are unforgiving, and the frigid winds cut through Jazz's champion hoodie like razor blades. He almost thought to turn back and surrender to the cold, but he knew this had to be done. His face and hands were numb by now, and he worried if he would be able to maintain a grip on his knife. He pulled his sleeves over his hands while he played the scenario over in his mind. Jazz crept onto the Baisley Projects grounds and settled on a bench in a playground amongst the buildings. From here he had a clear view of King's workers hustling across the street. He knew it was only a matter of time before Brenda showed up. She was on the block more often than other crackheads being that she ran errands for Breeze and copped for other heads so she could get in on their score. The problem was that the winds ripped through the buildings, making it feel twenty degrees colder, and the longer he sat there the more likely he would be noticed. As he sat on the bench, thoughts raced through his mind of what he was becoming: a cold-blooded murderer. He tried to rationalize to himself that this is what they made him. It wasn't his doing. He struggled to push the thoughts out of his mind, and at that moment he spotted her. Jazz recognized her walk more so than anything else; there's no mistaking a crackhead's walk. She made her way on the block and met with the two new workers to cop her drugs. It was then that Jazz noticed the all-too familiar faces of King's new soldiers, Angel and Sincere. But he couldn't allow that to dissuade him from his obligation. He had to eliminate the one person who could link him to the murders. He watched Brenda as she made her way back into the Projects toward him. He walked around the playground so that he could double back on her. Jazz tightened his hoodie around his face as he approached her rear. He allowed the knife to slide down from his sleeve into the grip of his hand right before he grabbed her around her neck. She gasped and belted out a single scream before Jazz tightened his grip. The scream echoed throughout the Projects and seemed to reach every building before fading away. He struggled to pull her into the jungle gym. She was surprisingly strong for a 115 lb. crackhead, but he knew he had to get her out of plain sight. At any moment someone could look out their apartment into the courtyard and witness what was going down. Jazz thrust the eight-inch knife into Brenda's side twice out of frustration to get her to stop fighting. Brenda's body went limp for the moment and he dragged her onto the rubber mats by the swings. He kneeled over her to finish the job but looked up with caution when the sounds of a couple of cars drag-racing down the block distracted him. In that moment Brenda regained some consciousness and spotted an empty 40 oz. beer bottle in her reach. With all that she had left, she grabbed the bottle and smashed it into the side of Jazz's face. A scar he would wear for the rest of his life. He was more stunned than hurt and wiped his hand over his face to check the severity of his wound. Brenda struggled to get to her feet and made it a few feet to the sliding boards before she collapsed. In an instant Jazz was back on her like a pit bull with the taste of blood. He grabbed her hair and pulled her head back, exposing her neck. As he slowly sliced her throat from left to right, he whispered in her ear, "You have spoken your last words, bitch."

As he headed back to the group home, he peeled off his blood-stained hoodie and jeans and discarded them into the corner trashcan. He layered the clothes with newspaper and lit the trashcan on fire. He made it back the last few blocks with only a t-shirt and basketball shorts. He slid back into the group home the same way he made it out, and after he showered he lay in his bunk bed playing the scene over in his head. From his bunk he looked out the window with a blank stare, and as it started to rain he grew confident that the rain would wash away any blood he might have left behind.

No sooner than the body was discovered, Detective Mills was at the group home standing over Jazz's bunk.

"You wanna tell me how you got that cut over the side of your face, kid?" Mills demanded. These were the words Jazz woke up to as he squinted his eyes and surveyed the room. He immediately recognized Detective Mills, who was about twelve inches from his face, and noticed the group-home social worker standing in the doorway. He sat up and felt a rush of pain shoot to the left side of his face where Brenda had clapped him with the bottle.

"Man, what the hell do you want from me?" Jazz snapped as he moaned from the pain.

Mills became flustered and his face turned fire red. "I want you to stop jerkin me around and tell me where you was at last night!" Mills snatched Jazz off the bunk bed and posted him against the closet door.

"Detective Mills!" Ms. Lyn, the group-home social worker, screamed.

Mills stepped into Jazz's face. "Don't fuck with me, boy, or I'll give you a matching scar on the other side of your face!"

"Detective Mills, that-will-be-enough! Now let him loose!" Ms. Lyn demanded.

Mills could tell by the look in Jazz's eyes that he had his man. There was a cold calm about Jazz's demeanor. It wasn't cockiness; it was just a calm about him like the intensity of the moment didn't affect him. Mills's glare shifted from Jazz and settled on Ms. Lyn. Mill's walkie-talkie broke the awkward silence in the room. *"This is base to unit four, unit four, come in,"* a female voice cracked over the speaker. Mills peeked down at the walkie-talkie and the intense expression on his face relaxed. He straightened himself up and walked out of the group home without saying a word.

Back at the scene of the murder, Detective Mills pushed his way through a crowd of spectators, making his way to the CSI team. The courtyard and playground were sectioned off, and Brenda's body was already on the way to the examiner's office for an official cause of death to be determined. CSI officers were littered about the scene, taking samples and collecting potential evidence. Although there were higher-ranking officers on the scene, Mills knew he would only converse and share his intel with one other person, Officer Susan Manelli. Officer Manelli was a six-year veteran of the force assigned to the CSI unit straight out of the academy. She'd graduated from John Jay College with a degree in forensic science. Although she came from a family of cops, most figured she would enter into a career of modeling and acting because of her stunning beauty. During college she actually did some commercial and print work to help pay for grad school. She and Mills were involved in a brief affair during her rookie year that gained him many enemies in the force. In part, because her brothers and father were still active in the department, but mostly because Mills just rubbed people the wrong way.

Although the affair was brief Mills never stopped loving Susan, and every time he saw her he felt a shower of emotions that he struggled with. He had too much pride to reveal his true feelings to her, so when they had to speak he would keep the conversation overtly professional. Before he approached her, he took a deep breath.

"Manelli, you find anything?" he said firmly.

"We have some blood samples but won't know the donor 'til we get the tests back from the lab. We're checking for prints, but it's gonna be tough; the rain washed away a lot of potential evidence," she replied in textbook form, leaving no room for "lingering innuendos." She barely made eye contact. She went through a rough time after their relationship was exposed. She was passed over for promotions that were given to her male counterparts with less experience and nowhere near her education level. They both felt burnt by the department because of their relationship, which was ultimately the demise of their love affair.

"Well, let me know what you come up with," Mills requested before walking away.

Manelli waited a few seconds before turning to watch Mills walk away in the distance. But by the time she looked up, he had already dissolved into the crowd. Her heart sank and she secretly cursed him out for leaving her heart in this condition.

When Mills returned to his car, he was met by Queens Assistant District Attorney Stephen Goldstein. Detective Mills and the district attorney's office had a love-hate relationship. Goldstein didn't necessarily agree with tactics the detective used to obtain his information, although he was certain it produced results.

"Stephen, how can I help you?" Mills sarcastically remarked.

"Mills, don't give me shit; I'm not in the mood. This is a disaster! The Jeffery Herns case is already circumstantial, and with my only witness chopped up across the Projects it doesn't freakin' help! Without this witness we have no case." Goldstein made sure to keep his voice down. Despite the amount of police in the area, it was clear that he was still uncomfortable being in the ghetto, a world away from his luxurious office.

Mills opened his car door with Goldstein still leaning on it. "Well, what'cha want from me, Stephen? I'm on it. But you know how this is gonna play out; a crackhead, murdered, in the Projects, in the middle of the night."

"I'll tell you what I want, Mills. This case wrapped up with a ribbon…..a freakin' ribbon, Mills!" Mills sped away in his unmarked car, leaving Goldstein standing in the street.

Later that night, Mills sat in his one-bedroom apartment in Howard Beach Queens drinking Jack Daniels. His phone rang ten times before he reached over and answered it.

"Mills," he answered, annoyed that someone was so persistent.

"Mills, this is Manelli. I'm at the lab and just got the results back from the tech."

He immediately sat up when he heard her voice. A part of him wished that the call wasn't business related.

"So what'cha got for me?"

"It's not good. The blood samples were too degraded for a positive match. I just sent a fax over to the D.A.'s office to notify them of our findings."

"What about prints? Any matches?"

"The rain made it almost impossible to lift any prints, and the ones we were able to get, from the size of them they're most likely children's fingerprints. I'm sorry, Mills, but at this point we don't have much to go on."

Mills knew that without this witness, the case on Jazz would fall apart. He felt defeated but didn't want to reveal his feelings to Manelli.

"Okay, uh…call me if anything turns up." Mills hung up the phone, fearing that she would hear the hesitation in his voice.

Mills asked Manelli to call him if anything turned up. But nothing ever did and the D.A.'s office was forced to drop the case against Jazz pending new evidence. Jazz's reputation in the hood became synonymous with being untouchable. It was common street knowledge that Jazz had committed these vicious murders and somehow got away with it. No one dared to oppose him from fear of turning up dead in some alley somewhere. He quickly became one of the most feared dudes in the ghetto. As he got older, Jazz worked on his physical appearance by lifting weights in the group home. He used some of the insurance money to cop a half a brick. He recruited most of his fellow group home members and even had some staff on the payroll. By '95 Jazz aged out of the group home but continued to control the house. By now he was supplying most of the lower-level drug dealers in South Queens, with the exception of King.

Although King despised Jazz, we managed to maintain our friendship over the years. I mean, let's be real, back in the day I was the one that stood up for Jeff and saved him from a lot of ass kickings. Every now and then Jazz and I would get together and shoot some pool. I could tell he looked forward to us getting together because his whole demeanor would change. He once told me that I was the only one he could be himself around, the only one he trusted. Which sounds crazy to me being that I was a lieutenant in King's crew and had the potential to set him up on any given day. At the same time I understood him. One of the hardest things about being in the drug, money, and murder business is not being able to trust anyone. Not being able to ever let your guard down, put down the rough exterior, and be yourself. That in itself could eat at your soul. So, however illogical it was, he looked to me for normalcy.

We'd usually meet at a Billard's in Forest Hills, Queens, around the corner from Midway Movie Theatre. This was mostly a Jewish and Russian community way outside of Jamaica. We figured it was neutral enough. Even though Jazz always came with a few soldiers, I always arrived alone. This would piss Sin off 'cause he figured I should've severed that friendship a long time ago, and even more so he felt it was too fuckin' risky.

Even though I would arrive earlier than Jazz he would always call ahead and have the table reserved and paid for. The table would always be accompanied with a bucket of Heineken's and a bottle of Hennessey.

"Ayo! A-gel!" Jazz yelled from the entrance of the Billard's. "A-gel" was a reluctant nickname that I obtained when I was a kid because of my curly hair. During the summers we'd cool off with the fire hydrant, and I guess when my hair was wet it appeared that I had gel in it. So the kids would call me A-gel rather than Angel. Yes, it was very corny, but fortunately the nickname only stuck with Jazz.

"What up, big man?" I replied sarcastically, referencing to how big he had gotten from weight lifting, an over-compensation from being so skinny when we were kids.

"Yeah, you know, you never know when you have to knock a nigga the fuck out!" Jazz joked as he flexed his bicep. We gave each other a pound and embraced like two brothers that hadn't seen each other in a while. "Now you know I'm gonna bust your ass so get your money ready."

"Nigga, just go ahead and rack 'em," I cracked back.

We shot pool for hours, drinking Heinekens and shots of Hennessey. Through the jokes, laughter, and reminiscing, we knew that once we hit the streets, we were on opposite sides of the battlefield.

Scene Seven

The summer nights in Jamaica Queens were always alive with energy, and the summer of 1995 was hotter than ever. We'd drive through the streets like we were royalty; no one could touch us. Chicks would break their necks to see who it was coming through the block. Niggas on every corner threw their hands up to say "Wassup!" And after we passed through, it was always some cornball ass nigga frontin', talkin' like he used to get money with us. King and Breeze drove matching BMW's 850 series. The paint job on those whips was so clean, the city lights reflected off the car like mirrors. You couldn't tell us shit! Sin rode with King, and I rode shotgun in Breeze's jet-black Beema. We pulled up to the Q Club off Jamaica Ave., the scene looking like a movie premier. Mutha fuckers were lined up around the corner to get in. Chicks dressed in their best booty dresses and pumps; it was a fuckin hoe-asis out there. Once we pulled up, honeys rushed the car wantn' to get down with the entourage. A bunch of cats made their way over to give us pounds and make bullshit conversation, hoping our shine would rub off on them. We walked straight into the club, giving pounds to the bouncers, hugs to the promoter, and shook hands with the owner. We made our way through the packed club to our reserved area. It felt like we were moving in slow motion. The music vibrated through my body as I resisted the urge to rap along with the lyrics. Breeze motioned to the server to bring over some bottles of Moet. The VIP area overlooked the dance floor, giving us a view of the whole club. You see, I wasn't only there to party and look cool. We had enemies. Amongst those that gave us fake handshakes and funny-style smiles were a lot of niggas plotting our downfall. There was no absence of tension, and we all felt it. It was me and Sin's job to watch the backs of Breeze and King. Sin always joked, "If we watchn' their backs, who the hell is watchn' ours." But he knew I would never let anything happen to him. I would give my life for him, as he would give his for me.

We had about seven or eight bitches in VIP with us. King lounged on the couch with two honeys, one on each side. Breeze was off to the side with a chick on his lap and a hand on her ass as she kissed on his neck. Sin posted up in the corner with this bad bitch, his hands all over her thick ass body. I don't know if it was the liquor or the strobe lights, but I could have sworn he had her tits out. I had this nice little red bone honey grinding on me. I'm in her ear heavy, talkin 'bout how I'm gonna blow her back out later. The DJ was gettin' it in mixin Jamaican tunes, and right on cue mutha fuckers lit up them blunts. I was on Henney straight all night, so by now my eyes were low and bloodshot. But through the music, liquor, and women, something wasn't right; something was off. I could feel it in the air. It was like in that instant right before something bad happens; it's a rush that shoots through your body. I forced my eyes wide to survey the club and pushed this bitch off me so I could stand up straight. My eyes focused on all the angles, anything that was out of place—like them bunch of dudes ice grillin at the table over on the other side of the floor, or them cats by the speakers with hot-ass hoodies on, not even paying attention to the half naked bitches standing next to them. I yelled over to Sin to get his attention, but he couldn't hear me over the music. When I made my way over to him, I glanced back and lost sight of the usual suspects. The table was empty and the speakers were abandoned. My eyes frantically searched the club, and my heart began to race as I reached for my pistol. Sin read the expression on my face and immediately drew his twin 9mm. From the corner of my eye, I saw a spark of light that could not be confused with strobes. I aimed my gun, desperately trying to locate the shooter; more shots blasted off from different locations and the club dropped to the floor. I felt the bullets impact the furniture around me. Some of the panicked clubbers tried to flee the club and caught stray rounds to the back and stumbled to the floor. A bouncer that was posted by the VIP section was shot in the face and collapsed on the stairs. One of the chicks that was over with King had her brains blown across the table. King took cover behind the remaining groupie as Breeze let off a few rounds before positioning himself behind the couch. Sin returned fire into the crowd, and the music was replaced by screams and chaos. In the darkness of the club, the strobes still flashed when one of the goons charged out of the scattering crowd toward us. I placed a bullet in his neck and blood sprayed across the projector screen still playing music videos.

"Sincere, let's get the fuck outta here!" I yelled as I made eye contact with Breeze, indicating for him to make an exit.

My command didn't faze Sin as he continued to blast his cannons simultaneously, dropping two of the thugs across the dance floor. Breeze eyed the fire exit behind the bar. He grabbed King by the arm, and they stumbled their way toward the exit, ducking to avoid the ricocheting bullets.

"Sin…Angel, WE-ARE-LEAVING!" Breeze demanded as he returned fire. We sprinted across the club, bullets at our heels. We dove over the bar and took cover. I motioned toward the fire exit, which was about five feet beyond the bar but enough out of cover to get our heads blown the fuck off. Our sprint to the bar distracted the shooters long enough for Breeze and King to make it through the exit. I reloaded and searched my memory for the last location of the shooters. "Angel, I'm out! I ain't got no more fuckin' bullets!" Had to think quickly; it wouldn't be long before they rushed the bar. I reached my arm over the bar top with my head still ducked down and fired some pointless shots to keep them back. I noticed the rack of reserve liquor aligned under the bar. I grabbed a couple of bottles of Puerto Rican rum and chucked it over the bar onto the dance floor. Sin looked at me like I was crazy. "Yo, what the fuck are you doing, making them a freakin Martini?"

"Just work with me!" I checked my clip and pulled back my action. *Two in the clip, one in the head.* "I have a plan." Still crouched down, I tossed a couple of tequilas to Sin and he flung 'em over, still not knowing what the hell was going on. I grabbed a roll of paper towels and lit it up with the bar lighter, peeked around the bar, and rolled the flaming paper towels onto the dance floor. There was an eerie silence that came over the room right before the dance floor and the surrounding carpet was set ablaze. The fire shot to the roof, giving us cover to make it to the exit. The fire engulfed one of the goons as he belched out a deathly scream. The remaining thugs let off fruitless rounds through the wall of flames as we made our exit. As we reached the door, Sin burst out, "Angel, get down!" I spun around in time to see the last two assassins breaking through the wall of fire using one of the wooden round tables as a shield. They came through blastin. One of the shots ripped through my shoulder, knocking me back into a stack of chairs along the wall. I lost my grip on the gun and it dropped in between the chairs. They raced toward me, and all I had the energy for was to toss a chair in their direction. I crumbled in defeat and at the last second Sin dove on me, knocking me out of the way. In that same motion he grabbed my gun from the chair and picked off one of the last two thugs. Sin immediately swung the pistol in the direction of the last thug, but he had gotten too close and they both grabbed each other and locked arms. As they struggled rounds squeezed off, blowing out a few strobe lights. Sin wrestled him down, freed his hand, and pressed the barrel to his forehead. *Click…click…click.* The gun was empty; Sin had emptied the last couple of rounds during the struggle. The thug struck Sin on the temple, gaining the advantage and pinning him on his back. I struggled to see through the dark smoke, but I was able to make out the thug going for his back-up gun. I grabbed one of the metal chairs with my good arm, ran from behind, and smacked it across his head. To be honest I was kind of surprised to see the side of his head was cracked open. Sin pushed the corpse off him, climbed to his feet, and wrapped my arm across his shoulder. We stumbled out the door coughing from smoke inhalation, finding ourselves in the alley out back. We picked up our heads and covered our eyes from blinding headlights of a car about twenty yards away pointed in our direction. I squinted my eyes, trying to identify the silhouette that exited the passenger side. I thought that it must be more troops from the assassination squad. My body fell limp on Sin's grip. For some reason, at that moment I felt a sense of pity for the club owner as flames burst out the windows. I pushed those crazy ass thoughts out of my mind and tried to come to terms that there was no way out of this alley. Suddenly the silhouette screamed out, "What the hell are ya'll niggas waiting for, we gotta get the fuck outta here." It was Breeze. They doubled back to pick us up. I could hear sirens in the distance as I climbed into the back seat resting my head on Sin's shoulder. I was fuckin exhausted. King pulled off at the same time the police and fire engines turned the corner.

King dropped us off at Mama's house with instructions to meet at the store the next afternoon.

"Hey? I'm gonna need ya'll to come to the store tomorrow around three o'clock. We have to figure this shit out." The look on King's face was unfamiliar; I'd never seen him so subdued.

We made our way to the basement through the back door. I went straight to the bathroom and peeled off my shredded clothes down to my boxers. My body was wasted and my lungs were on fire. It felt like I had been fed through a grinder and forced to swallow a bag of charcoal. I stared at my blackened face in the mirror, wiping my wound with a damp washcloth. I splashed a handful of cold water on my face, clearing my eyes of all the soot. As I refocused in the mirror, Sin was standing in the doorway behind me.

"How's your shoulder?" he asked through the reflection in the mirror.

"I'll be okay, it's not as bad as I thought; just a flesh wound."

Sin tossed me some bandages. "Here, put these on. Wrap it tight, it'll stop the bleeding."

"Thanks."

"Listen, Angel…tonight was pretty intense," Sin remarked in a consoling tone.

I glared at him through the mirror like he'd just made the understatement of a lifetime. "No shit!"

We both locked glares in the mirror with straight expressions. We held it about ten seconds and then burst into laughter. I guess we just broke down from all the nervous intense emotions that were built up throughout the night. Having a near-death experience would do that to a person. Still in laughter, we embraced in a brotherly hug.

"The important thing is that we held it down and had each other's back," I said.

Sin recited our lifelong motto. "The love you show me…"

I recalled, "…is the love I show you." And we both recited in unison, "50/50 luv…'til the sun burns out!"

"Angel?"

"Yeah?"

"Can you do me a favor?"

"Of course, anything, you name it, bra."

"If we gonna be doin all this huggin, can you go put some pants on!"

Laughing…Laughing…Laughing………Laughing.

Scene Eight

I lay in bed with only my thoughts to reason with, and even though my body was exhausted I couldn't sleep. And though I'd shared laughs with my brother, I was truly terrified. Not because of the certain repercussions that would come from our actions in the club, but of the line I had crossed tonight. Up until this point I had never killed anyone before. Sure, I had beaten, extorted, and terrorized people before. Hell, I'd even witnessed a few murders in my time. But to take someone's life, regardless of the circumstances, pays a toll on your psyche. My confliction was wearing on my soul as the dawn light pierced through the basement window, escaping a night that felt like a lifetime.

I spent years running the streets and experienced the good, the bad, and the ugly of it all. There was never a day that I didn't think to myself that there had to be more…more to life than struggle, poverty, and drug wars. If only I had the map that showed me the road leading to that better life. I've always felt torn between my love for the streets and my passion to leave it behind. Sincere seemed to absorb it all, the ills of the streets, and reveled in it. It didn't affect him…not the way it did me. But I'd always known since we were kids that we were built different. Not as far as being tough 'cause we were both tough as titanium and would go to war for each other in an instant. But like I mentioned earlier, every kid in the foster home had their own scars and crosses to bear, and Sincere was still weighed down from his.

Unlike Sin I was born into the foster home. My mother was adopted as a child, and I was raised alongside the foster kids of my generation. Sincere was brought into the home when he was around nine or ten years old along with his younger biological sister. We clicked immediately and became best friends—no scratch that, we became brothers. I had never met his biological mother and he never spoke about her. I remember one night, months after he'd been here, his mother made an unannounced visit. We were upstairs playing with our G.I. Joe men we'd boosted from the toy section of Macy's when Mama called Sin down to the living room. Instinctively I followed, figuring he was in trouble for something or another and wanted to witness the ass whippin. Sin paused at the bottom of the stairs when he noticed his mother sitting on the couch already with his sister. The resemblance was undeniable, and when she stood up to acknowledge him she stumbled into the end table, almost knocking the lamp over. She was damp with sweat and spoke in a slurred speech.

"Sincere, come give your mama a hug!" Sincere didn't move, and his surprised expression turned to anger.

"You don't hear me, boy? Get your ass over here and give yo mama a kiss. What! They already turned you against me...they ain't shit!...and you know what, little boy...you ain't shit either." His little sister tried to turn her mother's attention but got shoved away.

"You think you're better than me, don't you?" She paused for a few seconds, swaying back and forth, and broke into a superficial cry, "I know…I know I ain't nothin.… I know you ashamed of me…but I'm still your mama and you still my babies."

Sin turned his back on her and walked past me back up the stairs, and when our eyes met a single tear rolled down his eye. That would be the first and last time I would ever see him cry.

Her cries changed to menacing laughter. "Well go on then.… I don't give a fuck about you either. You too good for yo mama now! I ain't comin back so keep walkin'…."

My aunts tried to compose her but she violently pulled away. "Don't touch me! Don't fuckin touch me! Don't you ever mutha fuckin touch me! You don't have to say it…I know…I was leaving anyway." She stumbled out the door and got into a car that had been waiting for her with the engine still running. That was the last time I ever saw her, and years later she died of kidney failure due to alcoholism. Sin reluctantly attended her funeral, and till this day we've never spoke about that night.

The meeting at King's spot was brutal. He called everyone in from captain to soldier—everyone was accountable. Even those that weren't summoned called or sent word in good faith. No one wanted to be connected with this failed murder attempt.

After last night's shoot-out at the club, the streets were on alert and the police were on the hunt; like us, they wanted answers.

The streets were dead: nothing coming in and nothing going out. At times like this you just wanna lay low and chill, but a few of my people from my block convinced me to come hang out on Jamaica Ave. Jamaica Center is one of Queens' largest shopping areas, with about a mile length of streets lined with various stores, malls, and restaurants. And as always, the avenue was flooded with honeys. Niggas driving their freshly clean whips up and down the avenue bumpin the summer jams.... *It was all a dream, I used to read* Word Up *magazine*.... It was hot as hell that day, and I was even hotter 'cause I was wearing a champion hoodie to cover up the bandages on my shoulder. I tried to ignore the throbbing pain in my shoulder and kept my arm close to my body to avoid having people bumping it as they walked by. Hangin out with Fat Chase and the twins (Jason and Jayquan) made me feel normal again. They weren't affiliated in the drug game and we had been friends since we were kids. Besides that, they were just naturally funny ass dudes. We would just roast on each other all day as we browsed the avenue.

"Ayo, Angel? You didn't tell me yo moms drove a bus, you think you can get me some transfers?" Chase joked as the twins bust into a chuckle.

"Yo, Chase, I rather my moms drive a bus than to be as big as a fuckin bus, Ayo Twin, that bitch so fat I tried to walk around her and got lost."

"Ayo, Angel, don't be callin my moms no bitch!"

"Oh, my bad...that HOE is soo fat..." We bust out laughing.

Through the crowds of people walking past us, my eyes locked on a girl that illuminated out of the crowd. It was as if everyone around her was blurred and she was the only person in focus. She was beautiful; there was no way she was from South Side. The sight of her stopped me in mid-laughter. I tried to quickly regain my composure before she passed by, and the closer she got the more incredible she looked. She had a dark golden complexion like she was from some Caribbean island—hair jet black, straight like an Indian's that cascaded down her back. Her cheekbones were high, which gave her a mature look, and her chinky eyes were light brown and very intimidating. I was paralyzed. I tried but couldn't take my eyes off of her. I struggled to refocus my glance somewhere else; if she caught me staring at her, she might think I was some psycho dude that never saw a beautiful woman before.

I wanted to talk to her.
I needed to talk to her.
I had to say something.

Shit! Here she comes; I'm gonna miss my chance. My heart raced and my mind scrambled for the right words. I finally got the nerve to look up and say something, even though I still didn't know what to say.

"Damn!".... My heart dropped. She'd already passed and was a few paces past me. All I could do was turn around and get one last look to burn into my memory. Still walking in opposite directions, she turned and met my eyes. Our eyes locked and I fought not to turn away. It felt like I spent a lifetime in her glance. And then it happened; she smiled—an uncontrollable smile right before she looked away. A burst of adrenaline and confidence shot through my body. I about-faced and fought my way through the crowds toward her, leaving the twins and them behind. I caught up to her at the intersection and had to pause to catch my breath.

"Hey, how ya doing?"

She turned and looked me up and down as if we didn't just share a lifetime in each other's eyes. "Don't tell me you ran all the way down the block to ask me how I was doing," she said with a raised eyebrow. Her sharp sense of humor took me by surprise.

"You're right ma, I didn't fight my way through that crowd to ask you that. It's just that when we turned and noticed each other you smiled, and I just had to find out what that smile was about. If I had kept walking, I never would've known if that smile could have led to an opportunity to get to know you better. And if I had to live with that doubt, I'd be messed up for a while."

Walking alongside her, I tried to keep up with her pace as I maneuvered through the frantic shoppers. I paused and searched her face for a look of consideration.

"Straight up, ma, you are a beautiful woman, and I can't imagine what I can say that you haven't already heard before from a thousand other dudes. So hey, what can I say, I would just really like to get a chance to know you."

She paused and looked me up and down with a sly look on her face. "So, you're saying if you don't get a chance to get to know me you'll be messed up?"

"Yeah!"

"Messed up for how long?" she said with a grin.

"One…maybe two months. It wouldn't be easy to get over it, ma…. I'll tell you what, my summer would definitely be shot," I sarcastically remarked.

She broke into a girlish giggle and I fell in love. I knew it was crazy to feel that way, but it was something that washed over me like a warm shower. I knew then it would be hard for me not to have her in my life. She extended her hand. "My name is Zane… Zane Ortiz."

I shook her hand with a soft grip and held on longer than I should've. "I'm Angel."

She paused and raised both her eyebrows. "You don't have a last name, Angel?"

"Well, actually my full name is Victor Johnson, but everyone calls me Angel; a nickname my moms gave me when I was a baby. So, Ortiz? Is that Puerto Rican or…"

"No." She cut me off with a look like she was tired of that assumption. "My father is Jamaican and my mother is from Brazil."

"That's a unique mix."

"They met in England when my father's reggae band was performing at a pub my mother bar tendered at and the rest is history."

"Were you born out there?"

"Yeah, I stayed until I was thirteen, and then my mother moved to the States. My father didn't want to give up his dreams of being the next Bob Marley so he stayed."

I barely noticed that I'd walked her onto the York College campus, and it dawned on me that for someone that was born and raised out here, I'd never been on this campus, let alone any college campus.

I looked around to soak in the environment. "So, you go to school here?"

"Yes, and I'm late for class." She gave me a look like she needed to go as she glanced at her watch.

"Listen, I don't wanna hold you, ma, I just wanna finish our conversation. Do you think I can call you and maybe we can get together for lunch sometime?"

As she looked up at me, the sun caught her face and displayed the true brightness of her eyes. "Listen, Angel, I wanna be honest with you. I'm not looking for a relationship right now. You seem like a nice guy and all, but I'm just really trying to focus on my studies."

She seemed like she was almost apologizing, as if it just dawned on her that our easygoing conversation might have sent mixed signals. I had to say something quick before I lost the moment.

"I know exactly how you feel, sweetheart. I'm not ready for a committed relationship either, you know the last thing I need is for you to be calling me off the hook, poppin up at my crib, next thing I know I walk in my house and you'd be cooking collard greens with my mama." I shook my head sarcastically. "Nah, I couldn't deal with that." She laughed and I felt those emotions shower over me again. I didn't know what it was, but it felt like I'd been carrying a void inside that I wasn't aware of until now, and she somehow over the course of twenty minutes filled it perfectly. And I knew without her I would now forever be aware of that emptiness.

My smile fell from my face to show my sincerity. "I just wanna see you again...how can I see you again, Ms. Zane Ortiz?"

That sly look returned to her face and she said, "Well, you know what school I go to." She gestured at the York College logo. "You know what time I go to class..." She glanced at her watch. "...and if you watch me walk away, then you'll also know where my class is. So if you're as smart as I think you are, you'll figure out how to bump into me again."

She walked away and I indeed watched. Her body was bananas, thick like a Thunder cat, and she carried it like a woman. I clocked her as she walked into her class, and right before she entered she turned, looked, and gave me that genuine smile. I noticed the sign on the door, "Eng. Lit 101." The sign next to it read, "Report to the Millstein Bld. for late fall registration."

To be honest I still don't know how I graduated from high school, but I managed to pull it off. I guess I felt some sort of obligation to Mama since she was so disappointed by us being lost to the streets. She tried her best to get us back on the right track, but the truth is that a grandmother's discipline can keep a boy in line only for so long before you need the intervention of a strong male figure—whether it be a father, grandfather, or uncle, and where I'm from there's not too many of those in the household. My uncles that did live in the house with us were lowlifes; of my three uncles, there was an alcoholic crackhead, a heroin addict, and an overzealous Christian who was one of fifteen members of a storefront, house-of-prayer church. They were far from an all-star cast of male influences.

Mama never got to see me graduate; she died of cancer when I was sixteen. But she always said, "Child, at least get your high school diploma 'cause you never know when you're gonna need it." Those words proved to be prophetic 'cause without my diploma, I wouldn't have been able to make late registration into York College, and I wouldn't be sittin in Eng. Lit 101 looking at Zane sitting two rows ahead of me. The girl was so focused she didn't even notice me when she walked in, or maybe she didn't remember me. It had been a week since that fateful walk down the avenue. I made my way behind her and leaned over her chair. "I think I can get used to this."

I must have startled her 'cause she jumped when she turned to see who was whispering in her ear. "Angel, what are you doing here?" She smiled and looked around for the professor, who was still writing quotes on the blackboard for when class started.

"How did you find me?" she asked in a whisper.

"Find you? I'm just tryin to get my education on, girl. What ya think, I'm a stalker or something?"

She laughed. "No, for real, you have to get outta here before you get me in trouble."

"Nah, I think I'll stay and see what this whole college thing is about."

The professor began calling the attendance. "...James Anderson...Tawana Butler...Nichole Cox..."

"Okay, okay. I'll make a deal with you. If you leave now, I'll meet you after class," she said in desperation.

"I'm sorry, ma, I can't do that."

"What! Why?"

"...Jamel Fisher...Victor Johnson..."

"'Cause if I left I'd be marked absent." I raised my hand. "Present!"

She swung her head around to eyeball the professor. "What!"—not believing that he'd just called my name. She swung her head back to me. "You-are-not-in-my-class!" she said in amazement. A grin spread across her face.

I sat back in my chair with a smirk on my face. "Shhh...pay attention, I'm trying to get an 'A.'"

She laughed. "He's only calling the attendance, silly." The look she gave me at that moment told me she now knew that I wasn't the average dude and she would never underestimate me again.

Zane stayed true to her word and wouldn't agree to go on a date with me, although she agreed to be study partners for our English class. She introduced me to Barnes & Nobles, Star Bucks, and Au Bon Pain. I found myself spending more and more time on the college scene and less time on the block. She had me up in the Museum of Natural History, which was crazy. We'd talk into the night about philosophy, sociology, and politics. She fed me books on W.E.B. Du Bois, Che Guevara, and Malcom X. Even though she was three years older than I was, it was clear that she was mature beyond her age. There's not that many twenty-two-year-old women in South Jamaica that are beautiful and smart.

Over the past couple of months, I hadn't been on the block as much; I'd just lost the taste for it. Especially since Sincere got knocked last month, now he's doing a stint on the island, and things had gotten tense on the block. I knew it would catch up with me though, and the sight of King and Breeze walking up to my door wasn't a good sign. I ran to the basement to get my shit. I checked the clip, slapped the magazine back in, and cocked the chamber. Fear rushed through my body, and I realized that I hadn't carried my gun since the shoot-out at the club. Most of my time had been spent with Zane, and I would never expose her to this part of my life. I tucked the pistol in my jeans and covered the grip with my t-shirt before I opened the door.

"Hey wassup, King? What up, Breeze?" I wasn't sure what they wanted, but I can tell you through all the years I been fuckin with these cats, I can count on one hand how many times they'd been by my crib. When you're dealing with a paranoid fucker like King, you never know what he's thinking. Does he think I was part of the conspiracy to have him killed at the club? Does he think I snitched on him to help Sin's case? I don't know, but that's why I had my joint cocked at the ready in case this shit got ugly.

"What the hell you was doing, I been knockin at your door for ten minutes." King looked me up and down and then gazed over my shoulder into the house.

"I was sleeping, had to brush my teeth, didn't want to come to the door with the dragon." I searched their faces for a reaction.

"I hadn't seen you on the block for awhile and Breeze tells me you haven't been puttin in work. Now you suppose to be one of my top niggas. What am I suppose to think when you disappear on me like this?"

"Nah, I spoke to you a while back about me going back to school. That pretty much has been taking up most my time."

"The fuck I look like the United Negro College Fund! You ain't here for no school, you here to put work in, and now that ya brother's locked up you need be pickin up the slack."

The fear had left my body, and all that was left was rage and resentment. "Put work in? Nigga, all me and my brother been doing for the last five years is puttin in work for you. Don't even come at me like that, I'm not one of these newborn soldiers, I done made money for you and spilled blood for you. I ain't never get rich off this shit; you did! I stacked my chips enough to pay for college so I figure we even, no love lost. That shit that happen with Boogie is long and gone and at this point you have as much dirt on me as I have on you…so it's over!"

King charged at me in the doorway and we locked grips. "Nothing's over! It ain't over 'til I say it's over!"

We both reached for our guns, but Breeze jumped between us and grabbed our arms to prevent us from drawing our pistols. "Hold up! There ain't no need to take it there. I'm sure we can work something out." Breeze pulled King back and stepped toward me.

"Now, Angel, what is it that you want? What, you not fuckin with us anymore?"

"Listen B, things is getting crazy out here. Sincere got knocked on a gun charge, the shootout at the club was fucked, and we still don't know who the hell was behind that. I'm just saying it's time for me to get out."

King released a sarcastic exhale. "Well, baby boy, that's not altogether true. While you was running around with your pretty new girlfriend, word got back about who set us up at the club." My heart dropped when he mentioned Zane. Fear and anger rushed through me. The threat of Zane finding out about this life made me physically sick. My jaws clenched. King noticed the disgust in my face. "Oh, you didn't think I knew about your little slice of cake, huh. Yeah, she's a pretty lil' thang. You should know there's nothing that goes down in my hood that I don't know about. And if you like that, you're gonna love this. The hit at the club…ya boy Jazz was behind that." My expression turned to confusion. "Yeah, I have a little bird at the precinct who told me that them bodies they dragged out the club was linked back to Jazz's crew," King said in an arrogant tone.

"That's bullshit!" I didn't want to say why I thought it was bullshit. I always tried to downplay our friendship.

Why would Jazz order a hit on King if he knew I would be caught in the crossfire? My mind scrambled to make sense of it. And where was King going with this? He knew I wanted out the game, and despite my attempts to shadow my friendship with Jazz, King was aware that we were close. He knew at this point that any plans of retaliation could get back to Jazz.

"No, it's no bullshit, Angel. It was your boy that put that hit together, and being that the jury is still out on you you're gonna help me take him out."

"What! Nigga, you crazy. Are you forgetting I'm the one that shot up half the freakin club so we could get our asses out of there alive?" But I could see in King's eyes that none of that mattered. "Look, I told you I'm done with this."

"No, you're not done. You're not done at all." King stepped

toward me and closed the door I kept cracked open behind me. "Ya see, if you don't take Jazz out…that pretty little girlfriend of yours won't make it to walk down that aisle for graduation."

My body went numb. My first instinct was to put my gun to his head and blow his brains out. I fought to push the thought out of my head. Images of Zane flashed through my mind, and my eyes filled up with tears. I looked at Breeze, who was the only person who'd check King if he went too far, but he didn't.

"Don't fuck with me, 'A,' I want this thing done and I want it done soon. You're the only one that can get close to Jazz. You do this and you're free, free to leave the streets, free to be all you can be at that bullshit city college…" I strained not to let a tear flow from my eye. "…and don't worry, while you're putting in work, I'll keep an eye on that pretty little slice of cake of yours."

They walked away, got in their cars, and drove off. I collapsed in the doorway. I felt so defeated. I knew King was serious about taking Jazz out, and I knew he was crazy enough to hurt Zane if I didn't comply. I had to think of something; I had to get to Zane and make sure she was safe.

Scene Nine

I debated with myself in the cab ride over to Zane's house. Should I tell her about King's threats? Should I tell her about me being a drug dealer, a criminal, and a murderer? Should I tell her what had happened at the club? I didn't say much over the phone, but she could hear the stress in my voice. I said I needed to see her.

I couldn't allow Zane to be affected by my sins. She was different; she was better than this place. She didn't belong in my world. She was naive to the evils of the streets, and I had to protect her from that. Who was I kidding, I was madly in love with this woman, and I was sure she had love for me. All the time we spent together became more than we bargained for. In the beginning, she said she didn't want to get involved and I tried to respect her boundaries by not acting on the love I felt for her, but what do I do when I know she shares my love? She wasn't aware that I noticed the times she gazed at me when I wasn't looking, the way she let her guard down and let me into her heart. The times I hugged her goodbye and she melted in my arms. I wanted so badly to kiss her lips and tell her how I felt, but I knew I would eventually hurt her. If she knew the truth about me, she would never forgive me.

"Fifteen dollars," the cab driver demanded. The sound of the doors locking snapped me out of my deep thoughts. I focused my sight outside the car window into the Queens Village neighborhood. I had never been in this area before; every house had a manicured lawn and a driveway that led to a backyard. I double-checked the address and paid the man. I barely closed the door before he pulled off. I took a second to gather my thoughts and couldn't help but notice that the stars shone brighter on this side of Queens. This was a true suburb. I started to realize how Zane could be so out of touch with what went on in my world.

I knocked on the side door that led to her basement apartment. She once told me that her mother owned the house and rented her the basement, although I doubted she actually paid rent.

I was almost surprised that she answered the door. "Angel, come in." I made my way down the narrow staircase onto a carpeted floor. "Have a seat. Can I get you something to drink?"

"No, no thank you." I sunk into the Italian leather sofa and surveyed her apartment. I took notice to the African artifacts that hung on the walls, her stacked bookshelves that were no doubt the source of the books she fed me. My eyes settled on a framed picture of her and her father when she was a kid. It suddenly dawned on me that I was here to totally disrupt this girl's life. What I needed to tell her and warn her against was too horrific... what the hell was I doing here?

"Listen, Zane, I'm sorry for coming over here like this, so late and everything."

"No, it's okay, Angel. You sounded really upset over the phone. What's on your mind?"

"No, this is not a good idea." I got up to walk away and she grabbed my arm and pulled me close to her. I looked down at her and she was shorter than I remembered. She was dressed in a bathrobe and socks, and the scent of her hair drove me crazy. She pulled me back down to the sofa.

"So, how you doing, you okay?" I said in a sad attempt to change the subject.

"Now I know you didn't come all the way over here at one o'clock in the morning to ask me how I was doing." We both smiled.

"I need to tell you something, Zane." My expression flattened.

"So say it."

I paused and dropped my head. "I can't do this anymore... we...can't do this anymore."

Her smiled dropped from her face and her eyes watered up. "What are you talking about, Angel?"

"You know what I'm talking about. Us, being together all the time. Hanging out every day. It's becoming too much." I knew I had to push her away; it was the only way to protect her.

"Why are you talking like this? I don't understand. I thought..."

"I'm confused!...I just...I don't know what to do, every time we're together, I struggle with the truth."

"The truth? What truth?"

"The truth that I'm not the guy you think you know; college classes, trips to the museum, walks in the park. Zane, none of that is me; shit, I don't even recognize that person. Being around you, you showed me a person I could be; a person I want to be, but it's not the truth. I don't know, ma, we're just from two different worlds."

"You always say that, what does that mean?" she said in frustration.

"I've done a lot of bad things in my life, and I'm not exactly through the worst of it yet."

"Whatever you've done, Angel, it's in the past now and whatever you're going through I'll be there for you. And you're wrong, baby, you are the man I know…" She picked my head up to meet her eyes and put her hand on my cheek. "You have to be that man…because that's the man I fell in love with." A single tear ran down her face.

She moved closer into me, still stroking my face she led me to her lips. She quivered when I embraced her body and slowly massaged her tongue with mine. I kissed her deeply as she sucked on my bottom lip. Her mouth was so warm, it made my erection throb for her. She peeled off my shirt and I untied her robe; it slid off her body, and all that was left were her share bra and panties. Her breasts protruded out of her bra, and her flat stomach made her hips more pronounced. She took my hand and led me to the bedroom as we left a trail of clothing behind. My heart raced as if I'd never had sex before. I laid her on the quilt and moved down to the foot of the bed, sliding her socks off and gently kissing her toes, feet, and ankles. I took my time working my way up her leg and thigh. She moaned and caressed the back of my head as I brushed by her vagina with my mouth. I parted her lips with my tongue and her hips began to gyrate involuntarily. The deeper my tongue went, the more she gyrated. I sucked her lips and she gasped and released a deep exhale. I gently wrapped my lips and tongue around her clit and sucked rhythmically. She screamed out, moaned, gyrated…

"Oh my god… Oh my god…Angel…uh, uh, uh, uh." Her

grip on my head tightened. "Ohh, uhh, uhh…uhhhhhhh!" She let out an orgasmic scream.

My mouth made its way over her pelvis, belly button, and onto her dark supple nipples. She gripped my back as I engulfed her breast. She parted her legs and I accepted her invitation. Our eyes locked as I entered into her paradise. Her grip tightened as she whispered, "I'm scared, Angel…"

I held her tight and let her feel all of me inside of her. Without saying a word, she knew I would never let anything happen to her. Our deep strokes became more intense. She turned me on my back and straddled me, her beautiful hair cascaded over her face, and I felt myself about to explode. I let out a manly groan and she cried out for mercy. "Please!"

My phallus reached her spot and she shook with every stroke. As I climaxed, she released her orgasm and collapsed into my arms. We lay in each other's arms, and for that time I left my world behind…no streets, no death, and no King….

Scene Ten

I woke up to the sounds of eggs and bacon crackling in the frying pan. From the bed, I could see Zane in her small kitchen chefn' up some breakfast. I sat up and inhaled the aroma reminding me so much of Sunday mornings at Mama's house. I made my way to the kitchen and hugged her from behind. "I hope that ain't no pork bacon 'cause you know I don't be messing with that swine."

"No, Malcom X, it's turkey bacon," she cracked.

She smelled incredible. Her fresh scent was of a woman who'd just gotten out the shower, and her hair was still damp. She turned from the oven and pecked me on the lips.

"I left a towel, wash cloth, and toothbrush in the bathroom for you. Why don't you go clean up and I'll have breakfast ready when you get out?"

"Okay, ma, thanks." I looked in her eyes. "You know I love you, right?" I placed a kiss on her forehead and walked to the bathroom.

"And, oh, baby?" she called out. I turned in the bathroom doorway. "Make sure you use that toothbrush." She shook her head and gave me the stinky face.

We both broke into laughs. "You are a funny lady. Just make sure my eggs are fried hard, okay, Florida Evans?"

The shower washed over me but couldn't wash away the guilt I felt for not telling Zane that she was in danger.

How irresponsible could I be?

I tried to reason with myself that I could keep her safe. I could figure this out before things got ugly. I knew King wouldn't let me out the game unless I took Jazz out. King was notorious for making other people do his dirty work and for following through on his threat if they didn't comply. I had to think…had to make the right move here. First things first—I had to speak to Jazz. I needed to look him in the eyes and see if he was behind the hit at the club.

King was right—I was the only person that could get close to Jazz, but by now I was sure word had gotten back to him about the plot to retaliate. Shit, for all I knew this could be suicide going to Jazz's spot. He wasn't the type to ask questions first.

South Jamaica Housing Projects, a.k.a. Forty Projects, was a war zone. It wasn't a place you wanted to be unless you had to. These were the type of projects that made mutha fuckers in the hood be like "Damn this shit is ghetto." Bitches hanging out the window talkin' shit, kids playing in the streets with no freakin' parents in sight. One time I came out here and saw a baby in a freakin' walker going to the corner store by himself. Shit is crazy! Goddamn crackheads fighting with their ole lady in the staircase. It wasn't anything I wasn't used to, but it always hit a nerve. For Jazz it was good business, and was the reason why he converted one of the apartments into his office. He would always say, "Once you lose touch of the streets, the streets will end up touching you."

He had soldiers posted up in the lobby and hallway leading to his office. He could've easily had me taken out once I got in the building, so I figured since I made it to the door he was willing to talk. Before I knocked, the door bust open and one of his goons pulled me into the apartment. He pushed me against the wall and patted me down. He found the .380 Ruger in my belt holster and tucked it into his jacket. He turned me face forward and pushed me toward the hallway that led to the back room. I passed a room that was fully converted into an office, furnished with a big oak desk, computer, file cabinets, and an oversized leather chair with his name, "Jazz," inscribed onto it. There was no one in the office, and the sounds of weights clanging drew me to the room farthest to the back. This room was converted into a gym; the walls were lined with mirrors, which reflected the workout set, treadmill, and stationary bike. Jazz was on the bench pushin' what looked to be about 250 lbs. One of his boys was spotting him as he pushed up his last rep and mounted the weights. He sat up and wiped the sweat from his face. "Angel, what the hell you doing here, man?" Jazz said in an eerily calm voice.

"You know why I'm here," I said in frustration.

"Oh yeah, ya here to kill me, right?" he said sarcastically.

"Don't fuck with me, Jazz! Did you put that hit out on King or what?"

"So you're here on his behalf."

"No, I'm here on my fucking behalf, now tell me, did you put that hit out?"

Jazz walked to the window and turned his back to me. His posture slumped and he said in an apologetic tone, "You weren't supposed to be there…you or Sincere. I know Sincere don't really fuck with me like that, but I still wouldn't want him caught up in that shit. Despite how he feels I still have love for him; we all came up together, Angel. I just got some bad information. The word was that King and Breeze was gonna be at that club alone, maybe a couple of new soldiers, but not you."

And then it hit me. I wasn't supposed to be there. My mind went back to that time, and it all started coming together like the last pieces in a jigsaw puzzle. Me and Sin had hopped in the cars at the last minute that night. We'd planned to make a run out of town, but a couple of the new soldiers made the trip. Breeze had suggested they go instead of us, and it was Breeze who said we should hang out at the club that night. What the hell was going on?

"Breeze?" I asked with a confused look on my face. Jazz looked away with a guilty expression and ordered his soldiers out of the room.

Memories flashed through my mind of Breeze preventing Boogie and his crew from torturing a young Jeff on that pole, Breeze driving him to the hospital, vouching for Jeff and paying for his medical bills. The times I'd visited him in the hospital, I remembered seeing Breeze in the hallway but never put it together.

"Breeze approached me when I was still a kid," Jazz explained. "The time I was in the hospital. I was still recovering from what Boogie and his crew did to me…and…I was full of anger and vengeance and he used it. He used it to manipulate me into carrying out his deeds to achieve what he called his master plan."

"Master plan?"

"Yeah, Breeze outlined a plan to take out his own boss."

"King! But why?"

Jazz began to break it down to me. "He would first help build King's empire and at the same time be my advisor and silent partner. He fueled the rivalry between King and me. Hooked me up with my drug connects and basically taught me the game."

"So Breeze was playing both sides of the fence, but why? What did he have to gain? What was his play in all of this?" The more it was explained to me, the more questions I had.

"Breeze's plan from the beginning was to take out King once our business got big enough to rival his. After King was dead, we would combine forces and take over the city. Ya see, King would never allow Breeze to start up his own and become his competition. That's why he secretly backed me. King would have him killed if he ever caught wind of it. He knew Breeze was too valuable; Breeze was the brains behind the whole operation. Angel, always remember the true power of an empire never lies in its king, it's the puppet master that pulls his strings who really has control."

"Okay, Aristotle, if you knew he was pulling King's strings, didn't you figure he was doing the same to you?"

"Not at first. Like I said, I was just a kid getting more money than I'd ever seen in my life. After my uncle was killed…"

"Killed? I thought he died in the house fire?"

"Yeah, killed." Jazz let out a deep breath as if preparing to relieve himself of a deep, dark secret. "Back then Breeze got word that the cops were on to me about killing Boogie and Shakim."

"Damn, so you did kill 'em dudes." Jazz gave me a look like I should've known better. "I don't know, nigga, I thought it was an urban myth or some shit like that!"

"Anyway, Breeze knew detectives were on their way to question my uncle about what Crackhead Brenda told them. He told me I had to get rid of my uncle, it was the only way and he was right. My uncle would've sold me out for a bag of chips and a quarter-water. But when it came time to do it I couldn't, I couldn't even bring myself to walk in the house. I just stood there in front of the gate. Breeze must have followed and been watching me because he came out of nowhere, snatched the key from my hand, and went in. I heard some scuffling and Breeze came out a few minutes later. He knocked my uncle out and set the house on fire to cover it up. I was numb; I must have been in shock because I just sat on the curb until the fire trucks came."

It was all finally making sense to me. "So you killed Brenda to finish the job. With Brenda dead, the cops had no connection to you and the murders."

Jazz picked up a dumbbell and started curling it. "Ever since then we had this secret partnership. So when he said it was the right time to hit King, my only concern was to make sure you and Sincere was nowhere around when it went down. But rather than making sure you wasn't there, he made it his business to make sure that you were."

I walked to the window and gazed into the courtyard. "So he figured me and Sin would get taken out along with King." It hit me like a ton of bricks. "But what the fuck do I give a damn if he took King down; the hell with it!"

"Unfortunately Sincere didn't feel the same way. He made the mistake of telling Breeze of his intentions of one day taking over when King stepped down. That's all it took to sign his death warrant, and Breeze knew there was no way he could take Sincere out without taking you out too."

"Listen, Jazz, I'm done. I told King that I'm out the game."

"Yeah I heard, but with one exception. You have to kill me first, huh? Either that or he'll go after your girl, right? So what's your plan, Cochise?"

I stepped toward Jazz to look him in his eyes. "My only concern is Zane. If I have to kill King to keep her safe, then so be it."

I walked out, heading toward the front room where his crew was at. I spotted the cat that patted me down and took my hammer. He threw me a tough look and stepped in my path, blocking the exit. In one motion I grabbed his jacket, swept his foot, and slammed him on the floor. I dug in his jacket and grabbed my hammer. "Thanks for babysitting my bitch!"

Jazz's crew jumped to their feet at the same time Jazz entered the room. His expression was enough to cool them out. As I was leaving Jazz called out, "Angel...I'm sorry about your shoulder."

I paused but didn't turn around. "Listen, be careful with Breeze. You don't know him like I do...he's one sick son of a bitch!" I continued walking down the corridor. I knew our friendship would never be the same after this day, and he knew it too.

When I got home, Sincere was sitting in the living room as if he were waiting for me.

"What the hell! Sin, when did you...how the hell you get out?" The crib was uncharacteristically empty.

"That's not important right now, what's important is that I'm out." We embraced like two brothers back from separate wars. We talked for hours over a half-gallon of Henessy. He joked about shit that happened to him on the island, and I got him up to date with the streets.

"So what's this I hear about some college girl got your nose wide open." He grinned and took a sip of the VSOP.

"You gotta meet her, bra, she's the truth. She ain't like no other chick from this hood…she's an amazing woman."

Sin almost choked on his drink from laughing. "Now I know you're whipped. She got you using words like 'Amazing.' And now you're taking college courses?"

"I'll tell you what else too," I said in satisfaction.

"Yeah, what's that?"

"I'm out the game. I'm out for good."

Sin looked away as if he was disappointed and offered no response.

"What?" I barked in frustration. I wanted to tell him about the set up at the club, Breeze's secret alliance with Jazz, and King's death threats toward Zane. But I knew that would send him on a rampage, and that's one thing I didn't need right now. I was trying to do some damage control, and I didn't want Sin running crazy in the streets.

"You wasn't built for this life anyway, 'A,'" Sin replied, as if it took some time for him to accept it. "You're a smart dude, and if anybody could make it outta this shit it's you."

"That's where ya wrong, bra…we can both make it out."

"Nah, not this time, 'A.' All I got is these streets, and this game is my life. Besides, they got me dead in the wrong on these gun charges so I'm looking at three to five easy. Nah, bra, you go ahead. You make things right with your honey, she sounds like a good girl. You make sure she never finds out how we grew up, she won't understand."

Sincere had his own demons to exercise. What he didn't tell me was that King was the one who'd bailed him out of jail on the condition that he take out Jazz. King knew I would never go up against Jazz, so he promised Sin he'd let me loose if he did this one thing. It wasn't anything that my brother wouldn't do for me, and King knew it. What did Sin care? He figured he'd never liked Jazz in the first place, but getting close enough to kill him wouldn't be easy.

I couldn't keep this secret from Zane any longer. Every shred of common sense told me not to tell her, but I knew I couldn't go on deceiving her like this. By this time I'd been spending most of my time over at her crib, and she had been dropping hints that she wanted me to move in. Things were getting serious, and I needed to come clean.

I sat on the couch watching an episode of *The Honeymooners* while Zane lay in my arms. "Zane, we have to talk…"

"Talk? Talk about what?" Her voice cracked and she tried to conceal her concern.

"Sit up."

Her expression changed from concern to being upset. She paused, then took a deep breath. "Is this the part where you tell me that things are moving too fast and you think we need some space?" She cocked her head to the side and tightened her lips.

"No. This is the part where I tell you about my life…"

So I told her everything, from the time I witnessed Boogie's murder when I was a kid to the shoot-out at the club. I explained Breeze's plan to take over the drug game in Queens, and how he set my brother and me up to be killed. I told her that I tried to get out, but I knew King would keep his promise to have her killed. The more I told the story, the more fear filled her face. I dug in my jacket and put the hammer on the table.

The sound of the barrel hitting the glass startled her. She gasped. "Angel, what…"

"Listen, I want you to know I would never let anyone hurt you." I grabbed the hammer by the grip, ejected the cartridge, pulled back the action, and discharged the live round. "Here…I want you to hold this." Holding the barrel end I handed her the gun, but she just looked at me in shock.

"I can't take that."

"Why?"

"Baby, what's going on? Are you serious…this is too much…" She tried to accept it, and I could see that she tried to make sense of all that I'd told her. That was her beauty; she made sense of everything that was in her life…including me. But this was one thing that was not to be reasoned. In the streets it is what it is, for no rhyme or reason. I saw that it weighed heavy on her soul as she soaked it all in. The look on her face told me that despite all the madness, she was gonna stay by my side and hold me down. I had my doubts before, but women have this Geronimo quality about them when it comes to men that they're in love with; it's almost maternal in that way.

I laid the gun back on the table. "There is another option." I couldn't take her down this road. As quick as she decided to go all out for me was how swiftly it dawned on me to sacrifice us…our love…our relationship to assure her safety. I looked at her beautiful face as if it was for the first time and felt a rush of guilt for allowing her to be pulled into this unforgiving world of mine.

I grabbed the hammer, the clip, and left the round on the table. For some crazy reason, I wanted to leave something behind for her to remember me by. I threw on my jacket and darted toward the door without finishing my thought, with every intention to never come back. At first Zane just sat there with no expression, no doubt wrestling with the thought to stop me or let me leave. A part of me wanted her to stop me, but I knew it had to be this way. When I got to the door she was on me, grabbing at my leather Pelle Pelle jacket. She spun me around and looked up into my eyes with her intimidating glare. "You said there was another option…what is it?" She pierced through my eyes into my soul.

"There's no other option, baby…this is the only way…I have to deal with my demons alone."

"No, there is another way!" she barked in a chastising tone. "You can just leave it behind…just leave it all behind, baby. You don't owe them your life, you don't owe them anything. Stay here with me until the semester's done and we can work on getting a bigger place together, somewhere far from Queens." She wrapped her arms around my body and held me tight. My jacket engulfed her frame, and I rested my face on the top of her silky hair.

I whispered, "But Sincere…my brother…"

"I know you love him, Angel, but give him some time…soon he will see…"

"You don't know Sin; you don't know how we grew up."

"Baby, I don't care about your past, but I do care about your future…our future. The man I know…the man I love with all my heart…is the real Victor Johnson, you have to leave the boy behind." She stepped back to gauge my attention. "Life is like a book, sweetie…and now it's your time to move on to the next chapter." She slid my jacket off, reached into the small of my back, pulled the gun from my jeans and placed it on the end table. We made love that night, and I say love because for the first time in my life I felt the difference between having sex and making love....who am I kidding...this woman had me sprung.

We lay in bed with the moonlight painting our naked bodies blue, and I felt at peace—a peace I have never felt or thought possible. I have had sex with my share of women, but with Zane it was different. For a long time I believed I was incapable of expressing love, let alone receiving it. Emotionally I was broken, and the streets contributed to my detachment. For years I'd buried a secret so ominous, so disturbing that at times I thought it was just some terrible nightmare. I looked over to Zane. "Angel, what's wrong, baby?" Without explanation I unleashed demons that had eaten at me since I was a kid.

I knew when I decided to tell my story, I would have to revisit a hell I'd long ago buried deep inside my soul. A hell that always lay right beneath my surface. A wise person once told me that you can only bury your demons for so long before they pull you down; before you can truly move on, you must cleanse your soul....

Throughout my years at Mama's house, foster children would come and go; some were adopted and became family, and others were too broken to stay. Like I said before, every child bared their own demons, which were manifested into several behaviors: anger, isolation, promiscuity, pyromania, pedophilia, etc. As a child there's no way to process these things; you just adapt to your environment with no conception of how it would affect you in the future.

It was '84 when he came to the house. We all ran to the top of the staircase to peek down at the new kid. To us it was a new playmate, and depending on whether it was a girl or boy strengthened the battle of the sexes. We would always argue over who would have the TV, what shows to watch, or what games to play, so a new arrival was a big thing. Our anticipation became a quick disappointment when we realized he wasn't in our age group. This happened sometimes. Mama would get somebody that was close to aging out of the foster care system, and as a favor she would take them in for the agency. But even though he was older, he turned out to fit in just fine. He was quick to crack a joke and flash a funny face. He'd even play hide-and-go-seek with us.

His name was Robert Taylor. He was nineteen when he was transferred to Mama's house and had been in foster care since he was three. He was tall, dark with a slim build, and at first glance seemed to be the coolest dude ever. He sported shell tops, Lee jeans, BVD shirt, and a red Kangoo. This was pretty impressionable to a nine-year-old kid during the birth of the Hip-Hop era. I couldn't wait to step out into the hood with him; as far as I was concerned, he was fam now. Me and Black Rob, a nickname he quickly coined, hung out all the time. He taught me moves on the basketball court, gave me tips on how to pop locks, and was the funniest cat on the block. On my block, being funny was a necessity; I've seen kids go home in tears off of "Yo mama" jokes, and with Black Rob around, cats knew not to go there. It wasn't long before I began to emulate Rob; I dressed like him, talked like him, and acted like him. Finally, there was a normal dude in this crazy ass house.

With twelve kids, three aunts, three uncles, and Mama, the rooms were stacked. The girls had the attic and the boys shared a room with two bunk beds. We all loved to hang out on Rob's top bunk; he always had cool shit to do like G.I. Joe's, Marvel comics, and a box with a cassette player. We would all stay up late after curfew and go to sleep wherever we passed out at. This night was no different than any other night, other than that I ended up passing out on Rob's bed. It's the innocence of a child, the naïve manner and trusting heart of a kid...and then it happened. The one thing that would change my world forever, the moment I left my childhood as I knew it behind and would have to carry this evil inside me for the rest of my life.

He touched me...the way a man should never touch a boy.

Was I imagining this? Was I having a nightmare?

His grip was so deliberate...please let this be a mistake?

I turned over to protect my penis from any other mistaken brushes, but he touched me again. My heart pounded through the bunk bed. He placed his hand on my back and slid it down to my ass. I was terrified. I cracked my eyes open to see if maybe he was just dreaming, but as my pupils adjusted to the dark I could see Rob stroking himself as he touched me. I tried to pull away, but I couldn't move. My first thought was to hop out of the bed and run to Mama, but I was paralyzed with fear. This can't be happening. My nine-year-old mind struggled to understand what was going on, and I experienced confusion I never had nor would I ever feel again. Why was he doing this? I wanted to scream out but I didn't; I just lay there as he felt me up and finished his business.

Over the next few months, the molestation continued and became more intense. It became as common as a parent reading their child a bedtime story. I would never really fall asleep, and when I did I'd wake up to feel his hands in my pajamas or his penis rubbing on me. Day and night became two different worlds for me. During the day, life would go on as if nothing ever happened. He would revert back to the guy everyone liked and wanted to be around, and the night when everyone slept he was this predator that snuffed out every bit of innocence I had. I became so preoccupied with anxiety as day transitioned into night. My fear turned to rage, but strangely enough not towards Rob; ironically, I felt some sort of sick love for him. Not an intimate love, but a love one would have for their big brother. I looked up to him and didn't want to disappoint him. So I succumbed to the abuse and it became part of me. It was the only way my young mind could cope. But I still had anger and resentment toward the ones who were supposed to protect me and keep me safe from this living hell.

How could they not see what was going on? Could they not see it in my face…did they not hear it in my voice?

Maybe they just didn't care…maybe this was all my fault.

The episodes began to extend into the day. So now even the light offered no protection. Rob would coax me into the closet. "Little Angel," he would call me. "Come here, I wanna show you something." He would promise me things as he laid me on top of him and trained me how to hump him through his sweat pants. "Don't worry, Little Angel, I'ma gechu some G.I. Joe's… I'ma gechu Incredible Hulk…Don't worry…Don't worry, Little Angel…" He'd let me off of him when his pants got wet, and sometimes I would go to the bathroom and throw up Mama's breakfast. These were very dark moments in my life; most of the memories are blacked out, so I'm not sure what was the extent of the abuse. I just knew it wouldn't be long before I broke.

Over the next couple of years, it pushed my appetite for sex into overdrive. The abuse mixed with puberty was too much for me to handle. I would sneak into the attic into one of the girls' beds and violate them. I would touch their newly developed bodies and hump them through their piss-stained panties, my behavior compelled by the molestation. I needed to be reassured of my sexuality, I was so overwhelmed with guilt and confusion; I was so fucked up. This can't be right; this can't be the life of an eleven-year-old kid. I would study my friends, look 'em in the eyes, and search their face for that imprint of hell. Was this normal? Did this go on in their house? Why were they so happy? I wanted that happiness…I needed it. I would sleep over at my friend's house to escape and feel how it would be to be normal. One day I asked, "Ms. Williams, can I come and live with you?" She looked down at me, and with the most loving and sincere face she said, "Why, what's wrong, sweetie, you don't like where you live?" I wanted so much to tell her about my demons…about my fear of the night…about the circus of drugs, alcohol, and molestation at Mama's house. But I didn't. I sat there and looked at the world through jaded eyes. "Angel? You okay, sweetie… What is it, baby?" she spoke in her Southern belle accent. "You know you can talk to Ms. Williams… What's bothering you child?…"

Throughout the next year I did my best to avoid Black Rob, which isn't easy when you share a room with the son of a bitch. I took to the streets and spent more time there than at Mama's house. I stayed out late and became a student of the ghetto. I kicked it with the old heads and did my little dirt with the crew. One day when I got home from school, Black Rob's bed was stripped down and his dresser was empty—he was gone. And just like that, it was over. No more dirty promises, no more hiding, no more fear.

Sincere had clocked Jazz's routine for the past couple of weeks and felt confident about when and where he could strike.

Up to this point, he'd managed to conceal the fact that he was home from jail, which is damn near impossible to do in the hood. The hard part was trying to follow Jazz without being noticed. If he was gonna knock off Jazz, there were only two ways to do it: One, run up on him amongst his crew and start blastin, which gives you the element of surprise, and if you're lucky you'll get a kill shot off before one of his boys blows your head off, or two, find the weak link and figure out where he's most vulnerable in order to get in close enough for the kill and get out without getting detected. Sin opted for the second option.

Every Friday afternoon at 2 pm sharp, Jazz would enter Nu Tribe barbershop on the avenue for his weekly cut. Even though the shop was flooded he never waited; his appointments were locked. Nu Tribe is famous for attracting many politicians, business moguls, and celebrities, and their autographed portraits were displayed evenly throughout the shop. Anyone who was anyone got their hair cut at Nu Tribe, and that included powerful kingpins such as Jazz. The shop was part of the shopping mall, which offered two entrances, one from the street and another door on the opposite side of the shop that led directly into the mall.

Once Jazz stepped into the shop, he was greeted with pounds and hugs from the barbers and dudes from the hood waiting their turn to get in the chair. The owner came from the back to say, "What's up?" and make conversation, most likely about how Jazz was a good dude, and if he chose to he could make something out of himself if he went legit. Jazz flattered old man Simmons for the umpteenth time. He knew he didn't mean no harm, and for nothing else he respected old man Simmons for employing countless dudes from the hood and for being an all-out hustler…

on a legitimate level. Jazz settled into the barber's chair, not having to mention that he wanted a light taper with a two against. Music bleared through the speakers while dudes cracked jokes and told hood stories, never noticing the ominous figure standing outside the door leading into the mall.

Sin knew this was the only time he could strike without Jazz's soldiers being around, although they weren't far. They sat outside the door leading to the street and routinely played chess on a couple of crates perched up against the shop's plate glass window until Jazz finished his cut. Sin gave 'em some time to settle into their game and for the barber to start lining up Jazz's beard, when he would have to pull his head back to allow a sharp lineup. The time was now; Sin slid his hoodie over his head, pulled the drawstrings to cover his face, adjusted his dark shades, and gripped the hunting knife inside the pouch of his hoodie. He waited for the barber to spin the chair so Jazz's back would be facing him. Sin swiftly came through the door, and before anyone could realize that this wasn't a joke Sin had pistol-whipped the barber and wrapped his arm around Jazz's already exposed neck. He whispered something to Jazz before slitting his throat from ear to ear. He waved the nickel-plated nine at the few women in the shop who were screaming, and they quickly shut up. Sin backed out of the shop as swiftly as he'd entered and glimpsed at Jazz's bloody body jerking in the chair like a fish out of water. The word in the street was that Sin was in and out of the barbershop in less than sixty seconds. A cold-blooded killer…

Scene Eleven

King's ego couldn't stand for what he felt was a blatant disrespect to him. It had been a few weeks since our conversation about the terms of me getting out the game, and I hadn't been anywhere to be found. The fact that King got Sin out of jail to make the hit was irrelevant; it was the principle. I was given orders and didn't follow through. He knew I would never follow through on killing Jazz, but that wasn't the point—he could have gotten anyone to do that. King knew he had to give me an impossible ultimatum so I wouldn't leave. He viewed it as a sign of weakness in his so-called empire for me to leave the crew, especially now that mutha fuckers were trying to kill him. He couldn't stand the sense that things were falling apart around him: Sin getting locked up, me jumping ship, and Breeze ain't been acting the same since the club incident. He had to pull ranks—this wasn't the time to show weakness. He scanned the room and spotted Breeze just out the doorway on his cell phone; he appeared agitated. It bothered King that Breeze was seemingly involved in some other business that he was keeping from him. He was beggining to think that Breeze had something to do with the hit at the club, but he tried to remind himself of his paranoid nature and pushed those thoughts out of his mind.

From across the crowded store, Breeze finally turned around to allow King to make eye contact with him. King motioned for him to come over to the back of the counter. Breeze abruptly ended his call and pushed his way through the kids bunched up around the arcades. King buzzed him through the door and waited for it to slam in back of him.

"Have you heard from Angel?" he asked, already knowing the answer.

"Nah, I haven't heard nothing. A couple of people said they seen him on the campus, but other than that nothing."

King's temper fueled. He felt disrespected, ignored, and more so than anything else…powerless. He looked up at Breeze from his oversized chair. "I want you to find that pretty little bitch of his and bring her to me." He spun his chair halfway around and gazed out the window. "Angel is gonna come see me one way or another…."

With King's back turned to him, Breeze looked down on him with malice. He thought to himself that he could kill him right here and now and be done with it. He'd just got the wire that Sincere had taken care of Jazz at the barbershop, and with King out of the way, he could finally combine the two empires he'd worked on for years to build. But he knew better; over the years, Sincere had positioned himself to be as much the predecessor to King as he was. The thought angered him but was quickly replaced with a sly grin…he had plans for Sincere.

Detective Mills stood there staring at Jazz's bludgeoned body slumped in the barber's chair. Crime scene photographers snapped shots, and rookie detectives along with uniforms took statements from potential witnesses. A perimeter was set up outside as a crowd gathered around the window, trying to catch a glimpse of what was sure to be the hottest wire on the street. He couldn't pull his focus off the enormous gash that was so severe it slumped Jazz's head in an unnatural position. The force it must have took to cut clear through to the spine sent an unfamiliar feeling of nausea to Mills' stomach. One of the rookie detectives made his way over to Mills after interviewing a few of the witnesses. This immediately pissed Mills off. Any seasoned cop would know not to fuck with him while he was reviewing a crime scene.

Don't approach him…don't call him…and for damn sure don't talk to him. This was his process. He needed to block out everything to hear what the crime scene was telling him. But I guess this asshole didn't get the memo.

"So, what do you make of it? One of his 'homeboys' came in and pulled a Freddy Krueger?" Mills glanced at him with a frustrated look. It bothered him that the force was making it so easy for these kids to make detective fresh out of the academy. It never would have happened in his day. He looked uncomfortable in his suit, as if the last one he wore was at his high school graduation. The kid still had acne and chewed gum to cover up his halitosis. Mills could tell off the bat that he was the type that could hold a two-way conversation by himself.

"I interviewed four different witnesses, and they all gave different physical descriptions of the perp."

Mills tried his best to block him out and hoped that he would go away. He tried to refocus on the scene; he knew he didn't have much time before they removed the body. Mills remembered Jazz, a.k.a. Jeffery Herns. He remembered the skinny kid was good for the double homicides on Rockaway…and the crackhead that was killed in the project playground. He remembered the way those murders happened and couldn't help but notice the irony.

It was clear that Mills' ignoring him was offending the rookie. "So, Mills, do you even have an opinion on this one?" Mills let out a sigh, as if decompressing from his state of focus. He didn't work narcotics, but he was aware of Jazz's status in the Queens drug ring. And his detective intuitions told him this was only the beginning. He gave the rookie a sharp look. "You want my opinion, kid?"

"Yeah."

"Call your wife; let her know not to expect you home."

"What?"

Mills gave him a pat on the shoulder. "This is far from over…" He walked away, leaving the rookie behind, unsatisfied with what he saw. He knew he had to get ahead of this thing. Homicides in South Queens had nearly doubled in the past year, and the department had been overwhelmed. This one would be put on the shelf quick if there were no leads.

I'd been at Zane's for the past few weeks lying low. It's funny; she'd been taking care of me as a mother would. But it was more like she knew my state of mind needed fixin. She could see it in my eyes: I was anxious to get back to the streets. I didn't trust King, and this shit with Breeze had been eating away at me. It was becoming clear that I was not going to be able to move on until I tied this up.

Zane had been so happy since I decided to stay with her. Her smiles came so easily, and her energy was contagious. It was something about her that made me a better person, or at least try to be. At first I felt like I was imposing on her, but I realized that this was what she wanted…what she needed. Her father left a void that she was searching to fill. Her mother was never around. I had been here damn near a month and hadn't met her moms yet. I could imagine that she had had to pretty much raise herself; she didn't have any siblings, and from what I could see, not many friends either. She believed she had found all those things in me. That was why I loved her so much. I sat there watching her cook my favorite dinner, mashed potatoes, steak, and sweet corn.

She would turn around every now and then and flash that beautiful smile. "Are you hungry?" she yelled over from the kitchen. "You want a plate now or…"

"Girl, you better stop playing I'm starving. I'm so hungry I'm about to come over there and eat you up." Her face lit up and responded with a sly grin. "Well, I would love for you to come over here and try it." I hopped off the couch and into the kitchen, grabbed her from behind, and softly bit on her neck. She pulled away in laughter, turned and hugged me. I could die a thousand deaths and it wouldn't be equivalent to the pain I would feel if I lost Zane.

"Oh, I forgot to tell you Sincere called you earlier while you were at school."

"Oh word, I'm surprised he finally got around to calling his brother, as many messages I left him."

"What's going on with you two?"

"I don't know. Ever since I told him I was getting out the game and going back to school, he's been distant. I been trying to catch up with him, but ain't nobody in the hood seen him."

"Maybe you're just growing apart, baby," she said in a sympathetic voice. "I know it's hard, but you have to let him go…

you're trying to change your life and he's gonna end up bringing you down with him."

I was caught off guard by her words and immediately hated her for what she was saying. I hated myself for subconsciously agreeing with her. "What! What do you know? You don't know how it is. You don't have a brother…or a sister, so where you get off telling me to cut my brother off." I knew she was sensitive about not having siblings, but I just wanted her to feel the dagger of pain I felt. But her tone didn't falter. "Yeah, I don't know about having a brother, but I know about loyalty. I can see it in your eyes, baby, you're so full of loyalty it's blinding you. I would never tell you to cut your family off, but the things he was saying on the phone it just didn't make sense, it was crazy talk…all I'm saying is give 'em some room."

I looked away but I knew her words were sincere. "Yeah, maybe…so what he say?"

"Something about…don't worry he took care of things for you…and…now you can leave the streets behind…" She shook her head with a confused expression.

My mind scrambled to make sense of Sin's message. "Did he say anything else?"

"Uhh…he said something like…fifty-fifty love until the sun burns out… I told you he was talking crazy." My heart dropped as I figured it out. Zane saw right through my expression.

"I gotta go, I gotta find Sin!"

I tried to maintain my composure, but I could see the panic in her face. "What? What is it, baby?"

I rushed to the door and felt bad for a second as I glanced at my untouched plate on the stove.

"What is fifty-fifty love?…"

Halfway out the door, I turned and answered in a reluctant voice, "The love he shows me is the love I show him...until the sun burns out..."

The moment I closed the door behind me, panic filled my body.
Could he really have done it?
Did Sin really kill Jazz?
I knew he was crazy enough to do it; he'd do it for me even if I didn't want it done. In his mind he was sacrificing himself for my passage out of the hood. This was gonna cause a shit storm in the streets. I had to talk to him...who put 'em up to this?... King?... Breeze?... I had to figure out the angles.
The one place I knew I could find Sin was at his shorty's crib, Passion. Passion was your everyday hood rat chick. She just didn't give a fuck; she had a quick tongue and an even faster temper. She'd done cut up her share of bitches in the hood and even buck-fiftied a few niggas in her time. Cats in the streets called her Thug Passion. She would be a halfway decent-looking chick if she carried herself with a little more class, but Sin seemed to dig that raunchy shit. They'd been off and on for years and had a love-hate relationship. One time we were on the block hustlin, and Passion came out there flippin. She found out about some chick he'd been knockin down and was out there buggin. Putting her hands in his face, ripped off his shirt, and I think she even mushed him a couple of times. I told him, "Son, go ahead leave that bitch alone," and he damn near did until she grabbed his cell phone and threw it in the street, breaking it into pieces. He instantly flipped, dragged her ass into the street, and told her to get the hell off the block.He warned her, "If you don't get ya stupid

ass off the block I'ma shoot you!" She cursed him out with that sharp tongue of hers and said she wasn't going anywhere…and just like that…he shot her. Straight up shot her in the leg and made her limp her ass all the way to the hospital. I don't know what was more gangsta—that he shot this chick for being out of pocket, or that she held him down and never told the police what happened.

Passion lived in Baisley Projects, which was the last place I wanted to be, being that King still controlled a few apartments in the same building. But I figured while I was out here, I could catch up with some of my people and find out what was going on in the streets.

I had to bang on Passion's door for damn near fifteen minutes before that chick heard me over the loud-ass music pulsating from her apartment.

"Who is it?!" Passion screamed through the door before looking in the peephole.

"It's Angel…"

"Who?"

"Angel!" The music's volume shot down, there was a long pause, and two minutes later the door swung open.

"Oh, what's up, 'A,' I didn't know that was you."

"Sincere here?" I got right to the point. I didn't want to give her an opportunity to talk my fucking ear off.

"He's in the back…" She looked me up and down as I walked past her into and through the kitchen. Dirty dishes over piled the sink, and a box of cereal was knocked over on the counter. A foul odor came from the garbage as roaches scrambled through it, as if they sensed my presence. The living room was furnished with only a 52' screen television with a Play Station attached to it and a worn sofa pushed to the middle of the floor. The walls were no longer that generic project white. They were stained brown—no doubt from all the weed smoke that was blazed over the years. Children's toys were stacked in the corner beside a treadmill that hadn't been plugged in since The Fat Boys was on tour. I'd been here a hundred times before, but never having felt so disgusted with this place as I did now. I didn't want to be here. I wanted to be back in Queens Village where the streets were clean and the lawns were manicured. The houses were homes filled with families that loved each other and went on vacation to the Bahamas and shit. I wanted to be back in Zane's arms where everything felt right…but I couldn't have that…not right now…not until I finished this. So I pushed those thoughts out of my mind and made my way down the hallway toward the back room. I passed a room where Passion's two kids were squatted on the floor in a trance watching music videos. The strong aroma of that all too familiar chocolate teased my nose. It burned my eyes, and I immediately caught a contact. I knew the aroma originated from Sin pulling on that Sticky. Since I met Zane, I'd stopped smoking. It wasn't a conscious decision to stop, but like I said she's the type of honey that makes a brother wanna do right.

    I stepped into the doorway and leaned against the frame. Sin was laid back in a worn leather reclining chair with his signature twin nines on the end table. The table was littered with blunt guts, seeds from the weed, and a lighter. He tried not to notice me standing there, his glance set on the television playing an old Clint Eastwood western. I was bombarded with emotions and struggled to maintain my demeanor. I was so fucking pissed at him for starting this war—yes war, and nothing short of it. And I was smack dead in the middle. I glanced around the room before my eyes were arrested on him. The bed was just two mattresses stacked on top of each other. The closet doors had been torn off the hinges from wear and tear and exposed all the Timberland and Nike boxes neatly stacked. Behind it, leaned against the wall, was the M1 assault rifle we'd extorted from one of the bitch-ass, want-to-be gangsta cats in the hood.

Sin was always rugged and built for his size, but his body had taken on a man's frame, which protruded through his wife beater. A stint in jail often had that effect on a nigga. His dark complexion was smooth as night, and he had a strong jaw line. He was an intimidating figure even to those who were considered a friend. My stare was frozen on him, no doubt with disgust, still trying to figure this out. Sin finally met my stare, pulled the recliner upright, and took a long pull on his blunt. "What! What the fuck is your problem?... Why is you staring at me, Angel?" Sin blasted, but his words were laced with guilt.

"Because you fucked up! You fucked us up. What the hell were you thinking about? How long you think it's gonna take before the police figure this shit out and Jazz's crew is gonna put this one together blindfolded?"

"Fuck the police and fuck Jazz's boys." He slapped a clip in one of his nines and cocked it back. "Any one of them niggas can get it!"

"You always had to do shit your way, Sin, but not this time, this was the wrong move and you're taking me down with you."

"Taking you down with me?" He pulled off his Do Rag, exposing his perfect set of spinning waves, took another pull off his blunt, and talked through his exhale. "I did this shit for you, baby bro. We came into this thing together; two little niggas full of pain, full of hate, full of rage…man, I loved that about you… but…now…I don't even know you anymore." Shaking his head, he stood up and swiped the ashes off his sweatpants. "You wanted King to cut you loose, well there you have it…'cause I love you, bra…fifty-fifty love you until the sun burns out." Reading off our matching tattoo on his forearm.

"You know at first I really believed that shit, until I figured out your angle. You take out Jazz, get in favor with King over Breeze, now you're running the north side of Jamaica. Now you a boss…ain't that right, Sin? So you went in for blood but didn't know all the angles. Did you? You didn't know Breeze and Jazz had a secret alliance and that Breeze set us up to get taken out along with King in the club that night. And as far as King, that nigga is nothing but a manipulator always getting cats to do his dirt for him. I had plans for him…without having Jazz dead… without us ending up in the middle of a freakin war! You think you can trust King, you can't trust, dude! He'll just end up getting one of his young soldiers to set you up."

Sin knew what I was sayin was on the money, but he hated to lose an argument. "See, I knew you was gonna come over here on that shit."

"What shit?"

"You over here judging me, the way you talkin, the way you lookin at me, you freakin judging me!" Passion walked into the room as if she was looking for something in the dresser drawer, but no doubt being nosy. Sin stopped in mid-sentence and turned his attention to her. "What the fuck are you doing?"

"What…I'm looking for—"

"I don't care what you looking for, you don't see me in here arguing with my brother, the fuck outta here." Passion sucked her teeth, rolled her eyes, and stormed out of the room. I could hear her in the next room cussing about how this was her crib. Before Sin refocused his attention on me, he yelled out, "Yeah, but who pay all the fuckin bills in this dump? I do. So shut the fuck up and wash those dishes, you dirty bitch." He looked at me, shaking his head, and flashed the biggest smile that reminded me of when we were kids. "It's so hard to find good bitches these days."

"Cut it out, nigga, you know you love that girl." We busted out laughing, and for a second we were brothers again and forgot about all this crazy shit going on.

"Look man, I know you don't believe it, but you don't need this shit: these streets, this crack shit, none of it. I know you been stackin your chips, and I got a nice little chunk of change put aside too. I been talking to Zane and yo, this girl has a really good head on her shoulders…plus she's down for me. She said she be willing to transfer to a school down south if I wanted to make a move. I figure we put our money together and maybe get a two-family house. Shit, you can even bring Passion. I think a move would be good for her."

Half laughing he asked, "Yeah, and where would we go to cop this two-family house, Angel? Queens? Brooklyn?"

"Nah, I was thinking Virginia. You know Auntie and Cousin Rick is down there, so they could help walk us through it. I'm not saying it's gonna be easy, Sin, we both gonna have to start from the beginning with nothing, but at least we'll have a fresh start and get away from all this craziness. This life we living, Sin, is only gonna end us up in one of two places—locked up or in a casket—and I don't know about you, but I ain't in a rush to be in neither situation."

I could tell the idea was really sinking in. He imagined that new house, that new world, that new life. "It sounds good, bra, but what about this charge over my head?"

I thought for a minute and still a bit unsure, I answered, "Well, they ain't nothing much we can do about that one...they got you in the dead wrong on the possession charge. But listen, if you plead it down, and with it being your first charge I'm sure they won't give you more than three years, with good time you be out in eighteen months. That's just enough time for me and Zane to get down there, set up shop, and get on our feet. Then you can parole out to where we at."

Sin looked around the room as if considering leaving it all behind. "I don't know, 'A.' I don't know if that's for me."

"Come on, Sin!" I barked in frustration. "Do you trust me... Do-you-trust-me?"

He paused and looked at me with a smirk. "Of course I do, bra," he said reluctantly.

Not trusting his commitment I quipped, "I'm serious, Sincere...as of right now we done with this...all this shit." I gestured to the guns and drugs. "It's time to turn the page on the book of life."

He broke into a wide smile that he would only flash around me. "Okay, Aristotle, I'm serious too...here...I'm even gonna give you my twins in a gesture of good faith." Sin handed me both nines.

I tucked the joints in my jacket and looked over to the table. "What about the weed?"

"What about it, nigga...I agreed to give up the game, not the hash... Yo, Angel...get outta here, man, before I change my mind..." We laughed.

"Aiight, man, I'm outta here. Yo, my honey Zane invited you

over for dinner tomorrow. I really want you to meet her, she's a good girl…but don't be late 'cause she will get at you."

"I'm sure of it; I'll hit you in the morning for the info." We hugged, and while still embraced he reassured me, "I got a good feeling about this, bra."

Scene Twelve

Now that I had Sin on board, I just had to tie up a few loose strings. I had to get to King…try to reason with him. I needed to talk to Breeze. Maybe I could convince him to take the heat off of Sin; after all, he was just as responsible for Jazz's death—he knew about the hit and didn't say a word. Shit, he'd tried to get me and my brother killed, so as far as I'm concerned, he's lucky I ain't runnin up on him blastin. But I was trying to get out, not get in deeper, and there was too much blood on my hands as it is…had to make the right moves if I wanted to get out of this clean. But that was for another day…today my brother was coming out to Queens Village, hanging out with me and Zane and breaking bread with family. He aint never been out here either, so I was gonna meet him at the train station. I left Zane in the house working on dinner.

Sin was still skeptical about Angel's plan, but he seemed so passionate about the shit, how could he say no? Despite his indecisiveness, he knew it was a good plan. He decided he would take Zane up on her offer and come over for dinner. He'd let Angel map out the move to Virginia over a few shots of Patron, which he was sure would help him digest the idea of leaving South Side behind.

The sun was setting in the Projects as Sin was getting himself together for the trip to Queens Village. He was meeting Angel at the 125th Street & Jamaica Ave. station on the J line, and he was running late. They would normally meet at Jamaica Center station, but they both knew it was too risky. And Sin especially knew it; that's why he slid Uncle Ray's 25' in his jacket. He'd still held onto that pistol after all these years. It became sort of a momentum. Yeah, he gave Angel his twin niners as a show of faith, but he wasn't stupid. No way was he hitting the streets naked, not with half the hood out for blood. At this point he couldn't trust anyone; there was no way to tell who was friend or foe.

Passion walked into the back bedroom, sat on the bed, and eyed Sincere with a disgusted look. "Where the hell are you going?" She rolled her eyes but Sin continued to brush his waves and paid her no mind. She knew he was a born hustler, and you can't slow a hustler down—the harder you try, the harder they hustle. So him leaving abruptly was nothing new…something Passion dealt with over the years and knew it was the price of being a hustler's wifey. But tonight was different; it was something about the night that she didn't trust, but she knew if she told Sin he would brush it off, claiming that her ass was too superstitious. Even though she knew picking an argument wouldn't help, she couldn't control her emotions and damn sure never was able to control her tongue.

"I'm gettin' tired of this shit, Sincere. Every time I turn around you runnin' to them streets. You need to stay ya ass home."

Sin knew what all this bitchin was about…she wanted him to

dick her down before he left out, and on an average day he would oblige her, but he was running late to meet up with Angel and Zane; it was important for him not to make a bad impression. So he tried to ignore Passion as long as he could, but she knew how to push his buttons.

Passion said out loud to herself, "Probably going out there to fuck some skanky hoe...you better not bring no diseases back to this house with your *naassty* ass... Why you gettin' all dressed up for?"

Sin shot her a look that sent fear through her body and said in an uncharacteristically calm tone, "Look here, you crazy bitch... I'm going to see my brother and his new honey. I got a lot of shit on my mind right now, so the last thing I need is you in my face with the bullshit." His eye caught one of the kids running past the bedroom. He paused and took a deep breath. "Why don't you go cook the kids some freakin dinner for once? You feed them so much god damn Chinese food they gonna grow up to be Samoans." Before she could respond, he stormed out the door. He made his way through the courtyard toward the train station. The streets were dark and only illuminated by a streetlight in the distance. It was unnaturally quiet until some junkies bickering over a hit broke the silence. The autumn wind chilled the air and made its way through Sin's shirt. He cursed himself for forgetting his jacket back at Passion's crib. Not because of the cold, but more so for Uncle Ray's pistol that was in the jacket. He thought about going back but didn't want to hear this chick's mouth.

A bottle broke in the distance, and Sin noticed a dark, hooded image over his left shoulder...about fifty yards back.

Was he being followed?

He tried to process who would be following him, who would

be out to get him, but the list was too long. Sin felt so vulnerable, yet he pushed on. He fought every instinct to double back and flank his pursuer, but there was no time to embellish his paranoia.

He reached the train platform, gazed down the tracks, and glanced at his watch. A quarter to seven… "Shit!" Despite his attempts to ignore Passion, she still managed to set him back. Sin made his way down the end of the platform. He had to meet Angel at the rear exit of the 125th & Jamaica station, and he figured he'd get a jumpstart. The J train screamed into the station, and the few straphangers lingering on the platform stepped toward the iron horse. As Sin stepped onto the train, he noticed the same dark hooded image boarding a few cars away.

Was he going crazy, or was it just a coincidence that this dude was taking the same train. But why was this cat so ominous, so dark, and so menacing? Sin tried to rationalize that it was conceivable for this dude to be innocently taking the train. It would explain why he would be walking in the same direction. Maybe he wasn't being followed. He'd promised Angel that he would take a more positive approach, but still every street instinct told him different.

It was about a twenty-minute ride to his stop, and Sin tried to lose himself in the images of him and Angel in V.A. with their own crib. He almost laughed out loud with amusement and shook his head in an endearing way. He loved Angel…he always had to do things the hard way. Sin stared out the window into the Queens streets as the train cruised over the hood.

The conductor's voice cracked over the P.A. "*Next stop 125th Street…125th Street will be the next stop…this is a J train to Jamaica Center.*" Sin stood up and stretched his limbs; he stepped toward

ANGEL'S SIN

the doors and noticed that hooded dude making his way through the cars toward him. A burst of anger quickly took him over. "Fuck this!" Coincidence or not, he decided to take him out on the platform. Sin felt his pockets, searching for his switchblade; he flipped it open and slid it in his sleeve.

The train doors slid open, and they were the only two to exit onto the platform. Sin's heart raced as he mapped out his ambush in his mind. He could hear the footsteps behind him getting closer. He debated; should he stick him on the platform or hit him on the street. Sin gripped the blade's handle tight, ready to turn and thrust it into this unlucky bastard. He noticed the video cameras aligned on the platform and thought better to wait till he got to the street. They were about twenty feet from the rear exit: a rotating gate that led out onto a metal stairwell descending into the street.

I'd been at this damn station for the past half an hour, and I'd counted six downtown trains passing through here. I even asked this stupid ass token booth clerk if she'd seen anybody fitting Sin's description. I know this nigga Sin didn't stand me up and have me come all the way out here for nothin'.

Did he get here before me and leave? Did he get off at the wrong stop?... Nah, this son of a bitch stood me up... I couldn't believe this inconsiderate, California raisin mutha fucka. I'd wait to see if he was on this train pulling into the station; if not, I'm gone. Train conductor: *"This is 125th Street & Jamaica...125th & Jamaica...Next stop...Van Wyck..."*

The announcement triggered my memory. "Damn! I'm supposed to meet 'em at the rear exit," I whispered to myself.

I raced down the stairs into the streets and headed toward

the rear exit. I didn't like this feeling in my gut; something wasn't right. Tension choked the night.

Sin glanced over his shoulder again, and the hooded figure's pace had quickened. He now had no doubt that this dude was out for blood; adrenaline flashed through his body as he realized he was no longer being followed, but in fact being chased. It became a foot race to the rotating gates that exited the platform. Separated by only a few yards, the hooded figure reached inside his jacket as Sin entered into the rotating gates. Panic rushed his body, and his heart dropped when he noticed the two goons coming up the stairwell in front of him. He was trapped. Instinctively, Sin reached for his guns but they weren't there; he had relinquished them to Angel. The goons took aim at Sin with cannons, and the hooded figure, still on the platform behind him, pulled his pistol with the intent to kill. Caged into the rotating gate, Sin gripped the cold metal bars and didn't get a chance to brace himself before they opened fire. The first shots knocked him off his feet, and he struggled to pull himself up. He screamed out with every ounce of life he had left. "AAANGEEEL!!!" The rain of bullets ripped the flesh of his body, and a shot that connected to his face tore off his jaw. Sin's lifeless body slumped in the tight space between the bars.

I was halfway to the rear exit when I heard the shots. They ripped through the silent night and felt so close my first instinct was to duck and take cover, but I sprinted with everything I had to the rear exit. The array of shots continued without pause for thirty seconds, and I had already concluded that whoever was caught up in that wouldn't survive. This wasn't random fire, this wasn't a drive-by, this only meant one thing…it was a calculated hit. As I sprinted, my body filled with emotions and I fought to keep my composure. I grabbed the railing at the bottom of the stairs to stop my forward motion. I swung onto the stairwell and cleared the first five steps before I looked up.

It was Sin…slumped over…and undeniably dead.

"SINCERE!!!" My body went numb and I couldn't breathe. I floated over the rest of the stairs and pulled the gate forward to free his body. I cradled him, rocking back and forth like a nurturing mother; I cried uncontrollably.

With my last bit of energy, I pleaded through my tears. "Somebody!...help meeee…help meee!!...somebody, please!!" My cries fell on deaf ears.

I held and talked to my brother until the paramedics pulled me off of him. It wasn't till another train pulled into the station and people tried to exit before we were noticed perched on the stairs.

Detective Mills sat me in the backseat of his unmarked car, slammed the door, and sat in the driver's seat. He talked to me through the rearview mirror.

"Now, I know what'chu thinkin, son…you wanna kill the whole world right now; pretty much doesn't matter who…you just want blood. You figure someone has to pay for what happened to your brother."

I just sat there staring aimlessly into the night, soaked in Sin's blood, pieces of his face stuck to my shirt. I guess Mills was trying to warn me about the inevitable. He was right: people will die. Mills drove me to the station where they asked me a thousand questions before turning me loose right before dawn.

Zane sat at the kitchen table for hours, going through a range of emotions. Initially she was livid when Angel and Sin didn't get back in time to taste her lasagna, homemade garlic bread, and fresh salad. She'd slaved over the stove for hours, trying to make a good impression. She'd remembered when Angel mentioned that lasagna was his and Sincere's favorite. She even poured the Merlot in anticipation of their arrival. She had been excited to finally meet Sincere. She had seen how happy it made Angel to finally convince him to give up the streets and start a new life. Zane envied their relationship; Angel would tell her so many stories about how they grew up. They would laugh for hours, and although it made her feel closer to him, it always bothered her that she didn't have stories of her own to share. She didn't have any siblings, her cousins still lived overseas, and yeah, she had a few friends, but learned a long time ago everyone didn't share her loyalty. Her so-called friends would always tell her how beautiful she was and how she should be a model, but the compliments usually were accompanied with chuckles and under-breath remarks. Zane would always laugh it off and downplay it, quickly dismissing the jealousy and spitefulness. She would go above and beyond to try to show that she was a grounded and down-to-earth girl, but still there were always the whispers and rumors of her being stuck up or out for somebody's man. Truth is, she became to resent her looks; she resented the guys that tried to come on to her, knowing damn well she knew their girlfriends.

High school was difficult for her: she was an exceptional student, but socially she struggled to fit in. Everyone assumed that because she was beautiful things came easy for her, but it was exactly the opposite. She worked on losing her accent and learned all the slang words. It took a few years for her to realize that the problem wasn't her; the problem was these bitter, insecure bitches that couldn't be classy if their life depended on it. As a result Zane shied away and focused on her books, where she developed a taste for autobiographies and revolutionary figures.

Zane had to figure out life on her own. She wasn't close to her mother, who was the only relative she had in the States. It wasn't because she didn't want to have a bond with her mother; she longed for it, imagined it, and most of all needed it.

Her mother never got over the fact that her father chose his music career over keeping his family. She wasn't fully prepared to actually leave when she gave her husband the ultimatum, but her anger pushed her one step beyond the point she was ready for. The next thing she knew, she was on a plane with her thirteen-year-old daughter headed to the States. She still loved him, but she needed her independence—not only from him, but also from the dead-end life they were leading in London. He said he couldn't leave and pleaded with her to give him a few more years to get his band in mainstream. He knew reggae band music was on the verge of being widely accepted, and his band was in line to be one of the pioneering groups. But she no longer shared his vision, and with a student visa she found herself in Queens attending the local college for a nursing degree.

Zane's father made good on his promise, and his band became one of the premier reggae bands in Europe. She found out that her father had been sending money for her and her mother and purchased the house in Queens Village. When she became of age, her mother set up an account for her to directly receive her share of the payments, which only became one less reason to interact with her. She got to spend time with her father a few times when she was younger. His band came over to do some local gigs every few years, but it was nowhere near the bond she dreamed about.

She was madly in love with Angel; she loved his maturity and calm demeanor. It was something about when she was around him that made everything feel okay. The way he treated her was genuine. She'd never felt as comfortable around a man as she did with him. Her past boyfriends treated her like a trophy and never showed interest in any of her ambitions. She felt partially responsible for her bad experiences with guys; she tended to hook up with uptight dudes from well-to-do families that were so preoccupied with their own aspirations to rule the world, they forgot how to treat a woman. But Angel was different; he took his time with her, listened when she spoke, and intrigued her with his conversation. He was her friend, her brother, lover, and soul mate.

From the police station I walked back to Mama's house; I couldn't go back to Zane looking like this. I stopped at a phone booth. I had to call her…had to hear her voice. Despite it being six in the morning, Zane picked up on the first ring.

"Hello." I could hear the panic in her voice.

I let out a heavy exhale. "It's Angel."

"What do you want, Angel?" Her panic shifted to frustration. All she knew was that I'd stood her up for dinner and never made it back home. I wanted to explain everything that had happened, but my mind was too exhausted. A few select words were all I could get out.

"They killed him… They killed him, Zane… They're gonna have to pay…" My voice cracked and she heard the conviction in my tone.

"Oh my god, baby, what happened? Are you okay? Who was killed?" Her voice quivered in fear.

"Sincere is dead, baby. They killed my brother."

"Oh no, Angel, what happened to Sincere, oh my god… where are you?" She was distracted by footsteps walking into her driveway. Her windows in her basement apartment were at ground level.

"Zane, I have to go…"

"No, Angel. Don't go, come home, baby…come home to me…please…" She pleaded with me through her tears, but I had to go; I had to stay focused and her cries made me weak. I hung up and immediately picked the receiver back up.

"Hello…Hello…Zane!…" The connection was dead. I dropped my head in a moment of indecisiveness, but quickly shook it off and pushed on.

Besides, there was hell to pay, and today I'd be cashing in.

It took everything in me not to break down again when I got to our room in the basement at Mama's house. This was the place that Sin and I shared, and everything in here reminded me of a different memory of us. My rage held me together, and after a long shower I unlocked the closet to our heavy artillery. The Tech, the shotty, the four-fifth, a few nines—they were all coming with me.

No way could I walk around with all this heat on me, so I swiped Uncle Allen's keys off the kitchen counter and loaded up in his old '83 Volvo. I sped off without telling anyone in the house about Sin. It would only soak up my energy and slow me down. It wasn't till I drove a few blocks that it dawned on me that Sincere had wronged a lot of mutha fuckers, and it was a laundry list of niggas that wanted a piece of him. But once I singled out the cats that actually had the firepower, let alone the fuckin cojones to do what they did to my brother, the list was down to a few unlucky bastards.

I knew King had to know something about this shit, even if he wasn't directly involved. As far as the hood was concerned, we were still part of his crew unless he put the word out otherwise. Either way, he'd played a part in what had happened, and he had to answer for it.

I drove by King's store, not expecting to see much but I caught a humble; he was there receiving the morning delivery from the Hostess truck. I parked across the street and laid low until the deliveryman left. As I slid out of the car, a dark overcast took over the sky, the winds pulled on the fences, and garbage from the street made little tornadoes in the corners of the building. I secured the nine in my waist and switched off the safety. The gate was pulled down halfway over the storefront, so I ducked under and slowly pushed open the door. King's back was turned, stacking potato chips on the rack. I let the door slam behind me, and without turning around King barked, "Ya ass better had came back…you know you shorted me two boxes of Doritos." I ripped the glock from my waist and pistol-whipped him across the head, crashing him into the rack of potato chips. I was almost surprised that the one blow had knocked him out. I stood over his body with vengeance, remembering how he'd ruled over the hood through extortion, manipulation, and fear.

Like straight out of Stephen King's novel *Needful Things*, King turned the tenants of a project building against each other. Most the tenants were smoked out or on some sort of drug, but the few families that were trying to live a decent life despite their surroundings were a problem, or at least in King's opinion they had to get down or lay down.

Mr. Richards was your everyday God-fearing man who tended to see the good in everyone. He never said much, just invested his time into work, family, and church. For a fifty-year-old man, he still exuded youth and maintained his football build from his years at Grambling State. Unfortunately, Ms. Richards was an over-the-top Christian who used the phrase "Jesus Christ" like a lightning rod to strike down those whom she refuted. She spent most of her time peering out the window, cataloging the sins of the community. She probably spoke more than she should have, no doubt a trait she picked up being an usher at The House of Prayer Pentecostal Church. The Richards moved to the Baisley project tenements in the early seventies during the influx of Caribbeans coming to the States for a better living. So when King began to take over the building with drugs and intimidation, Ms. Richards' initial reaction was to lecture him on the sacrifices of Jesus and damnation. Her husband was able to settle her down, but he knew it wouldn't be long before she would revert back to spewing religious lecture.

It was late afternoon when King and I banged on the door of Apt. 3C. The building was alive with tenants returning home from work and kids playing in the hallway. A baby crying in an apartment down the hall caught my attention as Sheila finally answered the door.

"Yo, what the hell is your problem?" King barked. "It's damn near six o'clock and ya ass is still sleeping?"

Sheila leaned in the doorway halfway interested in what King was barking about. Her clothes that had once fitted her voluptuous frame hung off her now frail body. She spoke in a slurred speech and scratched while she talked.

"C'mon, Kevin... I'm not in the mood for you to be fucking with me right now... I just got my period, these freakin cramps are killin me..."

Shelia was the only person in the hood that called King by his government, and she knew it fucked with him. Years ago Kevin and Sheila was inseparable; they were together when King started in the game. Sheila was one of the baddest chicks in the hood. I remember as a youngn' all the getting-money-niggas were after her. At the time she was out of King's league, but he stayed persistent and gained her trust and loyalty. He was a master at manipulation. She held him down, stuck with him through his hustle, and even helped him move work out of town from time to time. She probably was the only girl he'd ever had true feelings for, but his greed and manipulative ways drove her to drugs. He'd pressured her to test his products—first Coke, and then freebase. By the time he took notice, she was a full-blown crackhead. He heard from Fat Chase that she was going across town suckin and fuckin them young hand-to-hand niggas for a hit. After a beat down that nearly killed her, King turned her apartment into a cook-up spot and put her on patrol. She was a liaison of sorts in the building, collecting money and distributing drugs from apartment to apartment. She was what we call a functional crackhead. The problem was that Sheila had a mouth on her and a tongue that cut like a blade.

"C'mon, hurry up, Kevin, I ain't got no time to be bullshittin' with you." She handed King a roll of cash wrapped in a rubber band.

King looked at the wad with distrust.

"It's all there, nigga. Fuck you looking like somebody stole your candy for?"

King backslapped her with the roll of money, poppin the rubber band and sending the bills raining down onto the hallway floor. Sheila collapsed into the doorway, regained her balance, and jolted toward King. She had as much fight in her as she had mouth. Her arms flailed like a broken windmill and caught King square in the jaw, scratching his left cheek. He grabbed Sheila by the throat, squeezing the air from her body. She choked and gagged, pulling at his arms to pry his grip loose. But he was relentless.

"Turn that girl a loose!" Ms. Richards shouted from across the hall.

King didn't budge, but her voice startled me and for some reason my senses heightened. The baby's cries became more pronounced, the couple arguing in 3E became more intense, and Sheila's gasps for air shot a cold chill through my body.

"In the name of Jesus Christ, young man, turn that girl a loose." Ms. Richards grabbed King by his jacket and tore his Pelle Pelle. Instinctively he turned and slapped her across the face, knocking her to the floor. Ms. Richards let out a high-pitched scream, and before she hit the floor Mr. Richards flew out of the apartment in a rage. King swiftly drew his 380 cal. and blasted one in his shoulder. Sheila gagged and tried to catch her breath.

"Pick up the fuckin money, bitch!" King demanded. Sheila scrambled to collect the bills. By this time, every apartment door on the floor was cracked with eyes peeking out. King holstered his burner and pulled out the hunting knife. He reached over to Ms. Richards and grabbed her by the ear. She screamed in agony, as her husband lay in her doorway barely conscious. King pressed the blade against her ear. He knew she was the one calling police and trying to organize the tenants against his reign over the building. King intended to make an example of Ms. Richards.

"You know whatcha problem is?" King lectured as he pressed the blade against Ms. Richards' ear. "You're too fuckin nosey! You hear too much!"

Ms. Richards' cries turned to religious rambling.

"Kevin…Kevin! Don't do it…please don't do it…" Shelia, in tears, pleaded with King.

The scene was surreal. "King, what the fuck?" I said nervously as my eyes shot around the hallway. I had no effect.

"Well I'm gonna help you with that hearing problem…" With one swift motion, King sliced her ear clean off. Blood shot across the wall and stung my face. I was in shock… I didn't move… I couldn't move. Ms. Richards lay balled in the corner crying in a deep moan, rocking back and forth reciting biblical scripture, her husband paralyzed from the bullet that had ripped through his spine. Sheila shook with fear and wept uncontrollably from the scene that unfolded in front of her eyes. He grabbed the wad of cash from Sheila's hand and made his way down the staircase as if he hadn't left behind a horrific scene.

I shook off the traumatic images that had stewed in my mind for years. It almost made me sick to know I had killed on his behalf, for his protection, for his dominance. I dragged his unconscious body to the back and tied him to the chair with box rope. The barrel of water attached to the cooler was heavier than I'd figured, but I managed to hoist it up over King's head and dump water down his throat until he woke up choking and gagging.

"You up now, you bitch ass nigga?" I emptied the rest of the barrel on his head and shook it to make sure every drop splashed him in the face.

"What the fuck?" King struggled to wipe his eyes on his shoulder to see who had got the drop on him. "Angel, what the fuck is you doing?"

"Shut up! Shut the hell up, King…I'm askin the fuckin questions, not you!"

"Ayo, Angel, you must be outside of your mind, you better cut me loose and I might consider not killing you." King saw from my expression that this was neither a game nor a joke, and I had full intentions on killing his ass if he didn't answer my questions correctly. Noticing that his threats had no impact, he conceded. "Angel, what the hell is this about, man?"

"What is this about?" I swung the double-barrel gauge from around my back, cocked it, and pressed the muzzle to his cheekbone. "You wrapped up fittin to die and you gonna have the audacity to play stupid."

"Okay, what? This is about Sincere…and you think I had him bodied, right? Wrong! Now why would I wanna kill one of my top lieutenants and why…you know what, can you take this fuckin barrel off my face already?" He looked up at me with a disgusted look—more disgusted with himself for getting caught sleeping. I stepped back a couple of feet with the muzzle still aimed at his cabbage.

"I don't have time for the bullshit, King, tell me what you know. And if I have the slightest feeling that you ain't on the up and up, I'm gonna blow your fuckin brains out the back of your melon."

"Listen here, you bitch made nigga, do you know who you fuckin with?" King barked.

I snatched the pistol from my waist, cocked it, and pressed it against his hand. "Actually I do…" I blasted a round through his hand and he growled through his teeth in pain.

"Yooou mutha fucka…yooou mutha fucka… ooooh…"

"I can do this all day, King, now tell me who had hands in killing my brother?" He growled some more and spoke through his teeth. "After I burn down yo mama's house…I'ma go out to Queens Village and have me a taste of that nice little slice a cake of yours…" King let out a devilish laugh.

Without hesitation, I swiftly let off a shot in his left kneecap. He yelled out in pain and his laughter turned to agonizing tears.

"Aiight! Aiight! You mutha fucka…stop that shit…"

"Tell me what I wanna know…who killed Sin?" He growled in pain and coughed up his breakfast. After catching his breath, he explained, "I bailed Sin outta prison…so he could take care of Jazz. I knew your bitch ass wouldn't do it and Sin was the only one crazy enough to take the chance."

I pressed the muzzle against his face as the rage ran through me. "You knew it was a suicide mission!" I fought back tears as the reality of Sin's death set in deeper. "There was no way he was gonna walk out of that. Jazz's goons are crazy, what the fuck was you thinking?"

King let out the same devilish laugh, but it was weaker now. "You right, I don't know how that crazy son of a bitch did it either, but he went in there and sliced that nigga Jazz damn near in half and walked out clean." I almost didn't realize that I was standing there with a stunned look on my face. "You still don't get it," King said through his groggy laugh. "Sin did it for you… you ungrateful piece of shit…he had no intentions on coming outta that barbershop alive. He freed you from the streets. Gave you a clean slate, and you couldn't protect him like he protected you."

"No...it's more to it. You don't do shit, King, unless you stand to gain from it." My rage subsided enough for me to see the angles.

King slumped his head down as sweat, tears, and saliva stretched to the floor. "Breeze...he was playing both sides of the fence. But you know what they say, 'Keep your friends close and your enemies closer.' Jazz was getting too powerful...it wasn't gonna be long before he shut me down." He paused between sentences, moaning in pain. "Oh, you son of a bitch...you gonna pay for this..." I pressed the barrel on his wounded hand still strapped to the armrest. "Everyone wanted me dead...there was no tellin who was friend or enemy. At some point Sin would've came for me just like Breeze set up the hit in the club." He laughed a pathetic laugh. "But you see, when you and ya brother took out Jazz's goons at the club, the only way Breeze could protect his secret was to play along with the escape." His voice dropped and his tone weakened. "You know, Angel? I'ma need a hospital pretty soon."

"Fuck a hospital! You still haven't told me shit. Who killed Sin...Jazz's goons or Breeze?..."

Jazz's soldiers...are Breeze's soldiers...put it together, Angel... who else could'a gave the order to take Sin out...Hey...Hey...I need a doctor..." King was right, but if Breeze put the hit out and King knew he was playing both sides, then he also knew and did nothing to stop it. The hell with him!

I wiped down the area as much as possible and checked for any of my footprints in the blood. As I walked away, King let out that devilish laugh that sent chills through me and yelled out, "He did it for you…for you, Angel…and now his sins are on you… HIS SINS ARE ON YOU!!"

I let the door slam on the way out as I had on the way in. As much as I tried, I couldn't get those words out of my head. My brother gave his life for me, and now I owned his sins. There was no escaping that. It had become a part of me…

I pulled up to Guy R. Brewer Blvd. and 109th Ave., which is about a block away from the Projects. I parked east, facing the buildings close enough to observe Jazz's goons going about their daily hustle. Breeze had assumed control over Jazz's crew, which meant that if these were the soon-to-be dead mutha fuckas that killed Sin, then the only one who could have put the hit out was Breeze.

It was a couple of hours before nightfall, and I decided that would be the best time to make my move. I reclined the seat just low enough to see over the dashboard and locked my sights on the building. The weight of the last sixteen hours had taken its toll on me, and I succumbed to the sleep that had been chasing me down like a lion on the hunt. I'm not sure when my thoughts transitioned to dreams, but images of me and my brother's lives flashed before me. When we were kids playing in the condemned H.P.D. houses, riding our bikes on the dirt hills, taking our girlfriends to the movies, and hanging with the crew. Those nostalgic images quickly turned to the terrifying flashes of my brother's murder. I could hear the gunshots that penetrated his body, and his screams jolted me back to consciousness as I woke up in a cold sweat. It took me a few seconds to slow my heart rate as I checked my windows and mirrors. It must have rained a bit when I was asleep because the streets were glossed and the blocks were empty. The night had darkened, and the overcast sat low over the buildings. I was barely able to see the front of the building but was able to make out two of Breeze's soldiers posted up by the door. I knew from prior visits to Jazz's spot that he posted two men in front of the building—a single man outside the apartment door and two more men inside the apartment. Over the years, I'd always joked to Jazz about his security being vulnerable from the rooftop. Either he was too cocky or too naïve, but he never made provisions to correct it, and I was betting that Breeze was also oblivious to this potential breach in his security.

My best route to the rooftop was through the adjacent building. From there I would cross over to Jazz's building and make my way down the rear staircase. By now I was sure Breeze had set up shop of his own in the apartment and was most likely there now. I was cursing myself for falling asleep because now I had no way of knowing if Breeze came back to the apartment or who else was in there, for that matter.

Jumping over to Jazz's roof was about a twenty-foot drop, and I remember thinking it didn't seem as steep from the street. The last thing I needed was to go to war with these goons with an injury. I took my time and calculated the jump. My days of jumping off of garage rooftops as a kid educated me on the technique of maneuvering steep jumps, although it had been quite a few years since I'd done it. I hopped off, dropped, and rolled into my landing, splashing the gravel underneath me. I rolled into a crouched position as if to take cover, and quietly laughed at myself for feeling like Sly Stone in *Rambo*. My smirk was quickly wiped away when I noticed a huge dog's bowl a couple of feet from where I'd landed. By the time I asked myself why would there be a dog's bowl on the roof, I figured it out. The reason

Jazz always laughed off my warnings about the roof was because he had a surprise for anyone who dared try to gain entry from up here. I knew off the bat what caliber of dog I was fixin to face. Jazz was notorious for his pit bull fights and was known to breed fighter dogs. I stayed in my crouch position and searched the roof with my eyes. The silence was eerie, and I strained to hear any shifts in the gravel. The fire door was about fifty feet from my position, and I had to decide whether to tiptoe to the door or break into a sprint. If this beast was asleep, maybe I could walk softly and not wake him, but if I did a Carl Lewis I had a better chance to make it through the door.

"Fuck it!"

I broke into a sprint, hell bent towards the door. Just when I began to feel foolish, convinced that there was nothing out here, I heard a low husky growl in the wind and an all too familiar fear shot up my spine.

I hate dogs! People always like to tell you, "Oh, he doesn't bite…" Screw that shit…if it's a dog, the mutha fucker bites. When I was in grade school, there was this big ass Doberman pinscher that was kept locked behind this tall ass fence in a driveway across the street from the school. This huge son of a bitch would bark all morning as we made our way into the school yard for lineup. Most the kids would cross the street to avoid even being near this mean bastard, but me and my crew would torment him. We'd kicked the fence, throw rocks, and mock his barks. He'd be so enraged he damn near cleared the six-foot fence that kept him imprisoned. I guess his owner got tired of our bullshit 'cause one morning as I rounded the corner, I noticed a bunch of my classmates climbed up the top of the school yard fence. I couldn't make out the warnings they were screaming out, but by the time I noticed the dragon's lair gate wide open, I had no time to react. This sadistic mother had left the fuckin gate open. I darted into the street but it was too late: the Doberman bit into my right ass cheek like a raw steak. I managed to avoid further damage with the help of my G.I. Joe book bag; unfortunately, Joe didn't make it out alive. Since that day I'd developed a primal fear for dogs, and now back on this rooftop I was once again confronted with my nemesis.

The growl was accompanied by the menacing sound of a chain being swept across the gravel. I maintained a full sprint and fell into a baseball slide toward the door. I immediately grabbed at the handle. "Shit! Chains? Who puts fuckin chains on a fire exit door?" The roof was poorly lit, and every shadow was threatening. I pressed my back against the metal door, anticipating anything to jump out at me. My first instinct was to pull the Ruger and pump a couple shots into anything that moved, but I knew that wouldn't be wise. Any shots would send Breeze's soldiers running to the roof. I reached down for my knife and unsnapped the guard. Again I heard the chains sweeping across the gravel, deep growls that sent fear straight through to my bones, but there was no sight of him. I felt like this beast was stalking me, waiting for me to make one wrong move, taunting me with his growls. "Show your face, you ugly ass mut!" I grunted and pierced through the darkness. I glanced down at the chain on the door, and in that moment a force sideswiped me. I crashed into the door and grabbed the beast by the collar. His barks were deafening and his jaws were massive. It was a freakin rottweiler, and his razor sharp teeth were inches from my face. This son of a bitch was massive, and it took everything in me to keep him from rippin my face off. I had to shut this dog up and quick. No way they don't hear all this fuckin barking; I'd give 'em minutes before they made their way up here. Gotta shut this mutt up. He lunged into me and slashed my face with his canines. I immediately felt the blood race down my face. I couldn't get to my knife without letting go of my grip, so I sacrificed my arm and stuffed my elbow down the beast's throat. I grunted in pain as he sunk his teeth into my arm, but at least he stopped all that goddamn barking. I reached my right arm across my left side and snatched the knife from its holster. In one motion I sliced the blade across the dog's body, but it didn't stop him from feasting on my arm. I continued to wrestle with the beast prying my arm from its jaws. I heard the chain rattling on the fire door. It was one of the goons coming to check the roof. I had to put this mutt out of its misery and fast. I firmed up my grip on the knife and lunged the blade into its neck. He belted out a high-pitched bark and fell limp. My arm was buried under the dead weight of the rottweiler pinning me down. The sound of the lock popping open quickly reminded me why I was on this freakin roof in the first place. I had to think fast. I was able to gain enough leverage and position my pistol under the dog's body. As the roof door swung open, I relaxed my body and played dead. The bulky silhouette paused a couple of steps onto the roof and raised his gun into the darkness. His eyes followed his aim as he swung it back and forth. Within seconds he spotted the bodies sprawled across the gravel. "What the fuck!" He cautiously crept over, his gun locked on my dead body. His gaze met my eyes, and satisfied that I was over he relaxed his pistol by his side. In that second I pumped two muffled shots from under the dog's body into his chest. As he collapsed to his knees his features became recognizable, and he was one big ugly ass son of a bitch. He gasped and regurgitated a mouth full of blood before dropping face first to the gravel.

I pulled myself up and felt a sharp pain shoot through my arm. I didn't escape this battle without paying for it. My jacket was torn to shit and my arm leaked with blood from deep gashes. I ripped my sleeve and wrapped my wounds tight before entering into the staircase. I walked softly down the two flights but moved quickly, knowing that someone would come looking for the dude I'd left on the roof. I peeked out the staircase into the hallway and saw one of the soldiers posted in front of the apartment door. I rolled an empty liquor bottle that was in the stairwell into the hallway to get his attention. He raised his head, and I stayed crouched down behind the door with the Ruger.

"Ayo, Diesel, that's you? He postured up. "C'mon, stop fuckin around, man. What's goin on up there? Is Beast fuckin with them pigeons again?" he spoke aloud as he approached the stairwell.

I thought to myself, Beast? Well what else would his name be?

When he opened the stairwell door, his ramblings were cut short with a .38 revolver pressed against his nuts.

"Drop the burner," I demanded.

His gun dropped to the cold concrete, and I tossed it over the railing. Still in my crouched position, I searched him from his ankles up till I was upright and sticking the pistol in his back. I walked him back down the hallway. "Now when we get to the door, you better give the right knocks or I'ma blow a hole in your back."

"Angel, you don't have to do this, man."

"Don't tell me what the fuck I don't have to do. But you better start telling me what you know about my brother's murder, and you have about ten seconds before I decide to put you under…"

"Listen, man… I didn't have anything to do with killing Sincere."

"Ain't Breeze running the crew now?"

In a nervous voice he replied, "Yeah, he took over after Sincere killed Jazz."

"What the hell you talking bout?" I yanked him by his collar and slammed him against the wall.

"C'mon, Angel, everybody in the hood knew Sin killed Jazz. It wasn't no fucking secret."

A sudden feeling of shame came over me and I changed the subject. "How many cats in the apartment?"

"Two, just two!"

"Breeze in there?"

"Nah, he ain't in there."

"Don't lie to me, Boss, I have no problem cutting your tongue out and shoving it up your ass! Now is Breeze in there…did he give the order to kill Sin?" I shoved the Ruger in his neck.

"Breeze ain't in the apartment, man!"

"Did he order the hit?" He locked his jaw and I smashed him in the face with the butt of the gun. "Did he order the hit?"

His face shook with anger and he spit out, "Of course he ordered the hit. He loved Jazz like a son and ya brother killed him."

Instinctively I wanted to defend my brother's actions, but there was no time for that now. I grabbed his collar and swung 'im around to the door. "Open it." I positioned myself on the side with the gun pressed against his gut. He banged on the door with a coded knock. I could hear the peephole slide open and closed.

There was a long pause, then a series of locks popped open, then another pause. I rested my weight on my rear leg, waiting to pounce on whoever opened the door. The metal-reinforced door cracked open slowly; his body flinched and shifted my attention. A double-barrel gauge flashed out the door and pumped a shot past my ear. I snatched Boss by the collar and swung him in front of me. The next shot caught him flush; the impact blew his chest out. I grimaced in pain as a few buck shots ripped through his flesh and found a home in my shoulder. "Uuuuhhhh." I used his body as cover, shoving his corpse in the doorway while squeezing off multiple rounds into the apartment. I stumbled into the front room and the metal door slammed behind me.

Complete darkness.

I positioned my back along the wall and tried to adjust my eyes to the blackness. My hand searched for a light switch, then decided not to waste my time. I'd better take cover. There were at least two more goons in here, and they had every intention on seeing me go down. I controlled my breathing and listened for movement. I remembered the layout of the place while I checked my wounds. I tucked the Ruger and drew Sin's twin 9mm's from my waist. I led my way through the darkness with extended arms and thought for sure they'd be able to hear my heart pumping through my chest. From the faint moonlight, I was able to make out one of the goons reflection off the bathroom door mirror. He was crouched in the tub behind the shower curtain, the barrel of his shotgun poked out, no doubt waiting for me to step into his line of fire. The shadows shielded me but I could see him clear as day. "I see youuu, you bastard..." I whispered. My grip tightened, and I unleashed fury into the bathroom. Bullets struck the door, breaking the mirror, ricocheted off the tub busting water pipes, raining water throughout the bathroom. I quickly reloaded and paused to watch for movement. Had to move closer, couldn't see through the shower of water spraying from the pipes. I inched in, aimed at the shower curtain that was riddled with holes but still hanging from its pole. Beads of water stung my face as I slowly moved the curtain to the side with my gun hand. In a second the double barrels showed its wicked face and I dove into the puddle on the tiled floor, just escaping the blast that blew a hole in the wall. The blast was deafening, and all I could hear was the high-pitched ringing in my ears. I pushed my back into the corner and blindly let off two shots in his direction. He crumbled through the curtain and slumped over the tub.

Just as I exhaled, my body tensed up. There was still one goon left. I pulled myself up and back into the hallway, where a closet door was blown off the frame by one of the buck shots meant for me. The door hung from a dead bolt lock and uncovered four keys of coke and several stacks of cash wrapped in plastic. My body ached and my first instinct was to grab the stack and bail out, but I had to finish the job.

I couldn't do this half ass.

Couldn't leave no loose ends.

So I pushed on down the hallway. Slowing my breathing with every step, I peeked into Jazz's office and cleared the room. One room left. The final door pierced at me with malice, and I knew there were more than weights and a flat bench behind it. The night was darker in this room, but that was quickly replaced by an excruciating pain that shot across my head. My body crashed into the treadmill from a blow to the back of my head. My gun flew across the room. The light switched on and I strained to adjust my eyes to the bulky figure standing over me. It was the same goon I'd slammed to the floor during my last meeting with Jazz. His gun was aimed at my center, and as he came closer he slowly raised it to my head. His eyes were red with anger when he spoke.

"You made a mistake coming back here, Angel. You shoulda took your bitch and left town when you had the chance." He let out a villainous laugh. "Come to think of it, I'm glad you stuck around. Now I could put you down like I watched ya brother go down." My eyes pierced at him with pure rage. The words drove the pain of my brother's death back to my gut. I pulled myself into a sitting position and leaned against the treadmill. I thought to go for the Ruger but wasn't sure if I'd reloaded it. "I shoulda took 'em out on the train, one on one when I had the chance…but that wasn't the plan, was it? No, Breeze was very specific about following him to the platform." He spoke as if he was talking to himself, embellishing in a time he would love to relive. "Son of a bitch just wouldn't go down…I mean I musta put six in him myself…huh…wasn't till Breeze hit him with that head shot that he finally slumped." He lost himself in the moment and I reached to grip the twenty-five pound dumbbell from under the treadmill. "But in the end your brother went down like all the rest of 'em…screaming for his life…he screamed and he screamed…he actually screamed for you…for you to come save him." He leaned down over me with the barrel pressed against my neck and whispered, "Just thought you would wanna know how ya brother went out before you joined him in a ditch."

I shifted my body, the same time smashing the dumbbell across his head. His head split open to the white meat, and his face quickly filled with deep red blood. He tried to pull himself off the floor and stumbled onto the flat bench. I grabbed a ten-pounder and pulverized his face. I swung till my arms burned with pain and every one of his teeth were scattered across the floor like skittles. With his lasts breaths he gurgled out the words, "Go ahead….kill me…you still won't be able to save your bitch…" He cracked a bloody smile. "Breeze got her number…" He faded.

Panic shot through me like a spear. "Zane!" I grabbed his limp body and tried to shake the life back into him. I needed answers.

"What have you done?! What-the-fuck-have-you-done?!" It wasn't till one of his eyes fell out that it hit me. I was interrogating a dead man.

I felt myself hyperventilating, my stomach twisted, and the room spun counterclockwise. I didn't know if it was my injuries setting in or the fear that they'd gotten to Zane. But whatever it was, I had to pull it together. I grabbed Jazz's gym bag, took a deep breath, and darted out of the room. On my way out of the apartment, I snatched the three bundles of cash wrapped in Saran Wrap and stuffed them in the bag.

Scene Thirteen

It was about a twenty-minute drive to Zane's house; I made it there in five. It was the longest five minutes of my life. When I pulled up to her house, I felt it in my bones, something wasn't right. The night had gotten colder and the winds wrestled with the trees, making an eerie whistling sound. The house was darker now. The lights that usually illuminated the walkway weren't on, nor was there any light coming from Zane's basement apartment. I didn't like it. I didn't like this feeling that came over me. My eyes darted back and forth as I approached the side door. I paused and pressed my ear against the door, waiting for several minutes for any indication of struggle.

Silence.

I checked my glock and slowly slid my key in the lock; every click sounded like an explosion. I cracked the door and again I listened.

Nothing.

My grip firmed up leading the way inside. Every step was placed with caution as my heart drummed my chest. I silently prayed to myself that Zane wasn't here, that maybe she had gotten away or maybe Breeze just wasn't that crazy to go after an innocent girl, but I couldn't shake this feeling; I knew she was in danger.

I reached the bottom of the stairs and strained my eyes to adjust to the darkness. Just as I was able to make out their silhouette, Breeze turned on the lamp beside the couch they sat on.

"Zane!" I screamed out in a panic.

My worst fear was realized: seeing Breeze sitting there with Zane in his clutches, her eyes swollen from crying and face filled with terror. Breeze secured his arm around her neck, gun pressed against her stomach. Her clothes were ripped, stretched out and hung off her body.

She tried to avoid looking at me. She was afraid I'd see right through her. Breeze had had his way with her and raped her repeatedly throughout the day. She blamed herself for opening the door. Breeze had told her that Angel was in danger and he'd come by to look out for him. When she'd cracked the door, he pushed his way in and wrestled her down. She tried to fight back with everything she had. She tried to fight like how Angel taught her to do, but he overpowered her.

I stood there with my sights aimed directly on Breeze, waiting for him to move his gun off her, waiting for him to make one wrong move. My gun hand shook with rage.

"Let her go, Breeze, this don't got shit to do with her and you know it."

He tightened his grip on her neck and shook his head. "Nah, 'A,' this has everything to do with her. We had a crew, we built an empire. And everybody had their place. You turned your back on the crew and let this bitch get in the way."

I shook my head. "When did you become so fucked in the head? You tried to freaking kill me in that club." Thoughts of

Sincere's lifeless body infiltrated me. My voice quivered. "You killed my brother, you mutha fucker! I just wanted out the game. I knew about your plans to take out King and form an alliance with Jazz. You were the one that committed treason; not me. Don't preach to me about an empire. What we had wasn't an empire; it was drugs, money, and bullshit. You want it you can have it, I'm done with it. I want out of this shit, Breeze." My voice dropped. "Jazz is dead, Sin is dead...just let her go, man, just let her go..."

Breeze stood up and pulled Zane up with him, still pressing the pistol against her body. He cracked a menacing smile. "Besides, I doubt you want her anymore, she's damaged goods now...but I was sure to loosen her ass up for you real good." He grabbed Zane by her face and ran his tongue up her cheek. Zane burst into tears; he had revealed to Angel the very one thing she dreaded. "Hey, it's not my fault...she begged for it..." With the barrel of his gun, he pulled her hair back from her face. "And how could I resist such a beautiful girl...but don't worry, I came in her ass...didn't wanna get any on the baby..." He circled her belly with the barrel.

I stood numb, not able to feel anything. My gun hand fell back to my side, and images of the rape flashed in my mind. I didn't want to believe him, but I knew it was true. I could see it in Zane's face she had been terrorized.

I blacked out, and for a second our eyes met and she knew what she had to do. Zane slung her head back crashing it into Breeze's nose. He jerked and released his grip.

"Get down!" I shouted to Zane as Breeze and I squeezed off rounds at each other. I dove behind the portable bar, checked if I was hit, and reloaded. I screamed out, "Zane, stay down!" I couldn't see her from my position and she didn't respond. "Zane?" I called out again but no response. From across the room, I could hear Breeze's menacing laughs. I called out to him. "What the hell happened to you, 'B'...were you always this twisted or did your screws just get knocked loose?" If he called out, I would be able to get a better feel for where he was.

"Sincere...he sliced up Jazz...he killed my brother...and destroyed my plans. So yeah, I took Sin out and ya girl is polished off too."

"What?"

"It's just me and you now, 'A,' your girl has left the building." I glanced from behind the bar and there she was...sprawled face first on the carpet. She got caught in the hail of bullets. I could see the carpet soaking in the blood from under her. "ZANE!!!" My heart pounded and it no longer mattered if I died. Simultaneously we both deserted our cover, firing at each other in this tiny apartment. Bullets ricocheted across the room, and I felt the fire of a slug rip into my leg. I charged at him, connecting a round into his shoulder that knocked him into the glass table, shattering it into pieces. Without hesitation, I leaped toward him but my injured leg gave out; I stumbled and crashed down on top of him. He smashed face first into the glass table, slicing deep into his face. I postured up over him, resting the barrel on his cheek. "It's over, Breeze, you lose." I pulled the trigger and the hammer clicked on an empty chamber.

"Click!"

Still pinned under me, Breeze grabbed the broken table leg and blindsided me. The flash of pain was blinding, knocking me on my back. Breeze switched his position, and now he was mounted. He reached for a shard of glass from the table and raised it over my head.

Zane struggled to open her eyes as she regained consciousness. She strained to focus the blurry images that were struggling a few feet from her. As she pulled herself upright, she winced in pain from the shot that had ripped through her side. She glanced at her wound for a heartbeat before her eyes articulated the images. She tried to call out to me but found no sound.

Still groggy from the blow, Breeze's words sounded muffled. "No, Angel...it's you...who loses..." The shard of glass he held over me reflected light from the window where dawn had just broke. The rays of light were beautiful. I was staring at inevitable death and I was at ease. There was no more struggling from me; my body had shut down from all the injuries it had sustained throughout the night...and death...it wouldn't be so bad. If there was a place after death, I looked forward to being there with Zane...Sincere...hell, even my man Jazz.

Breeze hoisted the razor-sharp glass in a motion to drive it straight through my throat. I locked sights with him. If he was to be the end of me, then he would have to look into a soul of a warrior. My body relaxed as he began to thrust down, and in that instant his head exploded. Blood and brain matter covered my face, and what was left of Breeze's head lay across my shoulder. The shard of glass missed my neck by inches and shattered across the floor.

Zane stood there shaking with the gun still tightly aimed at Breeze's body. During my struggle with Breeze, she had collected the gun that was knocked from my hand and rested a few inches from where she came to. It was the same gun I'd taught her how to use weeks earlier, when she reluctantly obliged me. I'd told her I hoped she would never have to use it but didn't want her not to know in case she had to. I taught her how to recognize the difference in weight of a loaded gun and an empty one, so she quickly realized the pistol had no ammo. Panic shot through her as she watched Breeze grab a glass and hold it over me. Zane spotted the single bullet I'd left on the mural when I was once willing to sacrifice our relationship for her safety. Ironically, it would be the one thing that saved us. She loaded the single round and stumbled toward where we were. The pain gripped her and she struggled not to faint. Her eyes widened, and with the rage of a raped woman she aimed and squeezed off a single shot to the back of Breeze's head.

She succumbed to her gunshot wound and dropped to the floor, laying lifeless amongst the bloody scene. I scrambled to my feet in desperation. "Zane!" I cradled her in my arms as the dawn sun pierced through the room. On my knees I looked up, praying to a God I'd never believed in.

Police crashed through the door and stormed the house. Still in my arms I stared at Zane, oblivious to the cops that circled me, guns drawn and flashlights blinding me. They shouted commands, "Put the girl down! Your hands behind your head! Do it now!" They pressed my face against the blood-soaked carpet and slapped a pair of cold metal cuffs around my wrist. I was left lying there while they searched the rest of the apartment. Paramedics rushed to put Zane on the gurney and into the ambulance. They covered her face with an oxygen mask and worked on her as they pushed past detectives. From the crowd Detective Mills emerged. "Stand him up." He gestured to a uniform. My shoulder burned with pain, and I felt the urge to pass out. He walked me out to another waiting ambulance and uncuffed me while they worked on my injuries.

I played it all back in my mind and tried to figure out where I went wrong. How could I have let this happen? Everyone I was meant to protect slipped through my fingers. I thought about what King had shouted to me as I walked out of his store, about me inheriting the sins of my brother. Now I'm thinking I'd always carried these demons deep inside my soul from childhood. The sins of Black Rob that tore into me, the sins of crackheads I sold death to, and the faces of men I'd murdered who looked back at me in the mirror.

"Victor…Victor Johnson…" Mills snapped me out of my Jacob's ladder and rested his hand on my shoulder in a consoling manner and shined an expression that was rare for him. "I just got word back from the E.R. at Jamaica. Ms. Ortiz is in surgery but they expect her to pull through. She's a strong girl."

Tears flooded my eyes as I held back the lump in my throat. "And…and what about the baby…"

"Victor…the baby's okay…"

A rush of emotions took me over and I bawled in the detective's arms.

"C'mon, I'll ride with you to the hospital, you're pretty banged up yourself." A sudden realization of the murder scene struck me and I searched his face, trying to get a take on his position. I straightened up. He must have noticed the concern in my face because he reassured me, "Did you and Ms. Ortiz live together in this house?"

I thought for a second to see where the detective was going with this. "Uh, yeah…we lived together."

"And that dead guy in there…he broke into your place with those guns?" Realizing what he meant, I went along with it. "Yes… Yes, Sir…"

"And I'm assuming he was killed in a struggle from you trying to protect yourself and Ms. Ortiz."

The pain of what he did to Zane weighed heavy on my heart. "Yeah...he was killed in the struggle." My tone faded off.

"Hey...and that's exactly what you write in your statement. You understand?" Mills instructed. He gave me a long look before settling back on the bench beside the gurney. The ambulance violently bounced as we raced to the hospital; the EMT steadied himself while he wrapped my leg, but my only thoughts were of Zane. When we arrived I quickly gathered myself in a wheelchair; I couldn't rest till I saw her. I struggled to free myself from the doctors and nurses trying to treat me, and Detective Mills stepped in. "It's okay, let 'im go." I made my way to the intensive care unit and rolled up to the nurse's station. "Zane...Zane Ortiz, which room is she in?" I asked in a panic. "23B...but excuse me, you can't..." I was off before the nurse finished her sentence. I rolled into the room and almost didn't recognize her; she was hooked up to so many machines. I pulled up beside the bed and gazed at her, but my guilt forced my head down on her lap. I had never felt love for anyone the way I felt for her. I rested my head against her belly and hugged her lap as my tears flowed onto the sheets. "Zane...I am sooo sorry, baby." I gently rocked her back and forth. "Could you... Would you ever forgive me?" The only sounds occupying the room's silence were the beeping heart monitor and air compressing. Just as I began to doubt myself Zane placed her soft hand on my head, and as she had done so many times before during my time of uncertainty, she once again caressed me like a wounded soul that needed forgiveness....

Scene Fourteen

The chimes on the door awoke King out of his slumber. He grimaced in pain, as the rope that bound him to the chair seemed to have set into his skin. He strained to yell out. "Breeze… is that you?" He coughed up blood and mucus, trying to get the words out. "I…I…need a doctor…" An image made its way to the back and stood a few feet from King. The single lightbulb that hung from the ceiling was too dim for King to identify this unfamiliar figure. "Who the hell are you?" The husky silhouette stood silent and stared down at King. "Listen, whoever the fuck you are…go call an ambulance! You don't see me bleeding to death over here?" The image stepped into the light and raised a twenty-two-caliber pistol to King's face.

The faint light illuminated part of the person's face, revealing her disfigured ear. "You… What the hell are you doing here?" She stood silent. "And what the hell you gonna do with that pistol? What's wrong, you can't hear me?… I told you get me a fuckin ambulance, bitch!" The small gun shook with intensity.

Instinctively, she said a prayer for the soon-to-be-departed. "May Jesus have mercy on your soul.…" With that she pulled back on the trigger.

"Noooo!" King screamed in panic. The firecracker-like shot echoed throughout the store and out into the street.

Zane ultimately made a full recovery of her injuries and gave birth to my son on the 17th of May. We followed through on our plans, moved to Springfield, Virginia, and made a new start. I used the eighty thousand I'd snatched from Jazz's spot to purchase a two-bedroom condo not far from my family. My injuries left me with a slight limp, a reminder of the life I'd left behind. But Zane and baby Sincere were the future I was never promised to have. So with that I move forward with the winds on my back. The days of Angel are long gone, buried away with my sins and the demons that chased me for years.

On the first day of fall in a grassy patch blanketed with red leaves, I dropped to my knee, looked up at Zane's beautiful face, still intimidated by her piercing eyes, and asked her to be Mrs. Victor Johnson. Tears rushed in her eyes, releasing a single tear of joy that raced off her cheek. She said, "Yes."

Special thanks to: The God inside of me for giving me the inspiration and energy to complete one of the hardest journeys I've traveled. To my mother Ana Sanchez who taught me the value of never giving up. To my father Vincent P. Sanchez Sr., I finally broke the cycle daddy; no more demons... I forgive you and forever love you (R.I.P.). My Grandmother Canzella "Mama" Johnson for raising generations of children with the biggest heart imaginable (R.I.P.). To all my family that was raised in Mama's House: Alvin, Jackie, Sonia, William, Willie, John, Albert, Blanche, Ana, Claude, Lisa, Kevin, lil Vicky, Brian, Mark, George, Tamika, Reggie, Keisha, Shakia, Big Vicky, Jamie, Richard, Carmen... To My daughters Imani and Nia for keeping daddy's heart pure; you girls are the reason why I strive to be the best. To Tawana Sharee Butler ,my love, you have inspired me beyond measures with your entreperneurial drive, your love and affection and motherhood. My cousin, Brian Johnson for introducing me to writing and word play; you're the best, my big brother! My uncle, Wadi Muhammad for teaching me too many life lessons for me to list and being a father figure when I most needed it. Greg "Itis" Davidson (DZYNE ID) for keeping me focused and being my right hand man throughout this journey... It's been real my dude!

Final thoughts: To my cousin Claude "CL" Wilson. Our lives and experiences has been the inspiration for Angel's Sin. As you may tell the Character Sin has been developed in your likeness.

Some plots and story lines in this book may hit close to home for some people in my close circle and I hope they'll understand that this was necessary for my process.

CPSIA information can be obtained at www.ICGtesting.com
Printed in the USA
236702LV00007B/145/P

திருவள்ளுவர் அருளிய திருக்குறள்

1. அறத்துப்பால்

1.1 பாயிரவியல்

1.1.1 கடவாழ்த்து

அகர முதல எழுத்தெல்லாம் ஆதி	
பகவன் முதற்றே உலகு.	1
கற்றதனால் ஆய பயனென்கொல் வாலறிவன்	
நற்றாள் தொழாஅர் எனின்.	2
மலர்மிசை ஏகினான் மாணடி சேர்ந்தார்	
நிலமிசை நீடுவாழ் வார்.	3
வேண்டுதல் வேண்டாமை இலானடி சேர்ந்தார்க்கு	
யாண்டும் இடும்பை இல.	4
இருள்சேர் இருவினையும் சேரா இறைவன்	
பொருள்சேர் புகழ்புரிந்தார் மாட்டு.	5
பொறிவாயில் ஐந்தவித்தான் பொய்தீர் ஒழுக்க	
நெறினின்றார் நீடுவாழ் வார்.	6
தனக்குவமை இல்லாதான் தாள்சேர்ந்தார்க் கல்லால்	
மனக்கவலை மாற்றல் அரிது.	7
அறவாழி அந்தணன் தாள்சேர்ந்தார்க் கல்லால்	
பிறவாழி நீந்தல் அரிது.	8
கோளில் பொறியின் குணமிலவே எண்குணத்தான்	
தாளை வணங்காத் தலை.	9
பிறவிப் பெருங்கடல் நீந்துவர் நீந்தார்	
இறைவன் அடிசேரா தார்.	10

1.1.2   வான்சிறப்பு

வான்நின்று உலகம் வழங்கி வருதலால்	
தான்அமிழ்தம் என்றுணரற் பாற்று.	11
துப்பார்க்குத் துப்பாய துப்பாக்கித் துப்பார்க்குத்	
துப்பாய தூஉம் மழை.	12
விண்இன்று பொய்ப்பின் விரிநீர் வியனுலகத்து	
உள்நின்று உடற்றும் பசி.	13
ஏரின் உழாஅர் உழவர் புயல்என்னும்	
வாரி வளங்குன்றிக் கால்.	14
கெடுப்பதூஉம் கெட்டார்க்குச் சார்வாய்மற் றாங்கே	
எடுப்பதூஉம் எல்லாம் மழை.	15
விசும்பின் துளிவீழின் அல்லால்மற் றாங்கே	
பசும்புல் தலைகாண்பு அரிது.	16

நெடுங்கடலும் தன்நீர்மை குன்றும் தடிந்தெழிலி
தான்நல்கா தாகி விடின். 17
சிறப்பொடு பூசனை செல்லாது வானம்
வறக்குமேல் வானோர்க்கும் ஈண்டு. 18
தானம் தவம்இரண்டும் தங்கா வியனுலகம்
வானம் வழங்கா தெனின். 19
நீர்இன்று அமையாது உலகெனின் யார்யார்க்கும்
வான்இன்று அமையாது ஒழுக்கு. 20

1.1.3. நீத்தார் பெருமை

ஒழுக்கத்து நீத்தார் பெருமை விழுப்பத்து
வேண்டும் பனுவல் துணிவு. 21
துறந்தார் பெருமை துணைக்கூரின் வையத்து
இறந்தாரை எண்ணிக்கொண் டற்று. 22
இருமை வகைதெரிந்து ஈண்டுஅறம் பூண்டார்
பெருமை பிறங்கிற்று உலகு. 23
உரனென்னும் தோட்டியான் ஓரைந்தும் காப்பான்
வரனென்னும் வைப்பிற்கோர் வித்து. 24
ஐந்தவித்தான் ஆற்றல் அகல்விசும்பு ளார்கோமான்
இந்திரனே சாலுங் கரி. 25
செயற்கரிய செய்வார் பெரியர் சிறியர்
செயற்கரிய செய்கலா தார். 26
சுவைஒளி ஊறுஓசை நாற்றமென ஐந்தின்
வகைதெரிவான் கட்டே உலகு. 27
நிறைமொழி மாந்தர் பெருமை நிலத்து
மறைமொழி காட்டி விடும். 28
குணமென்னும் குன்றேறி நின்றார் வெகுளி
கணமேயும் காத்தல் அரிது. 29
அந்தணர் என்போர் அறவோர்மற் றெவ்வுயிர் க்கும்
செந்தண்மை பூண்டொழுக லான். 30

1.1.4. அறன்வலியுறுத்தல்

சிறப்பு ஈனும் செல்வமும் ஈனும் அறத்தினூஉங்கு
ஆக்கம் எவனோ உயிர்க்கு. 31
அறத்தினூஉங்கு ஆக்கமும் இல்லை அதனை
மறத்தலின் ஊங்கில்லை கேடு. 32
ஒல்லும் வகையான் அறவினை ஓவாதே
செல்லும்வாய் எல்லாஞ் செயல். 33
மனத்துக்கண் மாசிலன் ஆதல் அனைத்து அறன்
ஆகுல நீர பிற. 34
அழுக்காறு அவாவெகுளி இன்னாச்சொல் நான்கும்
இழுக்கா இயன்றது அறம். 35
அன்றிவாம் என்னாது அறஞ்செய்க மற்றது
பொன்றுங்கால் பொன்றாத் துணை. 36
அறத்தாறு இதுவென வேண்டா சிவிகை
பொறுத்தானோடு ஊர்ந்தான் இடை. 37

வீழ்நாள் படாஅமை நன்றாற்றின் அஃதொருவன் வாழ்நாள் வழியடைக்கும் கல்.	38
அறத்தான் வருவதே இன்பம் மற்றெல்லாம் புறத்த புகழும் இல.	39
செயற்பால தோரும் அறனே ஒருவற்கு உயற்பால தோரும் பழி.	40

1.2. இல்லறவியல்

1.2.1. இல்வாழ்க்கை

இல்வாழ்வான் என்பான் இயல்புடைய மூவர்க்கும் நல்லாற்றின் நின்ற துணை.	41
துறந்தார்க்கும் துவ்வாதவர்க்கும் இறந்தார்க்கும் இல்வாழ்வான் என்பான் துணை.	42
தென்புலத்தார் தெய்வம் விருந்தொக்கல் தானென்றாங்கு ஐம்புலத்தாறு ஓம்பல் தலை.	43
பழியஞ்சிப் பாத்தூண் உடைத்தாயின் வாழ்க்கை வழியெஞ்சல் எஞ்ஞான்றும் இல்.	44
அன்பும் அறனும் உடைத்தாயின் இல்வாழ்க்கை பண்பும் பயனும் அது.	45
அறத்தாற்றின் இல்வாழ்க்கை ஆற்றின் புறத்தாற்றில் போஒய்ப் பெறுவ தெவன்?	46
இயல்பினான் இல்வாழ்க்கை வாழ்பவன் என்பான் முயல்வாருள் எல்லாம் தலை.	47
ஆற்றின் ஒழுக்கி அறனிழுக்கா இல்வாழ்க்கை நோற்பாரின் நோன்மை உடைத்து.	48
அறன் எனப் பட்டதே இல்வாழ்க்கை அஃதும் பிறன்பழிப்ப தில்லாயின் நன்று.	49
வையத்துள் வாழ்வாங்கு வாழ்பவன் வான்உறையும் தெய்வத்துள் வைக்கப் படும்.	50

1.2.2 வாழ்க்கைத் துணைநலம்

மனைக்தக்க மாண்புடையள் ஆகித்தற் கொண்டான் வளத்தக்காள் வாழ்க்கைத் துணை.	51
மனைமாட்சி இல்லாள்கண் இல்லாயின் வாழ்க்கை எனைமாட்சித் தாயினும் இல்.	52
இல்லதென் இல்லவள் மாண்பானால் உள்ளதென் இல்லவள் மாணாக் கடை?	53
பெண்ணின் பெருந்தக்க யாவுள கற்பென்னும் திண்மைஉண் டாகப் பெறின்.	54
தெய்வம் தொழாஅள் கொழுநன் தொழுதெழுவாள் பெய்யெனப் பெய்யு ம் மழை.	55
தற்காத்துத் தற்கொண்டாற் பேணித் தகைசான்ற சொற்காத்துச் சோர்விலாள் பெண்.	56
சிறைகாக்கும் காப்பெவன் செய்யும் மகளிர் நிறைகாக்கும் காப்பே தலை.	57

பெற்றாற் பெரின்பெறுவர் பெண்டிர் பெருஞ்சிறப்புப் புத்தேளிர் வாழும் உலகு.	58
புகழ்புரிந்த இல்லிலோர்க்கு இல்லை இகழ்வார்முன் ஏறுபோல் பீடு நடை.	59
மங்கலம் என்ப மனைமாட்சி மற்று அதன் நன்கலம் நன்மக்கட் பேறு.	60

1.2.3 புதல்வரைப் பெறுதல்

பெறுமவற்றுள் யாமறிவது இல்லை அறிவறிந்த மக்கட்பேறு அல்ல பிற.	61
எழுபிறப்பும் தீயவை தீண்டா பழிபிறங்காப் பண்புடை மக்கட் பெறின்.	62
தம்பொருள் என்பதம் மக்கள் அவர்பொருள் தம்தம் வினையான் வரும்.	63
அமிழ்தினும் ஆற்ற இனிதேதம் மக்கள் சிறுகை அளாவிய கூழ்.	64
மக்கள்மெய் தீண்டல் உடற்கின்பம் மற்று அவர் சொற்கேட்டல் இன்பம் செவிக்கு.	65
குழல் இனிது யாழ்இனிது என்பதம் மக்கள் மழலைச்சொல் கேளா தவர்.	66
தந்தை மகற்காற்று நன்றி அவையத்து முந்தி இருப்பச் செயல்.	67
தம்மின்தம் மக்கள் அறிவுடைமை மாநிலத்து மன்னுயிர்க் கெல்லாம் இனிது.	68
ஈன்ற பொழுதின் பெரிதுவக்கும் தன்மகனைச் சான்றோன் எனக்கேட்ட தாய்.	69
மகன்தந்தைக்கு ஆற்றும் உதவி இவன்தந்தை என்நோற்றான் கொல் எனும் சொல்.	70

1.2.4 அன்புடைமை

அன்பிற்கும் உண்டோ அடைக்குந்தாழ் ஆர்வலர் புன்கணீர் பூசல் தரும்.	71
அன்பிலார் எல்லாம் தமக்குரியர் அன்புடையார் என்பும் உரியர் பிறர்க்கு.	71
அன்போடு இயைந்த வழக்கென்ப ஆருயிர்க்கு என்போடு இயைந்த தொடர்பு.	73
அன்பு ஈனும் ஆர்வம் உடைமை அதுஈனும் நண்பு என்னும் நாடாச் சிறப்பு.	74
அன்புற்று அமர்ந்த வழக்கென்ப வையகத்து இன்புற்றார் எய்தும் சிறப்பு.	75
அறத்திற்கே அன்புசார் பென்ப அறியார் மறத்திற்கும் அஃதே துணை.	76
என்பி லதனை வெயில்போலக் காயுமே அன்பி லதனை அறம்.	77
அன்பகத் தில்லா உயிர்வாழ்க்கை வன்பார்கண் வற்றல் மரந்தளிர்த் தற்று.	78

புறத்துறுப் பெல்லாம் எவன்செய்யும் யாக்கை
அகத்துறுப்பு அன்பி லவர்க்கு. 79
அன்பின் வழியது உயிர்நிலை அஃதிலார்க்கு
என்புதோல் போர்த்த உடம்பு. 80

1.2.5. விருந்தோம்பல்

இருந்தோம்பி இல்வாழ்வ தெல்லாம் விருந்தோம்பி
வேளாண்மை செய்தற் பொருட்டு. 81
விருந்து புறத்ததாத் தானுண்டல் சாவா
மருந்தெனினும் வேண் டற்பாற் றன்று. 82
வருவிருந்து வைகலும் ஓம்புவான் வாழ்க்கை
பருவந்து பாழ்படுதல் இன்று. 83
அகனமர்ந்து செய்யாள் உறையும் முகனமர்ந்து
நல்விருந்து ஓம்புவான் இல். 84
வித்தும் இடல்வேண்டும் கொல்லோ விருந்தோம்பி
மிச்சில் மிசைவான் புலம். 85
செல்விருந்து ஓம்பி வருவிருந்து பார்த்திருப்பான்
நல்வருந்து வானத் தவர்க்கு. 86
இனைத்துணைத் தென்பதொன் றில்லை விருந்தின்
துணைத்துணை வேள்விப் பயன். 87
பரிந்தோம்பிப் பற்றற்றேம் என்பர் விருந்தோம்பி
வேள்வி தலைப்படா தார். 88
உடைமையுள் இன்மை விருந்தோம்பல் ஓம்பா
மடமை மடவார்கண் உண்டு. 89
மோப்பக் குழையும் அனிச்சம் முகந்திரிந்து
நோக்கக் குழையும் விருந்து. 90

1.2.6 இனியவைகூறல்

இன்சொலால் ஈரம் அளைஇப் படிறுஇலவாம்
செம்பொருள் கண்டார்வாய்ச் சொல். 91
அகன்அமர்ந்து ஈதலின் நன்றே முகனமர்ந்து
இன்சொலன் ஆகப் பெறின். 92
முகத்தான் அமர்ந்துஇனிது நோக்கி அகத்தானாம்
இன்சொ லினதே அறம். 93
துன்புறூஉம் துவ்வாமை இல்லாகும் யார்மாட்டும்
இன்புறூஉம் இன்சொ லவர்க்கு. 94
பணிவுடையன் இன்சொலன் ஆதல் ஒருவற்கு
அணியல்ல மற்றுப் பிற. 95
அல்லவை தேய அறம்பெருகும் நல்லவை
நாடி இனிய சொலின். 96
நயன் ஈன்று நன்றி பயக்கும் பயன்ஈன்று
பண்பின் தலைப்பிரியாச் சொல். 97
சிறுமையுள் நீங்கிய இன்சொல் மறுமையும்
இம்மையும் இன்பம் தரும். 98
இன்சொல் இனிதீன்றல் காண்பான் எவன்கொலோ
வன்சொல் வழங்கு வது? 99

இனிய உளவாக இன்னாத கூறல்
கனி இருப்பக் காய்கவர்ந் தற்று.   100

1.2.7   செய்ந்நன்றி அறிதல்

செய்யாமல் செய்த உதவிக்கு வையகமும்
வானகமும் ஆற்றல் அரிது.   101
காலத்தி னாற்செய்த நன்றி சிறிதெனினும்
ஞாலத்தின் மாணப் பெரிது.   102
பயன்தூக்கார் செய்த உதவி நயன்தூக்கின்
நன்மை கடலின் பெரிது.   103
தினைத்துணை நன்றி செயினும் பனைத்துணையாக்
கொள்வர் பயன்தெரி வார்.   104
உதவி வரைத்தன்று உதவி உதவி
செயப்பட்டார் சால்பின் வரைத்து.   105
மறவற்க மாசற்றார் கேண்மை துறவற்க
துன்பத்துள் துப்பாயார் நட்பு.   106
எழுமை எழுபிறப்பும் உள்ளுவர் தங்கண்
விழுமந் துடைத்தவர் நட்பு.   107
நன்றி மறப்பது நன்றன்று நன்றல்லது
அன்றே மறப்பது நன்று.   108
கொன்றன்ன இன்னா செயினும் அவர்செய்த
ஒன்றுநன்று உள்ளக் கெடும்.   109
எந்நன்றி கொன்றார்க்கும் உய்வுண்டாம் உய்வில்லை
செய்ந்நன்றி கொன்ற மகற்கு.   110

1.2.8   நடுவு நிலைமை

தகுதி எனவொன்று நன்றே பகுதியால்
பாற்பட்டு ஒழுகப் பெறின்.   111
செப்பம் உடையவன் ஆக்கஞ் சிதைவின்றி
எச்சத்திற் கேமாப்பு உடைத்து.   112
நன்றே தரினும் நடுவிகந்தாம் ஆக்கத்தை
அன்றே யொழிய விடல்.   113
தக்கார் தகவிலர் என்பது அவரவர்
எச்சத்தாற் காணப் படும்.   114
கேடும் பெருக்கமும் இல்லல்ல நெஞ்சத்துக்
கோடாமை சான்றோர்க் கணி.   115
கெடுவல்யான் என்பது அறிகதன் நெஞ்சம்
நடுவொரீஇ அல்ல செயின்.   116
கெடுவாக வையாது உலகம் நடுவாக
நன்றிக்கண் தங்கியான் தாழ்வு.   117
சமன்செய்து சீர்தூக்குங் கோல்போல் அமைந்தொருபால்
கோடாமை சான்றோர்க் கணி.   118
சொற்கோட்டம் இல்லது செப்பம் ஒருதலையா
உட்கோட்டம் இன்மை பெறின்.   119
வாணிகம் செய்வார்க்கு வாணிகம் பேணிப்
பிறவும் தமபோல் செயின்.   120

1.2.9. அடக்கமுடைமை

அடக்கம் அமரருள் உய்க்கும் அடங்காமை
ஆரிருள் உய்த்து விடும். — 121

காக்க பொருளா அடக்கத்தை ஆக்கம்
அதனினூஉங் கில்லை உயிர்க்கு. — 122

செறிவறிந்து சீர்மை பயக்கும் அறிவறிந்து
ஆற்றின் அடங்கப் பெறின். — 123

நிலையின் திரியாது அடங்கியான் தோற்றம்
மலையினும் மாணப் பெரிது. — 124

எல்லார்க்கும் நன்றாம் பணிதல் அவருள்ளும்
செல்வர்க்கே செல்வம் தகைத்து. — 125

ஒருமையுள் ஆமைபோல் ஐந்தடக்கல் ஆற்றின்
எழுமையும் ஏமாப் புடைத்து. — 126

யாகாவா ராயினும் நாகாக்க காவாக்கால்
சோகாப்பர் சொல்லிழுக்குப் பட்டு. — 127

ஒன்றானுந் தீச்சொல் பொருட்பயன் உண்டாயின்
நன்றாகா தாகி விடும். — 128

தீயினாற் சுட்டபுண் உள்ளாறும் ஆறாதே
நாவினாற் சுட்ட வடு. — 129

கதங்காத்துக் கற்றடங்கல் ஆற்றுவான் செவ்வி
அறம்பார்க்கும் ஆற்றின் நுழைந்து. — 130

1.2.10. ஒழுக்கமுடைமை

ஒழுக்கம் விழுப்பந் தரலான் ஒழுக்கம்
உயிரினும் ஓம்பப் படும். — 131

பரிந்தோம்பிக் காக்க ஒழுக்கம் தெரிந்தோம்பித்
தேரினும் அஃதே துணை. — 132

ஒழுக்கம் உடைமை குடிமை இழுக்கம்
இழிந்த பிறப்பாய் விடும். — 133

மறப்பினும் ஒத்துக் கொளலாகும் பார்ப்பான்
பிறப்பொழுக்கங் குன்றக் கெடும். — 134

அழுக்கா றுடையான்கண் ஆக்கம்போன்று இல்லை
ஒழுக்க மிலான்கண் உயர்வு. — 135

ஒழுக்கத்தின் ஒல்கார் உரவோர் இழுக்கத்தின்
ஏதம் படுபாக் கறிந்து. — 136

ஒழுக்கத்தின் எய்துவர் மேன்மை இழுக்கத்தின்
எய்துவர் எய்தாப் பழி. — 137

நன்றிக்கு வித்தாகும் நல்லொழுக்கம் தீயொழுக்கம்
என்றும் இடும்பை தரும். — 138

ஒழுக்க முடையவர்க்கு ஒல்லாவே தீய
வழுக்கியும் வாயாற் சொலல். — 139

உலகத்தோடு ஒட்ட ஒழுகல் பலகற்றும்
கல்லார் அறிவிலா தார். — 140

1.2.11. பிறனில் விழையாமை

பிறன்பொருளாள் பெட்டொழுகும் பேதைமை ஞாலத்து அறம்பொருள் கண்டார்கண் இல்.	141
அறன்கடை நின்றாருள் எல்லாம் பிறன்கடை நின்றாரின் பேதையார் இல்.	142
விளிந்தாரின் வேறல்லர் மன்ற தெளிந்தாரில் தீமை புரிந்து ஒழுகு வார்.	143
எனைத்துணையர் ஆயினும் என்னாம் தினைத்துணையும் தேரான் பிறனில் புகல்.	144
எளிதென இல்லிறப்பான் எய்துமெஞ் ஞான்றும் விளியாது நிற்கும் பழி.	145
பகைபாவம் அச்சம் பழியென நான்கும் இகவாவாம் இல்லிறப்பான் கண்.	146
அறனியலான் இல்வாழ்வான் என்பான் பிறனியலாள் பெண்மை நயவா தவன்.	147
பிறன்மனை நோக்காத பேராண்மை சான்றோர்க்கு அறனொன்றோ ஆன்ற வொழுக்கு.	148
நலக்குரியார் யாரெனின் நாமநீர் வைப்பின் பிறர்க்குரியாள் தோள்தோயா தார்.	149
அறன்வரையான் அல்ல செயினும் பிறன்வரையாள் பெண்மை நயவாமை நன்று.	150

1.2.12. பொறையுடைமை

அகழ்வாரைத் தாங்கும் நிலம்போலத் தம்மை இகழ்வார்ப் பொறுத்தல் தலை.	151
பொறுத்தல் இறப்பினை என்றும் அதனை மறத்தல் அதனினும் நன்று.	152
இன்மையுள் இன்மை விருந்தொரால் வன்மையுள் வன்மை மடவார்ப் பொறை.	153
நிறையுடைமை நீங்காமை வேண்டின் பொறையுடைமை போற்றி யொழுகப் படும்.	154
ஒறுத்தாரை ஒன்றாக வையாரே வைப்பர் பொறுத்தாரைப் பொன்போற் பொதிந்து.	155
ஒறுத்தார்க்கு ஒருநாளை இன்பம் பொறுத்தார்க்குப் பொன்றுந் துணையும் புகழ்.	156
திறனல்ல தற்பிறர் செய்யினும் நோநொந்து அறனல்ல செய்யாமை நன்று.	157
மிகுதியான் மிக்கவை செய்தாரைத் தாந்தம் தகுதியான் வென்று விடல்.	158
துறந்தாரின் தூய்மை உடையர் இறந்தார்வாய் இன்னாச்சொல் நோற்கிற் பவர்.	159
உண்ணாது நோற்பார் பெரியர் பிறர்சொல்லும் இன்னாச்சொல் நோற்பாரின் பின்.	160

1.2.13 அழுக்காறாமை

ஒழுக்காறாக் கொள்க ஒருவன்தன் நெஞ்சத்து அழுக்காறு இலாத இயல்பு.	161
விழுப்பேற்றின் அஃதொப்பது இல்லையார் மாட்டும் அழுக்காற்றின் அன்மை பெறின்.	162
அறன்ஆக்கம் வேண்டாதான் என்பான் பிறனாக்கம் பேணாது அழுக்கறுப் பான்.	163
அழுக்காற்றின் அல்லவை செய்யார் இழுக்காற்றின் ஏதம் படுபாக்கு அறிந்து.	164
அழுக்காறு உடையார்க்கு அதுசாலும் ஒன்னார் வழுக்கயேம் கேடென் பது.	165
கொடுப்பது அழுக்கறுப்பான் சுற்றம் உடுப்பதூஉம் உண்பதூஉம் இன்றிக் கெடும்.	166
அவ்வித்து அழுக்காறு உடையானைச் செய்யவள் தவ்வையைக் காட்டி விடும்.	167
அழுக்காறு எனஒரு பாவி திருச்செற்றுத் தீயுழி உய்த்து விடும்.	168
அவ்விய நெஞ்சத்தான் ஆக்கமும் செவ்வியான் கேடும் நினைக்கப் படும்.	169
அழுக்கற்று அகன்றாரும் இல்லை அஃதுஇல்லார் பெருக்கத்தில் தீர்ந்தாரும் இல்.	170

1.2.14. வெஃகாமை

நடுவின்றி நன்பொருள் வெஃகின் குடிபொன்றிக் குற்றமும் ஆங்கே தரும்.	171
படுபயன் வெஃகிப் பழிப்படுவ செய்யார் நடுவன்மை நாணு பவர்.	172
சிற்றின்பம் வெஃகி அறனல்ல செய்யாரே மற்றின்பம் வேண்டு பவர்.	173
இலமென்று வெஃகுதல் செய்யார் புலம்வென்ற புன்மையில் காட்சி யவர்.	174
அஃகி அகன்ற அறிவென்னாம் யார்மாட்டும் வெஃகி வெறிய செயின்.	175
அருள்வெஃகி ஆற்றின்கண் நின்றான் பொருள்வெஃகிப் பொல்லாத சூழக் கெடும்.	176
வேண்டற்க வெஃகியாம் ஆக்கம் விளைவயின் மாண்டற் கரிதாம் பயன்.	177
அஃகாமை செல்வத்திற்கு யாதெனின் வெஃகாமை வேண்டும் பிறன்கைப் பொருள்.	178
அறனிந்து வெஃகா அறிவுடையார்ச் சேரும் திறன்அரிந் தாங்கே திரு.	179
இறலீனும் எண்ணாது வெஃகின் விறல்ஈனும் வேண்டாமை என்னுஞ் செருக்கு.	180

1.2.15. புறங்கூறாமை

அறங்கூறான் அல்ல செயினும் ஒருவன்	
புறங்கூறான் என்றல் இனிது.	181
அறனழீஇ அல்லவை செய்தலின் தீதே	
புறனழீஇப் பொய்த்து நகை.	182
புறங்கூறிப் பொய்த்துயிர் வாழ்தலின் சாதல்	
அறங்கூற்றும் ஆக்கத் தரும்.	183
கண்ணின்று கண்ணறச் சொல்லினும் சொல்லற்க	
முன்னின்று பின்னோக்காச் சொல்.	184
அறஞ்சொல்லும் நெஞ்சத்தான் அன்மை புறஞ்சொல்லும்	
புன்மையாற் காணப் படும்.	185
பிறன்பழி கூறுவான் தன்பழி யுள்ளும்	
திறன்தெரிந்து கூறப் படும்.	186
பகச்சொல்லிக் கேளிர்ப் பிரிப்பர் நகச்சொல்லி	
நட்பாடல் தேற்றா தவர்.	187
துன்னியார் குற்றமும் தூற்றும் மரபினார்	
என்னைகொல் ஏதிலார் மாட்டு.	188
அறன்நோக்கி ஆற்றுங்கொல் வையம் புறன்நோக்கிப்	
புன்சொல் உரைப்பான் பொறை.	189
ஏதிலார் குற்றம்போல் தங்குற்றங் காண்கிற்பின்	
தீதுண்டோ மன்னும் உயிர்க்கு.	190

1.2.16. பயனில சொல்லாமை

பல்லார் முனியப் பயனில சொல்லுவான்	
எல்லாரும் எள்ளப் படும்.	191
பயனில பல்லார்முன் சொல்லல் நயனில	
நட்டார்கண் செய்தலிற் றீது.	192
நயனிலன் என்பது சொல்லும் பயனில	
பாரித் துரைக்கும் உரை.	193
நயன்சாரா நன்மையின் நீக்கும் பயன்சாராப்	
பண்பில்சொல் பல்லா ரகத்து.	194
சீர்மை சிறப்பொடு நீங்கும் பயனில	
நீர்மை யுடையார் சொலின்.	195
பயனில் சொல் பராட்டு வானை மகன்எனல்	
மக்கட் பதடி யெனல்.	196
நயனில சொல்லினுஞ் சொல்லுக சான்றோர்	
பயனில சொல்லாமை நன்று.	197
அரும்பயன் ஆயும் அறிவினார் சொல்லார்	
பெரும்பயன் இல்லாத சொல்.	198
பொருள்தீர்ந்த பொச்சாந்துஞ் சொல்லார் மருள்தீர்ந்த	
மாசறு காட்சி யவர்.	199
சொல்லுக சொல்லிற் பயனுடைய சொல்லற்க	
சொல்லிற் பயனிலாச் சொல்.	200

1.2.17. தீவினையச்சம்

தீவினையார் அஞ்சார் விழுமியார் அஞ்சுவர்
தீவினை என்னும் செருக்கு. 201
தீயவை தீய பயத்தலால் தீயவை
தீயினும் அஞ்சப் படும். 202
அறிவினுள் எல்லாந் தலையென்ப தீய
செறுவார்க்கும் செய்யா விடல். 203
மறந்தும் பிறன்கேடு சூழற்க சூழின்
அறஞ்சூழம் சூழ்ந்தவன் கேடு. 204
இலன் என்று தீயவை செய்யற்க செய்யின்
இலனாகும் மற்றும் பெயர்த்து. 205
தீப்பால தான்பிறர்கண் செய்யற்க நோய்ப்பால
தன்னை அடல்வேண்டா தான். 206
எனைப்பகை யுற்றாரும் உய்வர் வினைப்பகை
வீயாது பின்சென்று அடும். 207
தீயவை செய்தார் கெடுதல் நிழல்தன்னை
வீயாது அடிஉறைந் தற்று. 208
தன்னைத்தான் காதல னாயின் எனைத்தொன்றும்
துன்னற்க தீவினைப் பால். 209
அருங்கேடன் என்பது அறிக மருங்கோடித்
தீவினை செய்யான் எனின். 210

1.2.18. ஒப்புரவறிதல்

கைம்மாறு வேண்டா கடப்பாடு மாரிமாட்டு
என் ஆற்றுங் கொல்லோ உலகு. 211
தாளாற்றித் தந்த பொருளெல்லாம் தக்கார்க்கு
வேளாண்மை செய்தற் பொருட்டு. 212
புத்தே ளுலகத்தும் ஈண்டும் பெறலரிதே
ஒப்புரவின் நல்ல பிற. 213
ஒத்த தறவோன் உயிர்வாழ்வான் மற்றையான்
செத்தாருள் வைக்கப் படும். 214
ஊருணி நீர்நிறைந் தற்றே உலகவாம்
பேரறி வாளன் திரு. 215
பயன்மரம் உள்ளூர்ப் பழுத்தற்றால் செல்வம்
நயனுடை யான்கண் படின். 216
மருந்தாகித் தப்பா மரத்தற்றால் செல்வம்
பெருந்தகை யான்கண் படின். 217
இடனில் பருவத்தும் ஒப்புரவிற்கு ஒல்கார்
கடனறி காட்சி யவர். 218
நயனுடையான் நல்கூர்ந்தா னாதல் செயும்நீர
செய்யாது அமைகலா வாறு. 219
ஒப்புரவி னால்வரும் கேடெனின் அஃதொருவன்
விற்றுக்கோள் தக்க துடைத்து. 220

1.2.19. ஈகை

வறியார்க்கொன்று ஈவதே ஈகைமற் றெல்லாம் குறியெதிர்ப்பை நீர துடைத்து.	221
நல்லாறு எனினும் கொளல்தீது மேலுலகம் இல்லெனினும் ஈதலே நன்று.	222
இலனென்னும் எவ்வம் உரையாமை ஈதல் குலனுடையான் கண்ணே யுள.	223
இன்னாது இரக்கப் படுதல் இரந்தவர் இன்முகங் காணும் அளவு.	224
ஆற்றுவார் ஆற்றல் பசிஆற்றல் அப்பசியை மாற்றுவார் ஆற்றலின் பின்.	225
அற்றார் அழிபசி தீர்த்தல் அஃதொருவன் பெற்றான் பொருள்வைப் புழி.	226
பாத்தூண் மரீஇ யவனைப் பசியென்னும் தீப்பிணி தீண்டல் அரிது.	227
ஈத்துவக்கும் இன்பம் அறியார்கொல் தாமுடைமை வைத்திழக்கும் வன்க ணவர்.	228
இரத்தலின் இன்னாது மன்ற நிரப்பிய தாமே தமியர் உணல்.	229
சாதலின் இன்னாத தில்லை இனிததூஉம் ஈதல் இயையாக் கடை.	230

1.2.20. புகழ்

ஈதல் இசைபட வாழ்தல் அதுவல்லது ஊதியம் இல்லை உயிர்க்கு.	231
உரைப்பார் உரைப்பவை எல்லாம் இரப்பார்க்கொன்று ஈவார்மேல் நிற்கும் புகழ்.	232
ஒன்றா உலகத்து உயர்ந்த புகழல்லால் பொன்றாது நிற்பதொன் றில்.	233
நிலவரை நீள்புகழ் ஆற்றின் புலவரைப் போற்றாது புத்தேள் உலகு.	234
நத்தம்போல் கேடும் உளதாகும் சாக்காடும் வித்தகர்க் கல்லால் அரிது.	235
தோன்றின் புகழொடு தோன்றுக அஃதிலார் தோன்றலின் தோன்றாமை நன்று.	236
புகழ்பட வாழாதார் தந்நோவார் தம்மை இகழ்வாரை நோவது எவன்?	237
வசையென்ப வையத்தார்க் கெல்லாம் இசையென்னும் எச்சம் பெறாஅ விடின்.	238
வசையிலா வண்பயன் குன்றும் இசையிலா யாக்கை பொறுத்த நிலம்.	239
வசையொழிய வாழ்வாரே வாழ்வார் இசையொழிய வாழ்வாரே வாழா தவர்.	240

இல்லறவியல் முற்றிற்று

1.3 துறவறவியல்

1.3.1 அருளுடைமை

அருட்செல்வம் செல்வத்துள் செல்வம் பொருட்செல்வம்	
பூரியார் கண்ணும் உள.	241
நல்லாற்றாள் நாடி அருளாள்க பல்லாற்றால்	
தேரினும் அஃதே துணை.	242
அருள்சேர்ந்த நெஞ்சினார்க் கில்லை இருள்சேர்ந்த	
இன்னா உலகம் புகல்.	243
மன்னுயிர் ஓம்பி அருளாள்வார்க்கு இல்லென்ப	
தன்னுயிர் அஞ்சும் வினை.	244
அல்லல் அருளாள்வார்க்கு இல்லை வளிவழங்கும்	
மல்லன்மா ஞாலங் கரி.	245
பொருள்நீங்கிப் பொச்சாந்தார் என்பர் அருள்நீங்கி	
அல்லவை செய்தொழுகு வார்.	246
அருளில்லார்க்கு அவ்வுலகம் இல்லை பொருளில்லார்க்கு	
இவ்வுலகம் இல்லாகி யாங்கு.	247
பொருளற்றார் பூப்பர் ஒருகால் அருளற்றார்	
அற்றார்மற் றாதல் அரிது.	248
தெருளாதான் மெய்ப்பொருள் கண்டற்றால் தேரின்	
அருளாதான் செய்யும் அறம்.	249
வலியார்முன் தன்னை நினைக்க தான் தன்னின்	
மெலியார்மேல் செல்லு மிடத்து.	250

1.3.2. புலான்மறுத்தல்

தன்னூன் பெருக்கற்குத் தான்பிறிது ஊனுண்பான்	
எங்ஙனம் ஆளும் அருள்?	251
பொருளாட்சி போற்றாதார்க்கு இல்லை அருளாட்சி	
ஆங்கில்லை ஊன்தின் பவர்க்கு.	252
படைகொண்டார் நெஞ்சம்போல் நன்னூக்காது ஒன்றன்	
உடல்சுவை உண்டார் மனம்.	253
ருள்லது யாதெனின் கொல்லாமை கோறல்	
பொருளல்லது அவ்வூன் தினல்.	254
உண்ணாமை உள்ளது உயிர்நிலை ஊனுண்ண	
அண்ணாத்தல் செய்யாது அளறு.	255
தின்பொருட்டால் கொல்லாது உலகெனின் யாரும்	
விலைப்பொருட்டால் ஊன்தருவா ரில்.	256
உண்ணாமை வேண்டும் புலாஅல் பிறிதொன்றன்	
புண்ணது உணர்வார்ப் பெறின்.	257
செயிரின் தலைப்பிரிந்த காட்சியார் உண்ணார்	
உயிரின் தலைப்பிரிந்த ஊன்.	258
அவிசொரிந் தாயிரம் வேட்டலின் ஒன்றன்	
உயிர்செகுத் துண்ணாமை நன்று.	259
கொல்லான் புலாலை மறுத்தானைக் கைகூப்பி	
எல்லா உயிருந் தொழும்.	260

1.3.3 தவம்

உற்றநோய் நோன்றல் உயிர்க்குறுகண் செய்யாமை அற்றே தவத்திற் குரு.	261
தவமும் தவமுடையார்க்கு ஆகும் அதனை அஃதிலார் மேற்கொள் வது.	262
துறந்தார்க்குத் துப்புரவு வேண்டி மறந்தார்கொல் மற்றை யவர்கள் தவம்.	263
ஒன்னார்த் தெறலும் உவந்தாரை ஆக்கலும் எண்ணின் தவத்தான் வரும்.	264
வேண்டிய வேண்டியாங் கெய்தலால் செய்தவம் ஈண்டு முயலப் படும்.	265
தவஞ் செய்வார் தங்கருமஞ் செய்வார்மற் றல்லார் அவஞ்செய்வார் ஆசையுட் பட்டு.	266
சுடச்சுடரும் பொன்போல் ஒளிவிடும் துன்பஞ் சுடச்சுட நோற்கிற் பவர்க்கு.	267
தன்னுயிர் தான்அறப் பெற்றானை ஏனைய மன்னுயி ரெல்லாந் தொழும்.	268
கூற்றம் குதித்தலும் கைகூடும் நோற்றலின் ஆற்றல் தலைப்பட் டவர்க்குல்.	269
இலர்பல ராகிய காரணம் நோற்பார் சிலர்பலர் நோலா தவர்.	270

1.3.4. கூடாவொழுக்கம்

வஞ்ச மனத்தான் படிற்றொழுக்கம் பூதங்கள் ஐந்தும் அகத்தே நகும்.	271
வானுயர் தோற்றம் எவன்செய்யும் தன்னெஞ்சம் தான்அறி குற்றப் படின்.	272
வலியில் நிலைமையான் வல்லுருவம் பெற்றம் புலியின்தோல் போர்த்துமேய்ந் தற்று.	273
தவமறைந்து அல்லவை செய்தல் புதல்மறைந்து வேட்டுவன் புள்சிமிழ்த் தற்று.	274
பற்றற்றேம் என்பார் படிற்றொழுக்கம் எற்றெற்றென்று ஏதம் பலவுந் தரும்.	275
நெஞ்சின் துறவார் துறந்தார்போல் வஞ்சித்து வாழ்வாரின் வன்கணார் இல்.	276
புறங்குன்றி கண்டனைய ரேனும் அகங்குன்றி முக்கிற் கரியார் உடைத்து.	277
மனத்தது மாசாக மாண்டார் நீராடி மறைந்தொழுகு மாந்தர் பலர்.	278
கணைகொடிது யாழ்கோடு செவ்விதுஆங் கன்ன வினைபடு பாலால் கொளல்.	279
மழித்தலும் நீட்டலும் வேண்டா உலகம் பழித்தது ஒழித்து விடின்.	280

1.3.5. கள்ளாமை

எள்ளாமை வேண்டுவான் என்பான் எனைத்தொன்றும்	
கள்ளாமை காக்கதன் நெஞ்சு.	281
உள்ளத்தால் உள்ளலும் தீதே பிறன்பொருளைக்	
கள்ளத்தால் கள்வேம் எனல்.	282
களவினால் ஆகிய ஆக்கம் அளவிறந்து	
ஆவது போலக் கெடும்.	283
களவின்கண் கன்றிய காதல் விளைவின்கண்	
வீயா விழுமம் தரும்.	284
அருள்கருதி அன்புடைய ராதல் பொருள்கருதிப்	
பொச்சாப்புப் பார்ப்பார்கண் இல்.	285
அளவின்கண் நின்றொழுகல் ஆற்றார் களவின்கண்	
கன்றிய காத லவர்.	286
களவென்னும் காரறி வாண்மை அளவென்னும்	
ஆற்றல் புரிந்தார்கண்ட இல்.	287
அளவறேந்தார் நெஞ்சத் தறம்போல நிற்கும்	
களவறிந்தார் நெஞ்சில் கரவு.	288
அளவல்ல செய்தாங்கே வீவர் களவல்ல	
மற்றைய தேற்றா தவர்.	289
கள்வார்க்குத் தள்ளும் உயிர்நிலை கள்வார்க்குத்	
தள்ளாது புத்தே ளுளகு.	290

1.3.6. வாய்மை

வாய்மை எனப்படுவது யாதெனின் யாதொன்றும்	
தீமை இலாத சொலல்.	291
பொய்மையும் வாய்மை யிடத்த புரைதீர்ந்த	
நன்மை பயக்கும் எனின்.	292
தன்நெஞ் சறிவது பொய்யற்க பொய்த்தபின்	
தன்நெஞ்சே தன்னைச் சுடும்.	293
உள்ளத்தார் பொய்யா தொழுகின் உலகத்தார்	
உள்ளத்து எல்லாம் உளன்.	294
மனத்தொடு வாய்மை மொழியின் தவத்தொடு	
தானஞ்செய் வாரின் தலை.	295
பொய்யாமை அன்ன புகழில்லை எய்யாமை	
எல்லா அறமுந் தரும்.	296
பொய்யாமை பொய்யாமை ஆற்றின் அறம்பிற	
செய்யாமை செய்யாமை நன்று.	297
புறந்தூய்மை நீரான் அமையும் அகந்தூய்மை	
வாய்மையால் காணப் படும்.	298
எல்லா விளக்கும் விளக்கல்ல சான்றோர்க்குப்	
பொய்யா விளக்கே விளக்கு.	299
யாமெய்யாக் கண்டவற்றுள் இல்லை எனைத்தொன்றும்	
வாய்மையின் நல்ல பிற.	300

1.3.7   வெகுளாமை

செல்லிடத்துக் காப்பான் சினங்காப்பான் அல்லிடத்துக்	
காக்கின்என் காவாக்கால் என்?	301
செல்லா இடத்துச் சினந்தீது செல்லிடத்தும்	
இல்அதனின் தீய பிற.	302
மறத்தல் வெகுளியை யார்மாட்டும் தீய	
பிறத்தல் அதனான் வரும்.	303
நகையும் உவகையும் கொல்லும் சினத்தின்	
பகையும் உளவோ பிற.	304
தன்னைத்தான் காக்கின் சினங்காக்க காவாக்கால்	
தன்னையே கொல்லுஞ் சினம்.	305
சினமென்னும் சேர்ந்தாரைக் கொல்லி இனமென்னும்	
ஏமப் புணையையச் சுடும்.	306
சினத்தைப் பொருளென்று கொண்டவன் கேடு	
நிலத்தறைந்தான் கைபிழையா தற்று.	307
இணர்எரி தோய்வன்ன இன்னா செயினும்	
புணரின் வெகுளாமை நன்று.	308
உள்ளிய தெல்லாம் உடனெய்தும் உள்ளத்தால்	
உள்ளான் வெகுளி எனின்.	309
இறந்தார் இறந்தார் அனையர் சினத்தைத்	
துறந்தார் துறந்தார் துணை.	310

1.3.8   இன்னாசெய்யாமை

சிறப்பீனும் செல்வம் பெறினும் பிறர்க்கு இன்னா	
செய்யாமை மாசற்றார் கோள்.	311
கறுத்துஇன்னா செய்தவக் கண்ணும் மறுத்தின்னா	
செய்யாமை மாசற்றார் கோள்.	312
செய்யாமல் செற்றார்க்கும் இன்னாத செய்தபின்	
உய்யா விழுமந் தரும்.	313
இன்னாசெய் தாரை ஒறுத்தல் அவர்நாண	
நன்னயஞ் செய்து விடல்.	314
அறிவினான் ஆகுவ துண்டோ பிறிதின்நோய்	
தந்நோய்போல் போற்றாக் கடை.	315
> இன்னா எனத்தான் உணர்ந்தவை துன்னாமை	
வேண்டும் பிறன்கண் செயல்.	316
எனைத்தானும் எஞ்ஞான்றும் யார்க்கும் மனத்தானாம்	
மாணாசெய் யாமை தலை.	317
தன்னுயிர்க்கு ஏன்னாமை தானறிவான் என்கொலோ	
மன்னுயிர்க்கு இன்னா செயல்.	318
பிறர்க்கின்னா முற்பகல் செய்யின் தமக்கு இன்னா	
பிற்பகல் தாமே வரும்.	319
நோயெல்லாம் நோய்செய்தார் மேலவாம் நோய்செய்யார்	
நோயின்மை வேண்டு பவர்.	320

1.3.9 கொல்லாமை

அறவினை யாதெனின் கொல்லாமை கோறல்	
பிறவினை எல்லாந் தரும்.	321
பகுத்துண்டு பல்லுயிர் ஓம்புதல் நூலோர்	
தொகுத்தவற்றுள் எல்லாந் தலை.	322
ஒன்றாக நல்லது கொல்லாமை மற்றதன்	
பின்சாரப் பொய்யாமை நன்று.	323
நல்லாறு எனப்படுவது யாதெனின் யாதொன்றும்	
கொல்லாமை சூழும் நெறி.	324
நிலைஅஞ்சி நீத்தாருள் எல்லாம் கொலைஅஞ்சிக்	
கொல்லாமை சூழ்வான் தலை.	325
கொல்லாமை மேற்கொண் டொழுகுவான் வாழ்நாள்மேல்	
செல்லாது உயிருண்ணுங் கூற்று.	326
தன்னுயிர் நீப்பினும் செய்யற்க தான்பிறிது	
இன்னுயிர் நீக்கும் வினை.	327
நன்றாகும் ஆக்கம் பெரிதெனினும் சான்றோர்க் குக்	
கொன்றாகும் ஆக்கங் கடை.	328
கொலைவினைய ராகிய மாக்கள் புலைவினையர்	
புன்மை தெரிவா ரகத்து.	329
உயிர் உடம்பின் நீக்கியார் என்ப செயிர் உடம்பின்	
செல்லாத்தீ வாழ்க்கை யவர்.	330

1.3.10 நிலையாமை

நில்லாத வற்றை நிலையின என்றுணரும்	
புல்லறி வாண்மை கடை.	331
கூத்தாட்டு அவைக் குழாத் தற்றே பெருஞ்செல்வம்	
போக்கும் அதுவிளிந் தற்று.	332
அற்கா இயல்பிற்றுச் செல்வம் அதுபெற்றால்	
அற்குப ஆங்கே செயல்.	333
நாளென ஒன்றுபோற் காட்டி உயிர் ஈரும்	
வாளது உணர்வார்ப் பெறின்.	334
நாச்செற்று விக்குள்மேல் வாராமுன் நல்வினை	
மேற்சென்று செய்யப் படும்	335
நெருநல் உளனொருவன் இன்றில்லை என்னும்	
பெருமை உடைத்துஇவ் வுலகு.	336
ஒருபொழுதும் வாழ்வது அறியார் கருதுப	
கோடியும் அல்ல பல.	337
குடம்பை தனித்து ஒழியப் புள்பறந் தற்றே	
உடம்பொடு உயிரிடை நட்பு.	338
உறங்கு வதுபோலுஞ் சாக்காடு உறங்கி	
விழிப்பது போலும் பிறப்பு.	339
புக்கில் அமைந்தின்று கொல்லோ உடம்பினுள்	
துச்சில் இருந்த உயிர்க்கு.	340

1.3.11 துறவு

யாதனின் யாதனின் நீங்கியான் நோதல்	
அதனின் அதனின் இலன்.	341
வேண்டின் உண் டாகத் துறக்க துறந்தபின்	
ஈண்டுஇயற் பால பல.	342
அடல்வேண்டும் ஐந்தன் புலத்தை விடல்வேண்டும்	
வேண்டிய வெல்லாம் ஒருங்கு.	343
இயல்பாகும் நோன்பிற்கொன்று இன்மை உடைமை	
மயலாகும் மற்றும் பெயர்த்து.	344
மற்றும் தொடர்ப்பாடு எவன்கொல் பிறப்பறுக்கல்	
உற்றார்க்கு உடம்பும் மிகை.	345
யான் எனது என்னும் செருக்கு அறுப்பான் வானோர்க்கு	
உயர்ந்த உலகம் புகும்.	346
பற்றி விடாஅ இடும்பைகள் பற்றினைப்	
பற்றி விடாஅ தவர்க்கு.	347
தலைப்பட்டார் தீரத் துறந்தார் மயங்கி	
வலைப்பட்டார் மற்றை யவர்.	348
பற்றற்ற கண்ணே பிறப்பறுக்கும் மற்று	
நிலையாமை காணப் படும்.	349
பற்றுக பற்றற்றான் பற்றினை அப்பற்றைப்	
பற்றுக பற்று விடற்கு.	350

1.3.12 மெய்யுணர்தல்

பொருளல்ல வற்றைப் பொருளென்று உணரும்	
மருளானாம் மாணாப் பிறப்பு.	351
இருள்நீங்கி இன்பம் பயக்கும் மருள்நீங்கி	
மாசறு காட்சி யவர்க்கு.	352
ஐயத்தின் நீங்கித் தெளிந்தார்க்கு வையத்தின்	
வானம் நணிய துடைத்து.	353
ஐயுணர்வு எய்தியக் கண்ணும் பயமின்றே	
மெய்யுணர்வு இல்லா தவர்க்கு.	354
எப்பொருள் எத்தன்மைத் தாயினும் அப்பொருள்	
மெய்ப்பொருள் காண்பது அறிவு.	355
கற்றீண்டு மெய்ப்பொருள் கண்டார் தலைப்படுவர்	
மற்றீண்டு வாரா நெறி.	356
ஓர்த்துள்ளம் உள்ளது உணரேன் ஒருதலையாப்	
பேர்த்துள்ள வேண்டா பிறப்பு.	357
பிறப்பென்னும் பேதைமை நீங்கச் சிறப்பென்னும்	
செம்பொருள் காண்பது அறிவு.	358
சார்புணர்ந்து சார்பு கெடஒழுகின் மற்றழித்துச்	
சார்தரா சார்தரு நோய்.	359
காமம் வெகுளி மயக்கம் இவைமூன்றன்	
நாமம் கெடக்கெடும் நோய்.	360

1.3.13   அவாவறுத்தல்

அவாஎன்ப எல்லா உயிர்க்கும் எஞ் ஞான்றும்
தவாஅப் பிறப்பீனும் வித்து.   361
வேண்டுங்கால் வேண்டும் பிறவாமை மற்றது
வேண்டாமை வேண்ட வரும்.   362
வேண்டாமை அன்ன விழுச்செல்வம் ஈண்டில்லை
ஆண்டும் அஃதொப்பது இல்.   363
தூஉய்மை என்பது அவாவின்மை மற்றது
வாஅய்மை வேண்ட வரும்.   364
அற்றவர் என்பார் அவாஅற்றார் மற்றையார்
அற்றாக அற்றது இலர்.   365
அஞ்சுவ தோரும் அறனே ஒருவனை
வஞ்சிப்ப தோரும் அவா.   366
அவாவினை ஆற்ற அறுப்பின் தவாவினை
தான்வேண்டு மாற்றான் வரும்.   367
அவா இல்லார்க் கில்லாகுந் துன்பம் அஃதுண்டேல்
தவாஅது மேன்மேல் வரும்.   368
இன்பம் இடையறா தீண்டும் அவவென்னும்
துன்பத்துள் துன்பங் கெடின்.   369
ரா இயற்கை அவாநீப்பின் அந்நிலையே
பேரா இயற்கை தரும்.   370

1.4   ஊழியல்
1.4.1.   ஊழ

ஆகூழால் தோன்றும் அசைவின்மை கைப்பொருள்
போகூழால் தோன்றும் மடி.   371
பேதைப் படுக்கும் இழவூழ் அறிவகற்றும்
ஆகலூழ் உற்றக் கடை.   372
நுண்ணிய நூல்பல கற்பினும் மற்றுந்தன்
உண்மை யறிவே மிகும்.   373
இருவேறு உலகத்து இயற்கை திருவேறு
தெள்ளிய ராதலும் வேறு.   374
நல்லவை எல்லாஅந் தீயவாம் தீயவும்
நல்லவாம் செல்வம் செயற்கு.   375
பரியினும் ஆகாவாம் பாலல்ல உய்த்துச்
சொரியினும் போகா தம.   376
வகுத்தான் வகுத்த வகையல்லால் கோடி
தொகுத்தார்க்கு துய்த்தல் அரிது.   377
துறப்பார்மன் துப்புர வில்லார் உறற்பால
ஊட்டா கழியு மெனின்.   378
நன்றாங்கால் நல்லவாக் காண்பவர் அன்றாங்கால்
அல்லற் படுவ தெவன்?   379
ஊழிற் பெருவலி யாவுள மற்றொன்று
சூழினுந் தான்முன் துழும்.   380

ஊழியல் முற்றிற்று
அறத்துப்பால் முற்றிற்று

2. பொருட்பால்

2.1 அரசியல்

2.1.1 இறைமாட்சி

படைகுடி கூழ்அமைச்சு நட்பரண் ஆறும் உடையான் அரசருள் ஏறு.	381
அஞ்சாமை ஈகை அறிவூக்கம் இந்நான்கும் எஞ்சாமை வேந்தர்க் கியல்பு.	382
தூங்காமை கல்வி துணிவுடைமை இம்மூன்றும் நீங்கா நிலனான் பவர்க்கு.	383
அறனிழுக்கா தல்லவை நீக்கி மறனிழுக்கா மானம் உடைய தரசு.	384
இயற்றலும் ஈட்டலுங் காத்தலும் காத்த வகுத்தலும் வல்ல தரசு.	385
காட்சிக் கெளியன் கடுஞ்சொல்லன் அல்லனேல் மீக்கூறும் மன்னன் நிலம்	386
இன்சொலால் ஈத்தளிக்க வல்லார்க்குத் தன்சொலால் தான்கண் டனைத்திவ் வுலகு.	387
முறைசெய்து காப்பாற்றும் மன்னவன் மக்கட்கு இறையென்று வைக்கப் படும்.	388
செவிகைப்பச் சொற்பொறுக்கும் பண்புடை வேந்தன் கவிகைக்கீழ்த் தங்கும் உலகு.	389
கொடையளி செங்கோல் குடியோம்பல் நான்கும் உடையானாம் வேந்தர்க் கொளி.	390

2.1.2 கல்வி

கற்க கசடறக் கற்பவை கற்றபின் நிற்க அதற்குத் தக.	391
எண்ணென்ப ஏனை எழுத்தென்ப இவ்விரண் டும் கண்ணென்ப வாழும் உயிர்க்கு.	392
கண்ணுடையர் என்பவர் கற்றோர் முகத்திரண்டு புண்ணுடையர் கல்லா தவர்.	393
உவப்பத் தலைக்கூடி உள்ளப் பிரிதல் அனைத்தே புலவர் தொழில்.	394
உடையார்முன் இல்லார்போல் ஏக்கற்றுங் கற்றார் கடையரே கல்லா தவர்.	395
தொட்டனைத் தூறும் மணற்கேணி மாந்தர்க்குக் கற்றனைத் தூறும் அறிவு.	396
யாதானும் நாடாமால் ஊராமால் என்னொருவன் சாந்துணையுங் கல்லாத வாறு.	397
ஒருமைக்கண் தான் கற்ற கல்வி ஒருவற்கு எழுமையும் ஏமாப் புடைத்து.	398
தாமின் புறுவது உலகின் புறக் கண்டு காமுறுவர் கற்றறிந் தார்.	399
கேடில் விழுச்செல்வம் கல்வி யொருவற்கு மாடல்ல மற்றை யவை.	400

2.1.3 கல்லாமை

அரங்கின்றி வட்டாடி யற்றே நிரம்பிய நூலின்றிக் கோட்டி கொளல்.	401
கல்லாதான் சொற்கா முறுதல் முலையிரண்டும் இல்லாதாள் பெண்காமுற் றற்று.	402
கல்லா தவரும் நனிநல்லர் கற்றார்முன் சொல்லா திருக்கப் பெறின்.	403
கல்லாதான் ஒட்பம் கழியநன் றாயினும் கொள்ளார் அறிவுடை யார்.	404
கல்லா ஒருவன் தகைமை தலைப்பெய்து சொல்லாடச் சோர்வு படும்.	405
உளரென்னும் மாத்திரையர் அல்லால் பயவாக் களரனையர் கல்லா தவர்.	406
நுண்மாண் நுழைபுலம் இல்லான் எழில்நலம் மண்மாண் புனைபாவை யற்று.	407
நல்லார்கண் பட்ட வறுமையின் இன்னாதே கல்லார்கண் பட்ட திரு.	408
மேற்பிறந்தா ராயினும் கல்லாதார் கீழ்ப்பிறந்தும் கற்றார் அனைத்திலர் பாடு.	409
விலங்கொடு மக்கள் அனையர் இலங்குநூல் கற்றாரோடு ஏனை யவர்.	410

2.1.4 கேள்வி

செல்வத்துட் செல்வஞ் செவிச்செல்வம் அச்செல்வம் செல்வத்து ளெல்லாந் தலை.	411
செவகேக்குண வில்லாத போழ்து சிறிது வயிற்றுக்கும் ஈயப் படும்.	412
செவியுணவிற் கேள்வி யுடையார் அவியுணவின் ஆன்றாரோ டொப்பர் நிலத்து.	413
கற்றில னாயினுங் கேட்க அஃதொருவற்கு ஒற்கத்தின் ஊற்றாந் துணை.	414
இழுக்கல் உடையுழி ஊற்றுக்கோல் அற்றே ஒழுக்க முடையார்வாய்ச் சொல்.	415
எனைத்தானும் நல்லவை கேட்க அனைத்தானும் ஆன்ற பெருமை தரும்.	416
பிழைத் துணர்ந்தும் பேதைமை சொல்லா ரிழைத்துணர்ந் தீண்டிய கேள்வி யவர்.	417
கேட்பினுங் கேளாத் தகையவே கேள்வியால் தோட்கப் படாத செவி.	418
நுணங்கிய கேள்விய ரல்லார் வணங்கிய வாயின ராதல் அரிது.	419
செவியிற் சுவையுணரா வாயுணர்வின் மாக்கள் அவியினும் வாழினும் என்?	420

2.1.5 அறிவுடைமை

அறிவற்றங் காக்குங் கருவி செறுவார்க்கும் உள்ளழிக்க லாகா அரண்.	421
சென்ற இடத்தால் செலவிடா தீதொரீஇ நன்றின்பால் உய்ப்ப தறிவு.	422
எப்பொருள் யார்யார்வாய்க் கேட்பினும் அப்பொருள் மெய்ப்பொருள் காண்ப தறிவு.	423
எண்பொருள வாகச் செலச்சொல்லித் தான்பிறர்வாய் நுண்பொருள் காண்ப தறிவு.	424
உலகம் தழீஇய தொட்பம் மலர்தலும் கூம்பலும் இல்ல தறிவு.	425
எவ்வ துறைவது உலகம் உலகத்தோடு அவ்வ துறைவ தறிவு.	426
அறிவுடையார் ஆவ தறிவார் அறிவிலார் அஃதறி கல்லா தவர்.	427
அஞ்சுவ தஞ்சாமை பேதைமை அஞ்சுவது அஞ்சல் அறிவார் தொழில்.	428
எதிரதாக் காக்கும் அறிவினார்க் கில்லை அதிர வருவதோர் நோய்.	429
அறிவுடையார் எல்லா முடையார் அறிவிலார் என்னுடைய ரேனும் இலர்.	430

2.1.6 குற்றங்கடிதல்

செருக்குஞ் சினமும் சிறுமையும் இல்லார் பெருக்கம் பெருமித நீர்த்து.	431
இவறலும் மாண்பிறந்த மானமும் மாணா உவகையும் ஏதம் இறைக்கு.	432
தினைத்துணையாங் குற்றம் வரினும் பனைத்துணையாக் கொள்வர் பழிநாணு வார்.	433
குற்றமே காக்க பொருளாகக் குற்றமே அற்றந் த்ரூஉம் பகை.	434
வருமுன்னர்க் காவாதான் வாழ்க்கை எரிமுன்னர் வைத்தூறு போலக் கெடும்.	435
தன்குற்றம் நீக்கிப் பிறர்குற்றங் காண்கிற்பின் என்குற்ற மாகும் இறைக்கு?	436
செயற்பால செய்யா திவறியான் செல்வம் உயற்பால தன்றிக் கெடும்.	437
பற்றுள்ளம் என்னும் இவறன்மை எற்றுள்ளும் எண்ணப் படுவதொன் றன்று.	438
வியவற்க எஞ்ஞான்றும் தன்னை நயவற்க நன்றி பயவா வினை.	439
காதல காதல் அறியாமை உய்க்கிற்பின் ஏதில ஏதிலார் நூல்.	440

2.1.7 பெரியாரைத் துணைக்கோடல்

அறநறிந்து மூத்த அறிவுடையார் கேண்மை	
திறனறிந்து தேர்ந்து கொளல்.	441
உற்றநோய் நீக்கி உறாஅமை முற்காக்கும்	
பெற்றியார்ப் பேணிக் கொளல்.	442
அரியவற்று எல்லாம் அரிதே பெரியாரைப்	
பேணித் தமராக் கொளல்.	443
தம்மிற் பெரியார் தமரா ஒழுகுதல்	
வன்மையு ளெல்லாந் தலை.	444
சூழ்வார்கண் ணாக ஒழுகலான் மன்னவன்	
சூழ்வாரைக் சூழ்ந்து கொளல்.	445
தக்கா ரினத்தனாய்த் தானொழுக வல்லானைச்	
செற்றார் செய்க்கிடந்த தில்.	446
இடிக்குந் துணையாரை யாள்வரை யாரே	
கெடுக்குந் தகைமை யவர்.	447
இடிப்பாரை இல்லாத ஏமரா மன்னன்	
கெடுப்பா ரிலானுங் கெடும்.	448
முதலிலார்க ஊதிய மில்லை மதலையாஞ்	
சார்பிலார்க் கில்லை நிலை.	449
பல்லார் பகை கொளலிற் பத்தடுத்த தீமைத்தே	
நல்லார் தொடர்கை விடல்.	450

2.1.8 சிற்றினஞ்சேராமை

சிற்றினம் அஞ்சும் பெருமை சிறுமைதான்	
சுற்றமாச் சூழ்ந்து விடும்.	451
நிலத்தியல்பால் நீர்திரிந் தற்றாகும் மாந்தர்க்கு	
இனத்தியல்ப தாகும் அறிவு.	452
மனத்தானாம் மாந்தர்க் குணர்ச்சி இனத்தானாம்	
இன்னான் எனப்படுஞ் சொல்.	453
மனத்து எதுபோலக் காட்டி ஒருவற்கு	
இனத்துள தாகும் அறிவு.	454
மனந்தூய்மை செய்வினை தூய்மை இரண்டும்	
இனந்தூய்மை தூவா வரும்.	455
மனந்தூயார்க் கெச்சநன் றாகும் இனந்தூயார்க்கு	
இல்லைநன் றாகா வினை.	456
மனநலம் மன்னுயிர்க் காக்கம் இனநலம்	
எல்லாப் புகழும் தரும்.	457
மனநலம் நன்குடைய ராயினும் சான்றோர்க்கு	
இனநலம் ஏமாப் புடைத்து.	458
மனநலத்தின் ஆகும் மறுமைமற் றஃதும்	
இனநலத்தின் ஏமாப் புடைத்து.	459
நல்லினத்தி னூங்குந் துணையில்லை தீயினத்தின்	
அல்லற் படுப்பதூஉம் இல்.	460

2.1.9 தெரிந்துசெயல்வகை

அழிவதூஉம் ஆவதூஉம் ஆகி வழிபயக்கும் ஊதியமும் சூழ்ந்து செயல்.	461
தெரிந்த இனத்தொடு தேர்ந்தெண்ணிச் செய்வார்க்கு அரும்பொருள் யாதொன்றும் இல்	462
ஆக்கம் கருதி முதலிழக்கும் செய்வினை ஊக்கார் அறிவுடை யார்.	463
தெளிவி லதனைத் தொடங்கார் இளிவென்னும் ஏதப்பாடு அஞ்சு பவர்.	464
வகையறச் சூழா தெழுதல் பகைவரைப் பாத்திப் படுப்பதோ ராறு.	465
செய்தக்க அல்ல செயக் கெடும் செய்தக்க செய்யாமை யானுங் கெடும்.	466
எண்ணித் துணிக கருமம் துணிந்தபின் எண்ணுவம் என்பது இழுக்கு.	467
ஆற்றின் வருந்தா வருத்தம் பலர்நின்று போற்றினும் பொத்துப் படும்.	468
நன்றாற்ற லுள்ளுந் தவறுண்டு அவரவர் பண்பறிந் தாற்றாக் கடை.	469
எள்ளாத எண்ணிச் செயல்வேண்டும் தம்மோடு கொள்ளாத கொள்ளாது உலகு.	470

2.1.10 வலியறிதல்

வினைவலியும் தன்வலியும் மாற்றான் வலியும் துணைவலியும் தூக்கிச் செயல்.	471
ஒல்வ தறிவது அறிந்ததன் கண்தங்கிச் செல்வார்க்குச் செல்லாதது இல்.	472
உடைத்தம் வலியறியார் ஊக்கத்தின் ஊக்கி இடைக்கண் முரிந்தார் பலர்.	473
அமைந்தாங் கொழுகான் அளவறியான் தன்னை வியந்தான் விரைந்து கெடும்.	474
பீலிபெய் சாகாடும் அச்சிறும் அப்பண்டஞ் சால மிகுத்துப் பெயின்.	475
நுனிக்கொம்பர் ஏறினார் அஃதிறந் தூக்கின் உயிர்க்கிறுதி ஆகி விடும்.	476
ஆற்றின் அறவறிந்து ஈக அதுபொருள் போற்றி வழங்கு நெறி.	477
ஆகாறு அளவிட்டி தாயினுங் கேடில்லை போகாறு அகலாக் கடை.	478
அளவறந்து வாழாதான் வாழ்க்கை உளபோல இல்லாகித் தோன்றாக் கெடும்.	479
உளவரை தூக்காத ஒப்புர வாண்மை வளவரை வல்லலைக் கெடும்.	480

2.1.11 காலமறிதல்

பகல்வெல்லும் கூகையைக் காக்கை இகல்வெல்லும் வேந்தர்க்கு வேண்டும் பொழுது.	481
பருவத்தோடு ஒட்ட ஒழுகல் திருவினைத் தீராமை ஆர்க்குங் கயிறு.	482
அருவினை யென்ப உளவோ கருவியான் காலம் அறிந்து செயின்.	483
ஞாலம் கருதினுங் கைகூடுங் காலம் கருதி இடத்தாற் செயின்.	484
காலம் கருதி இருப்பர் கலங்காது ஞாலம் கருது பவர்.	485
ஊக்க முடையான் ஒடுக்கம் பொருதகர் தாக்கற்குப் பேருந் தகைத்து.	486
பொள்ளென ஆங்கே புறம்வேரார் காலம்பார்த்து உள்வேர்ப்பர் ஒள்ளி யவர்.	487
செறுநரைக் காணின் சுமக்க இறுவரை காணின் கிழக்காம் தலை.	488
எய்தற் கரியது இயைந்தக்கால் அந்நிலையே செய்தற் கரிய செயல்.	489
கொக்கொக்க கூம்பும் பருவத்து மற்றதன் குத்தொக்க சீர்த்த இடத்து.	490

2.1.12 இடனறிதல்

தொடங்கற்க எவ்வினையும் எள்ளற்க முற்றும் இடங்கண்ட பின்அல் லது.	491
முரண்சேர்ந்த மொய்ம்பி னவர்க்கும் அரண்சேர்ந்தாம் ஆக்கம் பலவுந் தரும்.	492
ஆற்றாரும் ஆற்றி அடுப இடனறிந்து போற்றார்கண் போற்றிச் செயின்.	493
எண்ணியார் எண்ணம் இழப்பர் இடனறிந்து துன்னியார் துன்னிச் செயின்.	494
நெடும்புனலுள் வெல்லும் முதலை அடும்புனலின் நீங்கின் அதனைப் பிற.	495
கடலோடா கால்வல் நெடுந்தேர் கடலோடும் நாவாயும் ஓடா நிலத்து.	496
அஞ்சாமை அல்லால் துணைவேண்டா எஞ்சாமை எண்ணி இடத்தால் செயின்.	497
சிறுபடையான் செல்லிடம் சேரின் உறுபடையான் ஊக்கம் அழிந்து விடும்.	498
சிறைநலனும் சீரும் இலரெனினும் மாந்தர் உறைநிலத்தோடு ஒட்டல் அரிது.	499
காலாழ் களரில் நரியடும் கண்ணஞ்சா வேலாள் முகத்த களிறு.	500

2.1.13 தெரிந்துதெளிதல்

அறம்பொருள் இன்பம் உயிரச்சம் நான்கின் திறந்தெரிந்து தேறப் படும்.	501
குடிபிறந்து குற்றத்தின் நீங்கி வடுப்பரியும் நாணுடையான் சுட்டே தெளிவு.	502
அரியகற்று ஆசற்றார் கண்ணும் தெரியுங்கால் இன்மை அரிதே வெளிறு.	503
குணம்நாடிக் குற்றமும் நாடி அவற்றுள் மிகைநாடி மிக்க கொளல்.	504
பெருமைக்கும் ஏனைச் சிறுமைக்கும் தத்தம் கருமமே கட்டளைக் கல்.	505
அற்றாரைத் தேறுதல் ஓம்புக மற்றவர் பற்றிலர் நாணார் பழி.	506
காதன்மை கந்தா அறிவறியார்த் தேறுதல் பேதைமை எல்லாந் தரும்.	507
தேரான் பிறனைத் தெளிந்தான் வழிமுறை தீரா இடும்பை தரும்.	508
தே றற்க யாரையும் தேராது தேர்ந்தபின் தேறுக தேறும் பொருள்.	509
தேரான் தெளிவும் தெளிந்தான்கண் ஐயுறவும் தீரா இடும்பை தரும்.	510

2.1.14 தெரிந்துவினையாடல்

நன்மையும் தீமையும் நாடி நலம்புரிந்த தன்மையான் ஆளப் படும்.	511
வாரி பெருக்கி வளம்படுத்து உற்றவை ஆராய்வான் செய்க வினை.	512
அன்பறிவு தேற்றம் அவாவின்மை இந்நான்கும் நன்குடையான் கட்டே தெளிவு.	513
எனைவகையான் தேறியக் கண்ணும் வினைவகையான் வேறாகும் மாந்தர் பலர்.	514
அறிந்தாற்றிச் செய்கிற்பாற்கு அல்லால் வினைதான் சிறந்தானென்று ஏவற்பார் றன்று.	515
செய்வானை நாடி வினைநாடிக் காலத்தோடு எய்த உணர்ந்து செயல்.	516
இதனை இதனால் இவன்முடிக்கும் என்றாய்ந்து அதனை அவன்கண் விடல்.	517
வினைக் குரிமை நாடிய பின்றை அவனை அதற்குரிய நாகச் செயல்.	518
வினைக்கண் வினையுடையான் கேண்மையே றாக நினைப்பானை நீங்கும் திரு.	519
நாடோறும் நாடுக மன்னன் வினைசெய்வான் கோடாமை கோடா துலகு.	520

2.1.15 சுற்றந்தழால்

பற்றற்ற கண்ணும் பழைமைபா ராட்டுதல் சுற்றத்தார் கண்ணே உள.	521
விருப்பறாச் சுற்றம் இயையின் அருப்பறா ஆக்கம் பலவும் தரும்.	522
அளவளா வில்லாதான் வாழ்க்கை குளவளாக் கோடின்றி நீர்நிறைந் தற்று.	523
சுற்றத்தால் சுற்றப் படஒழுகல் செல்வந்தான் பெற்றத்தால் பெற்ற பயன்.	524
கொடுத்தலும் இன்சொலும் ஆற்றின் அடுக்கிய சுற்றத்தால் சுற்றப் படும்.	525
பெருங்கொடையான் பேணான் வெகுளி அவனின் மருங்குடையார் மாநிலத்து இல்.	526
காக்கை கரவா கரைந்துண்ணும் ஆக்கமும் அன்னநீ ரார்க்கே உள.	527
பொதுநோக்கான் வேந்தன் வரிசையா நோக்கின் அதுநோக்கி வாழ்வார் பலர்.	528
தமராகிக் தற்றுறந்தார் சுற்றம் அமராமைக் காரணம் இன்றி வரும்.	529
உழைப்பிரிந்து காரணத்தின் வந்தானை வேந்தன் இழைத் திருந்து எண்ணிக் கொளல்.	530

2.1.16 பொச்சாவாமை

இறந்த வெகுளியின் தீதே சிறந்த உவகை மகிழ்ச்சியிற் சோர்வு.	531
பொச்சாப்புக் கொல்லும் புகழை அறிவினை நிச்ச நிரப்புக் கொன் றாங்கு.	532
பொச்சாப்பார்க் கில்லை புகழ்மை அதுஉலகத்து எப்பால்நூ லோர்க்கும் துணிவு.	533
அச்ச முடையார்க்கு அரணில்லை ஆங்கில்லை பொச்சாப் புடையார்க்கு நன்கு.	534
முன்னுறக் காவாது இழுக்கியான் தன்பிழை பின்னூறு இரங்கி விடும்.	535
இழுக்காமை யார்மாட்டும் என்றும் வழுக்காமை வாயின் அதுவொப்பது இல்.	536
அரியஎன்று ஆகாத இல்லைபொச் சாவாக் கருவியால் போற்றிச் செயின்.	537
புகழ்ந்தவை போற்றிச் செயல்வேண்டும் செய்யாது இகழ்ந்தார்க்கு எழுமையும் இல்.	538
இகழ்ச்சியின் கெட்டாரை உள்ளுக தாந்தம் மகிழ்ச்சியின் மைந்துறும் போழ்து.	539
உள்ளியது எய்தல் எளிதுமன் மற்றுந்தான் உள்ளியது உள்ளப் பெறின்.	540

2.1.17 செங்கோன்மை

ஓர்ந்துகண் ணோடாது இறைபுரிந்து யார்மாட்டும்
தேர்ந்துசெய் வஃதே முறை. 541
வானோக்கி வாழும் உலகெல்லாம் மன்னவன்
கோல் நோக்கி வாழுங் குடி. 542
அந்தணர் நூற்கும் அறத்திற்கும் ஆதியாய்
நின்றது மன்னவன் கோல். 543
குடிதழீஇக் கோலோச்சும் மாநில மன்னன்
அடிதழீஇ நிற்கும் உலகு. 544
இயல்புளிக் கோலோச்சும் மன்னவன் நாட்ட
பெயலும் விளையுளும் தொக்கு. 545
வேலன்று வென்றி தருவது மன்னவன்
கோலதூஉங் கோடா தெனின். 546
இறைகாக்கும் வையகம் எல்லாம் அவனை
முறைகாக்கும் முட்டாச் செயின். 547
எண்பதத்தான் ஓரா முறைசெய்யா மன்னவன்
தண்பதத்தான் தானே கெடும். 548
குடிபுறங் காத்தோம்பிக் குற்றம் கடிதல்
வடுவன்று வேந்தன் தொழில். 549
கொலையிற் கொடியாரை வேந்தொறுத்தல் பைங்கூழ்
களைகட் டதனொடு நேர். 550

2.1.18 கொடுங்கோன்மை

கொலைமேற்கொண் டாரிற் கொடிதே அலைமேற்கொண்டு
அல்லவை செய்தொழுகும் வேந்து. 551
வேலொடு நின்றான் இடுவென் றதுபோலும்
கோலொடு நின்றான் இரவு. 552
நாடொறும் நாடி முறைசெய்யா மன்னவன்
நாடொறும் நாடு கெடும். 553
கூழுங் குடியும் ஒருங்கிழக்கும் கோல்கோடிச்
சூழாது செய்யும் அரசு. 554
அல்லற்பட்டு ஆற்றாது அழுதகண் ணீரன்றே
செல்வத்தைத் தேய்க்கும் படை. 555
மன்னர்க்கு மன்னுதல் செங்கோன்மை அஃதின்றேல்
மன்னாவாம் மன்னர்க் கொளி. 556
துளியின்மை ஞாலத்திற்கு எற்றற்றே வேந்தன்
அளியின்மை வாழும் உயிர்க்கு. 557
இன்மையின் இன்னாது உடைமை முறைசெய்யா
மன்னவன் கோற்கீழ்ப் படின். 558
முறைகோடி மன்னவன் செய்யின் உறைகோடி
ஒல்லாது வானம் பெயல். 559
ஆபயன் குன்றும் அறுதொழிலோர் நூல்மறப்பர்
காவலன் காவான் எனின். 560

2.1.19 வெருவந்தசெய்யாமை

தக்காங்கு நாடித் தலைச்செல்லா வண்ணத்தால்
ஒத்தாங்கு ஒறுப்பது வேந்து. 561
கடிதோச்சி மெல்ல எறிக நெடிதாக்கம்
நீங்காமை வேண்டு பவர். 562
வெருவந்த செய்தொழுகும் வெங்கோல நாயின்
ஒருவந்தம் ஒல்லைக் கெடும். 563
இறைகடியன் என்றுரைக்கும் இன்னாச்சொல் வேந்தன்
உறைகடுகி ஒல்லைக் கெடும். 564
அருஞ்செவ்வி இன்னா முகத்தான் பெருஞ்செல்வம்
பேய்க்கண் டன்னது உடைத்து. 565
கடுஞ்சொல்லன் கண்ணிலன் ஆயின் நெடுஞ்செல்வம்
நீடின்றி ஆங்கே கெடும். 566
கடுமொழியும் கையிகந்த தண்டமும் வேந்தன்
அடுமுரண் தேய்க்கும் அரம். 567
இனத்தாற்றி எண்ணாத வேந்தன் சினத்தாற்றிச்
சீரிற் சிறுகும் திரு. 568
செருவந்த போழ்திற் சிறைசெய்யா வேந்தன்
வெருவந்து வெய்து கெடும். 569
கல்லார்ப் பிணிக்கும் கடுங்கோல் அதுவல்லது
இல்லை நிலக்குப் பொறை. 570

2.1.20 கண்ணோட்டம்

கண்ணோட்டம் என்னும் கழிபெருங் காரிகை
உண்மையான் உண்டிவ் வுலகு. 571
கண்ணோட்டத் துள்ளது உலகியல் அஃதிலார்
உண்மை நிலக்குப் பொறை. 572
பண்என்னாம் பாடற்கு இயைபின்றேல் கண்என்னாம்
கண்ணோட்டம் இல்லாத கண். 573
உளபோல் முகத்தெவன் செய்யும் அளவினால்
கண்ணோட்டம் இல்லாத கண். 574
கண்ணிற்கு அணிகலம் கண்ணோட்டம் அஃதின்றேல்
புண்ணென்று உணரப் படும் 575
மண்ணோ டியைந்த மரத்தனையர் கண்ணோ
டியைந்துகண் ணோடா தவர். 576
கண்ணோட்டம் இல்லவர் கண்ணிலர் கண்ணுடையார்
கண்ணோட்டம் இன்மையும் இல். 577
கருமம் சிதையாமல் கண்ணோட வல்லார்க்கு
உரிமை உடைத்திவ் வுலகு. 578
ஒறுத்தாற்றும் பண்பினார் கண்ணும்கண் ணோடிப்
பொறுத்தாற்றும் பண்பே தலை. 579
பெயக்கண்டும் நஞ்சுண் டமைவர் நயத்தக்க
நாகரிகம் வேண்டு பவர். 580

2.1.21 ஒற்றாடல்

ஒற்றும் உரைசான்ற நூலும் இவையிரண்டும் தெற்றென்க மன்னவன் கண்.	581
எல்லார்க்கும் எல்லாம் நிகழ்பவை எஞ்ஞான்றும் வல்லறிதல் வேந்தன் தொழில்.	582
ஒற்றினான் ஒற்றிப் பொருள்தெரியா மன்னவன் கொற்றங் கொளக்கிடந்தது இல்.	583
வினைசெய்வார் தம்சுற்றம் வேண்டாதார் என்றாங்கு அனைவரையும் ஆராய்வது ஒற்று.	584
கடாஅ உருவொடு கண்ணஞ்சாது யாண்டும் உகாஅமை வல்லதே ஒற்று.	585
துறந்தார் படிவத்த ராகி இறந்தாராய்ந்து என்செயினும் சோர்விலது ஒற்று.	586
மறைந்தவை கேட்கவற் றாகி அறிந்தவை ஐயப்பாடு இல்லதே ஒற்று.	587
ஒற்றொற்றித் தந்த பொருளையும் மற்றுமோர் ஒற்றினால் ஒற்றிக் கொளல்.	588
ஒற்றெற் றுணராமை ஆள்க உடன்மூவர் சொற்றொக்க தேறப் படும்.	589
சிறப்பறிய ஒற்றேன்கண் செய்யற்க செய்யின் புறப்படுத்தான் ஆகும் மறை.	590

2.1.22 ஊக்கமுடைமை

2.1.23 மடியின்மை

குடியென்னும் குன்றா விளக்கம் மடியென்னும் மாசூர மாய்ந்து கெடும்.	601
மடியை மடியா ஒழுகல் குடியைக் குடியாக வேண்டு பவர்.	602
மடிமடிக் கொண்டொழுகும் பேதை பிறந்த குடிமடியும் தன்னினும் முந்து.	603
குடிமடிந்து குற்றம் பெருகும் மடிமடிந்து மாண்ட உஞற்றி லவர்க்கு.	604
நெடுநீர் மறவி மடிதுயில் நான்கும் கெடுநீரார் காமக் கலன்.	605
படியுடையார் பற்றமைந்தக் கண்ணும் மடியுடையார் மாண்பயன் எய்தல் அரிது.	606
இடிபுரிந்து எள்ளுஞ் சொல் கேட்பர் மடிபுரிந்து மாண்ட உஞற்றி லவர்.	607
மடிமை குடிமைக்கண் தங்கின்தன் ஒன்னார்க்கு அடிமை புகுத்தி விடும்.	608
குடியாண்மை யுள்வந்த குற்றம் ஒருவன் மடியாண்மை மாற்றக் கெடும்.	609
மடியிலா மன்னவன் எய்தும் அடியளந்தான் தாஅய தெல்லாம் ஒருங்கு.	610

2.1.24 ஆள்வினையுடைமை

அருமை உடைத்தென்று அசாவாமை வேண்டும் பெருமை முயற்சி தரும்.	611
வினைக்கண் வினைகெடல் ஓம்பல் வினைக்குறை தீர்ந்தாரின் தீர்ந்தன்று உலகு.	612
தாளாண்மை என்னும் தகைமைக்கண் தங்கிற்றே வேளாண்மை என்னுஞ் செருக்கு.	613
தாளாண்மை இல்லாதான் வேளாண்மை பேடிகை வாளாண்மை போலக் கெடும்.	614
இன்பம் விழையான் வினைவிழைவான் தன்கேளிர் துன்பம் துடைத்தூன்றும் தூண்.	615
முயற்சி திருவினை ஆக்கும் முயற்றின்மை இன்மை புகுத்தி விடும்.	616
மடியுளாள் மாமுகடி என்ப மடியிலான் தாளுளாள் தாமரையி னாள்.	617
பொறியின்மை யார்க்கும் பழியன்று அறிவறிந்து ஆள்வினை இன்மை பழி.	618
தெய்வத்தான் ஆகா தெனினும் முயற்சிதன் மெய்வருத்தக் கூலி தரும்.	619
ஊழையும் உப்பக்கம் காண்பர் உலைவின்றித் தாழாது உஞற்று பவர்.	620

2.1.25 இடுக்கணழியாமை

இடுக்கண் வருங்கால் நகுக அதனை அடுத்தூர்வது அஃதொப்ப தில்.	621
வெள்ளத் தனைய இடும்பை அறிவுடையான் உள்ளத்தின் உள்ளக் கெடும்.	622
இடும்பைக்கு இடும்பை படுப்பர் இடும்பைக்கு இடும்பை படாஅ தவர்.	623
மடுத்தவா யெல்லாம் பகடன்னான் உற்ற இடுக்கண் இடர்ப்பாடு உடைத்து.	624
அடுக்கி வரினும் அழிவிலான் உற்ற இடுக்கண் இடுக்கட் படும்.	625
அற்றேமென்று அல்லற் படுபவோ பெற்றேமென்று ஓம்புதல் தேற்றா தவர்.	626
இலக்கம் உடம்பிடும்பைக் கென்று கலக்கத்தைக் கையாறாக் கொள்ளாதாம் மேல்.	627
இன்பம் விழையான் இடும்பை இயல்பென்பான் துன்பம் உறுதல் இலன்.	628
இன்பத்துள் இன்பம் விழையாதான் துன்பத்துள் துன்பம் உறுதல் இலன்.	629
இன்னாமை இன்பம் எனக்கொளின் ஆகுந்தன் ஒன்னார் விழையுஞ் சிறப்பு.	630

அரசியல் முற்றிற்று

2.2. அங்கவியல்

2.2.1 அமைச்சு

கருவியும் காலமும் செய்கையும் செய்யும் அருவினையும் மாண்டது அமைச்சு.	631
வன்கண் குடிகாத்தல் கற்றறிதல் ஆள்வினையோடு ஐந்துடன் மாண்டது அமைச்சு.	632
பிரித்தலும் பேணிக் கொளலும் பிரிந்தார்ப் பொருத்தலும் வல்ல தமைச்சு.	633
தெரிதலும் தேர்ந்து செயலும் ஒருதலையாச் சொல்லலும் வல்லது அமைச்சு.	634
அறனறிந்து ஆன்றமைந்த சொல்லானெஞ் ஞான்றும் திறனறிந்தான் தேர்ச்சித் துணை.	635
மதிநுட்பம் நூலோடு உடையார்க்கு அதிநுட்பம் யாவுள முன்நிற் பவை.	636
செயற்கை அறநேந்தக் கடைத்தும் உலகத்து இயற்கை அறிந்து செயல்.	637
அறிகொன்று அறியான் எனினும் உறுதி உழையிருந்தான் கூறல் கடன்.	638
பழுதெண்ணும் மந்திரியின் பக்கதுள் தெவ்வோர் எழுபது கோடி உறும்.	639
முறைப்படச் சூழ்ந்தும் முடிவிலவே செய்வர் திறப்பாடு இலா அ தவர்.	640

2.2.2 சொல்வன்மை

நாநலம் என்னும் நலனுடைமை அந்நலம் யாநலத்து உள்ளதூஉம் அன்று.	641
ஆக்கமுங் கேடும் அதனால் வருதலால் காத்தோம்பல் சொல்லின்கட் சோர்வு.	642
கேட்டார்ப் பிணிக்கும் தகையவாய்க் கேளாரும் வேட்ப மொழிவதாம் சொல்.	643
திறனறிந்து சொல்லுக சொல்லை அறனும் பொருளும் அதனினூஉங்கு இல்.	644
சொல்லுக சொல்லைப் பிறிதோர்சொல் அச்சொல்லை வெல்லுஞ்சொல் இன்மை அறிந்து.	645
வேட்பத்தாஞ் சொல்லிப் பிறர்சொல் பயன்கோடல் மாட்சியின் மாசற்றார் கோள்.	646
சொலல்வல்லன் சோர்விலன் அஞ்சான் அவனை இகல்வெல்லல் யார்க்கும் அரிது.	647
விரைந்து தொழில்கேட்கும் ஞாலம் நிரந்தினிது சொல்லுதல் வல்லார்ப் பெறின்.	648
பலசொல்லக் காமுறுவர் மன்றமா சற்ற சிலசொல்லல் தேற்றா தவர்.	649
இணருழ்த்தும் நாறா மலரனையர் கற்றது உணர விரித்துரையா தார்.	650

2.2.3 வினைத்தூய்மை

துணைநலம் ஆக்கம் தரூஉம் வினைநலம் வேண்டிய எல்லாந் தரும்.	651
என்றும் ஒருவுதல் வேண்டும் புகழொடு நன்றி பயவா வினை.	652
ஓஓதல் வேண்டும் ஒளிமாழ்கும் செய்வினை ஆஅதும் என்னு மவர்.	653
இடுக்கண் படினும் இளிவந்த செய்யார் நடுக்கற்ற காட்சி யவர்.	654
எற்றென்று இரங்குவ செயற்க செய்வானேல் மற்றன்ன செய்யாமை நன்று.	655
ஈன்றாள் பசிகாண்பான் ஆயினுஞ் செயற் க சான்றோர் பழிக்கும் வினை.	656
பழிமலைந்து எய்திய ஆக்கத்தின் சான்றோர் கழிநல் குரவே தலை.	657
கடிந்த கடிந்தொராஅர் செய்தார்க்கு அவைதாம் முடிந்தாலும் பீழை தரும்.	658
அழக் கொண்ட எல்லாம் அழப்போம் இழப்பினும் பிற்பயக்கும் நற்பா லவை.	659
சலத்தால் பொருள்செய்தே மார்த்தல் பசுமண் கலத்துள்நீர் பெய்திரீஇ யற்று.	660

2.2.4 வினைத்திட்பம்

வினைத்திட்பம் என்பது ஒருவன் மனத்திட்பம் மற்றைய எல்லாம் பிற.	661
ஊறொரால் உற்றபின் ஒல்காமை இவ்விரண்டின் ஆறென்பர் ஆய்ந்தவர் கோள்.	662
கடைக்கொட்கச் செய்தக்க தாண்மை இடைக்கொட்கின் எற்றா விழுமந் தரும்.	663
சொல்லுதல் யார்க்கும் எளிய அரியவாம் சொல்லிய வண்ணம் செயல்.	664
வீறெய்தி மாண்டார் வினைத்திட்பம் வேந்தன்கண் ஊறெய்தி உள்ளப் படும்.	665
எண்ணிய எண்ணியாங்கு எய்து எண்ணியார் திண்ணியர் ஆகப் பெறின்.	666
உருவுகண்டு எள்ளாமை வேண்டும் உருள்பெருந்தேர்க்கு அச்சாணி அன்னார் உடைத்து.	667
கலங்காது கண்ட வினைக்கண் துளங்காது தூக்கங் கடிந்து செயல்.	668
துன்பம் உறவரினும் செய்க துணிவாற்றி இன்பம் பயக்கும் வினை.	669
எனைத்திட்பம் எய் தியக் கண்ணும் வினைத்திட்பம் வேண்டாரை வேண்டாது உலகு.	670

2.2.5 வினைசெயல்வகை

சூழ்ச்சி முடிவு துணிவெய்தல் அத்துணிவு தாழ்ச்சியுள் தங்குதல் தீது.	671
தூங்குக தூங்கிச் செயற்பால தூங்கற்க தூங்காது செய்யும் வினை.	672
நல்லுும்வா யெல்லாம் வினைநன்றே ஒல்லாக்கால் செல்லும்வாய் நோக்கிச் செயல்.	673
வினைபகை என்றிரண்டின் எச்சம் நினையுங்கால் தீயெச்சம் போலத் தெறும்.	674
பொருள்கருவி காலம் வினையிடனொடு ஐந்தும் இருள்தீர எண்ணிச் செயல்.	675
முடிவும் இடையூறும் முற்றியாங்கு எய்தும் படுபயனும் பார்த்துச் செயல்.	676
செய்வினை செய்வான் செயன்முறை அவ்வினை உள்ளறிவான் உள்ளம் கொளல்.	677
வினையான் வினையாக்கிக் கோடல் நனைகவுள் யானையால் யானையாத் தற்று.	678
நட்டார்க்கு நல்ல செயலின் விரைந்ததே ஒட்டாரை ஒட்டிக் கொளல்.	679
உறைசிறியார் உள்நடுங்கல் அஞ்சிக் குறைபெறின் கொள்வர் பெரியார்ப் பணிந்து.	680

2.2.6 தூது

அன்புடைமை ஆன்ற குடிப்பிறத்தல் வேந்தவாம் பண்புடைமை தூதுரைப்பான் பண்பு.	681
அன்பறிவு ஆராய்ந்த சொல்வன்மை தூதுரைப்பார்க்கு இன்றி யமையாத மூன்று.	682
நூலாருள் நூல்வல்லன் ஆகுதல் வேலாருள் வென்றி வினையுரைப்பான் பண்பு.	683
அறிவுரு வாராய்ந்த கல்விஇம் மூன்றன் செறிவுடையான் செல்க வினைக்கு.	684
தொகச் சொல்லித் தூவாத நீக்கி நகச்சொல்லி நன்றி பயப்பதாந் தூது.	685
கற்றுக்கண் அஞ்சான் செலச்சொல்லிக் காலத்தால் தக்கது அறிவதாம் தூது.	686
கடனறிந்து காலங் கருதி இடனறிந்து எண்ணி உரைப்பான் தலை.	687
தூய்மை துணைமை துணிவுடைமை இம்மூன்றின் வாய்மை வழியுரைப்பான் பண்பு.	688
விடுமாற்றம் வேந்தர்க்கு உரைப்பான் வடுமாற்றம் வாய்சேரா வன்க ணவன்.	689
இறுதி பயப்பினும் எஞ்சாது இறைவற் கு உறுதி பயப்பதாம் தூது.	690

2.2.7 மன்னரைச் சேர்ந்தொழுதல்

அகலாது அணுகாது தீக்காய்வார் போல்க இகல்வேந்தர்ச் சேர்ந்தொழுகு வார்.	691
மன்னர் விழைப விழையாமை மன்னரால் மன்னிய ஆக்கம் தரும்.	692
போற்றின் அரியவை போற்றல் கடுத்தபின் தேற்றுதல் யார்க்கும் அரிது.	693
செவிச்சொல்லும் சேர்ந்த நகையும் அவித்தொழுகல் ஆன்ற பெரியா ரகத்து.	694
எப்பொருளும் ஓரார் தொடரார்மற் றப்பொருளை விட்டக்கால் கேட்க மறை.	695
குறிப்பறிந்து காலங் கருதி வெறுப்பில வேண்டுப வேட்பச் சொலல்.	696
வேட்பன சொல்லி வினையில எஞ்ஞான்றும் கேட்பினும் சொல்லா விடல்.	697
இளையர் இனமுறையர் என்றிகழார் நின்ற ஒளியோடு ஒழுகப் படும்.	698
கொளப்பட்டேம் என்றெண்ணிக் கொள்ளாத செய்யார் துளக்கற்ற காட்சி யவர்.	699
பழையம் எனக்கருதிப் பண்பல்ல செய்யும் கெழுதகைமை கேடு தரும்.	700

2.2.8 குறிப்பறிதல்

கூறாமை நோக்கே குறிப்பறிவான் எஞ்ஞான்றும் மாறாநீர் வையக் கணி.	701
ஐயப் படாஅது அகத்தது உணர்வானைத் தெய்வத்தோ டொப்பக் கொளல்.	702
குறிப்பிற் குறிப்புணர் வாரை உறுப்பினுள் யாது கொடுத்தும் கொளல்.	703
குறித்தது கூறாமைக் கொள்வாரோ டேனை உறுப்போ ரனையரால் வேறு.	704
குறிப்பிற் குறிப்புணரா வாயின் உறுப்பினுள் என்ன பயத்தவோ கண்?	705
அடுத்தது காட்டும் பளிங்குபோல் நெஞ்சம் கடுத்தது காட்டும் முகம்.	706
முகத்தின் முதுக்குறைந்தது உண்டோ உவப்பினும் காயினும் தான்முந் துறும்.	707
முகம்நோக்கி நிற்க அமையும் அகம்நோக்கி உற்ற துணர்வார்ப் பெறின்.	708
பகைமையும் கேண்மையும் கண்ணுரைக்கும் கண்ணின் வகைமை உணர்வார்ப் பெறின்.	709
நுண்ணியம் என்பார் அளக்குங்கோல் காணுங்கால் கண்ணல்லது இல்லை பிற.	710

2.2.9 அவையறிதல்

அவையறிநது ஆராய்ந்து சொல்லுக சொல்லின்
தொகையறிந்த தூய்மை யவர். 711
இடைதெரிந்து நன்குணர்ந்து சொல்லுக சொல்லின்
நடைதெரிந்த நன்மை யவர். 712
அவையறியார் சொல்லல்மேற் கொள்பவர் சொல்லின்
வகையறியார் வல்லதூஉம் இல். 713
ஒளியார்முன் ஒள்ளிய ராதல் வெளியார்முன்
வான்சுதை வண்ணம் கொளல். 714
நன்றென்ற வற்றுள்ளும் நன்றே முதுவருள்
முந்து கிளவாச் செறிவு. 715
ஆற்றின் நிலைதளர்ந் தற்றே வியன்புலம்
ஏற்றுணர்வார் முன்னர் இழுக்கு. 716
கற்றறிந்தார் கல்வி விளங்கும் கசடறச்
சொல்தெரிதல் வல்லார் அகத்து. 717
உணர்வ துடையார்முன் சொல்லல் வளர்வதன்
பாத்தியுள் நீர்சொரிந் தற்று. 718
புல்லவையுள் பொச்சாந்தும் சொல்லற்க நல்லவையுள்
நன்குசலச் சொல்லு வார். 719
அங்கணத்துள் உக்க அமிழ்தற்றால் தங்கணத்தார்
அல்லார்முன் கோட்டி கொளல். 720

2.2.10 அவையஞ்சாமை

வகையறிந்து வல்லவை வாய்சோரார் சொல்லின்
தொகையறிந்த தூய்மை யவர். 721
கற்றாருள் கற்றார் எனப்படுவர் கற்றார்முன்
கற்ற செலச்சொல்லு வார். 722
பகையகத்துச் சாவார் எளியர் அரியர்
அவையகத்து அஞ்சா தவர். 723
கற்றார்முன் கற்ற செலச்சொல்லித் தாம்கற்ற
மிக்காருள் மிக்க கொளல். 724
ஆற்றின் அளவறிந்து கற்க அவையஞ்சா
மாற்றங் கொடுத்தற் பொருட்டு. 725
வாளொடென் வன்கண்ணர் அல்லார்க்கு நூலொடென்
நுண்ணவை அஞ்சு பவர்க்கு. 726
பகையகத்துப் பேடிகை ஒள்வாள் அவையகத்து
அஞ்சு மவன்கற்ற நூல். 727
பல்லவை கற்றும் பயமிலரே நல்லவையுள்
நன்கு செலச்சொல்லா தார். 728
கல்லா தவரின் கடையென்ப கற்றறிந்தும்
நல்லா ரவையஞ்சு வார். 729
உளரெனினும் இல்லாரொடு ஒப்பர் களன்அஞ்சிக்
கற்ற செலச்சொல்லா தார். 730

அமைச்சியல் முற்றிற்று

2.3 அங்கவியல்

2.3.1 நாடு

தள்ளா விளையுளும் தக்காரும் தாழ்விலாச்	
செல்வரும் சேர்வது நாடு.	731
பெரும்பொருளால் பெட்டக்க தாகி அருங்கேட்டால்	
ஆற்ற விளைவது நாடு.	732
பொறையொருங்கு மேல்வருங்கால் தாங்கி இறைவற்கு	
இறையொருங்கு நேர்வது நாடு.	733
உறுபசியும் ஓவாப் பிணியும் செறுபகையும்	
சேரா தியல்வது நாடு.	734
பல்குழுவும் பாழ்செய்யும் உட்பகையும் வேந்தலைக்கும்	
கொல்குறும்பும் இல்லது நாடு.	735
கேடறியாக் கெட்ட இடத்தும் வளங்குன்றா	
நாடென்ப நாட்டின் தலை.	736
இருபுனலும் வாய்ந்த மலையும் வருபுனலும்	
வல்லரணும் நாட்டிற்கு உறுப்பு.	737
பிணியின்மை செல்வம் விளைவின்பம் ஏமம்	
அணியென்ப நாட்டிவ் வைந்து.	738
நாடென்ப நாடா வளத்தன நாடல்ல	
நாட வளந்தரு நாடு.	739
ஆங்கமை வெய்தியக் கண்ணும் பயமின்றே	
வேந்தமை வில்லாத நாடு.	740

2.3.2 அரண்

ஆற்று பவர்க்கும் அரண்பொருள் அஞ்சித்தற்	
போற்று பவர்க்கும் பொருள்.	741
மணிநீரும் மண்ணும் மலையும் அணிநிழற்	
காடும் உடைய தரண்.	742
உயர்வகலம் திண்மை அருமைஇந் நான்கின்	
அமைவரண் என்றுரைக்கும் நூல்.	743
சிறுகாப்பிற் பேரிடத்த தாகி உறுபகை	
ஊக்கம் அழிப்ப தரண்.	744
கொளற்கரிதாய்க் கொண்டகூழ்த் தாகி அகத்தார்	
நிலைக்கெளிதாம் நீரது அரண்.	745
எல்லாப் பொருளும் உடைத்தாய் இடத்துதவும்	
நல்லாள் உடையது அரண்.	746
முற்றியும் முற்றா தெறிந்தும் அறைப்படுத்தும்	
பற்றற் கரியது அரண்.	747
முற்றாற்றி முற்றி யவரையும் பற்றாற்றிப்	
பற்றியார் வெல்வது அரண்.	748
முனைமுகத்து மாற்றலர் சாய வினைமுகத்து	
வீறெய்தி மாண்ட தரண்.	749
எனைமாட்சித் தாகியக் கண்ணும் வினைமாட்சி	
இல்லார்கண் இல்லது அரண்.	750

2.3.3 பொருள்செயல்வகை

பொருளல் லவரைப் பொருளாகச் செய்யும் பொருளல்லது இல்லை பொருள்.	751
இல்லாரை எல்லாரும் எள்ளுவர் செல்வரை எல்லாரும் செய்வர் சிறப்பு.	752
பொருளென்னும் பொய்யா விளக்கம் இருளறுக்கும் எண்ணிய தேயத்துச் சென்று.	752
அறன்ஈனும் இன்பமும் ஈனும் திறனறிந்து தீதின்றி வந்த பொருள்.	754
அருளொடும் அன்பொடும் வாராப் பொருளாக்கம் புல்லார் புரள விடல்.	755
உறுபொருளும் உல்கு பொருளும்தன் ஒன்னார்த் தெறுபொருளும் வேந்தன் பொருள்.	756
அருளென்னும் அன்பீன் குழவி பொருளென்னும் செல்வச் செவிலியால் உண்டு.	757
குன்றேறி யானைப் போர் கண்டற்றால் தன்கைத்தொன்று உண்டாகச் செய்வான் வினை.	758
செய்க பொருளைச் செறுநர் செருக்கறுக்கும் எஃகதனிற் கூரிய தில்.	759
ஒண்பொருள் காழ்ப்ப இயற்றியார்க்கு எண்பொருள் ஏனை இரண்டும் ஒருங்கு.	760

2.3.4 படைமாட்சி

உறுப்பமைந்து ஊறஞ்சா வெல்படை வேந்தன் வெறுக்கையுள் எல்லாம் தலை.	761
உலைவிடத்து ஊறஞ்சா வன்கண் தொலைவிடத்துத் தொல்படைக் கல்லால் அரிது.	762
ஒலித்தக்கால் என்னாம் உவரி எலேப்பகை நாகம் உயிர்ப்பக் கெடும்.	763
அழிவின்றி அறைபோகா தாகி வழிவந்த வன்க ணதுவே படை.	764
கூற்றுடன்று மேல்வரினும் கூடி எதிர்நிற்கும் ஆற்ற லதுவே படை.	765
மறமானம் மாண்ட வழிச்செலவு தேற்றம் எனநான்கே ஏம படைக்கு.	766
தார்தாங்கிச் செல்வது தானை தலைவந்த போர்தாங்கும் தன்மை அறிந்து.	767
அடல்தகையும் ஆற்றலும் இல்லெனினும் தானை படைத்தகையால் பாடு பெறும்.	768
சிறுமையும் செல்லாத் துனியும் வறுமையும் இல்லாயின் வெல்லும் படை.	769
நிலைமக்கள் சால உடைத்தெனினும் தானை தலைமக்கள் இல்வழி இல்.	770

2.3.5 படைச்செருக்கு

என்னைமுன் நில்லன்மின் தெவ்விர் பலரென்னை முன்நின்று கல்நின் றவர்.	771
கான முயலெய்த அம்பினில் யானை பிழைத்தவேல் ஏந்தல் இனிது.	772
பேராண்மை என்ப தறுகண்ஒன் றுற்றக்கால் ஊராண்மை மற்றதன் எஃகு.	773
கைவேல் களிற்றொடு போக்கி வருபவன் மெய்வேல் பறியா நகும்.	774
விழித்தகண் வேல்கொண டெறிய அழித்திமைப்பின் ஒட்டன்றோ வன்க ணவர்க்கு.	775
விழுப்புண் படாதநாள் எல்லாம் வழுக்கினுள் வைக்கும்தன் நாளை எடுத்து.	776
சுழலும் இசைவேண்டி வேண்டா உயிரார் கழல்யாப்புக் காரிகை நீர்த்து.	777
உறின்உயிர் அஞ்சா மறவர் இறைவன் செறினும் சீர்குன்றல் இலர்.	778
இழைத்தது இகவாமைச் சாவாரை யாரே பிழைத்தது ஒறுக்கிற் பவர்.	779
புரந்தார்கண் நீர்மல்கச் சாகிற்பின் சாக்காடு இரந்துகோள் தக்கது உடைத்து.	780

2,3.6 நட்பு

செயற்கரிய யாவுள நட்பின் அதுபோல் வினைக்கரிய யாவுள காப்பு.	7811
நிறைநீர நீரவர் கேண்மை பிறைமதிப் பின்னீர பேதையார் நட்பு.	782
நவில்தொறும் நூல்நயம் போலும் பயில்தொறும் பண்புடை யாளர் தொடர்பு.	783
நகுதற் பொருட்டன்று நட்டல் மிகுதிக்கண் மேற்சென்று இடித்தற் பொருட்டு.	784
புணர்ச்சி பழகுதல் வேண்டா உணர்ச்சிதான் நட்பாங் கிழமை தரும்.	785
முகநக நட்பது நட்பன்று நெஞ்சத்து அகநக நட்பது நட்பு.	786
அழிவி னவைநீக்கி ஆறுய்த்து அழிவின்கண் அல்லல் உழப்பதாம் நட்பு.	787
உடுக்கை இழந்தவன் கைபோல ஆங்கே இடுக்கண் களைவதாம் நட்பு.	788
நட்பிற்கு வீற்றிருக்கை யாதெனின் கொட்பின்றி ஒல்லும்வாய் ஊன்றும் நிலை.	789
இனையர் இவரெமக்கு இன்னம்யாம் என்று புனையினும் புல்லென்னும் நட்பு.	790

2.3.7 நட்பாராய்தல்

நாடாது நட் டலிற் கேடில்லை நட்பின் வீடில்லை நட்பாள் பவர்க்கு.	791
ஆய்ந்தாய்ந்து கொள்ளாதான் கேண்மை கடைமுறை தான்சாம் துயரம் தரும்.	792
குணமும் குடிமையும் குற்றமும் குன்றா இனனும் அறிந்தியாக்க நட்பு.	793
குடிப்பிறந்து தன்கண் பழிநாணு வானைக் கொடுத்தும் கொளல்வேண்டும் நட்பு.	794
அழச்சொல்லி அல்லது இடித்து வழக்கறிய வல்லார்நடபு ஆய்ந்து கொளல்.	795
கேட்டினும் உண்டோர் உறுதி கிளைஞரை நீட்டி அளப்பதோர் கோல்.	796
ஊதியம் என்பது ஒருவற்குப் பேதையார் கேண்மை ஒரீஇ விடல்.	797
உள்ளற்க உள்ளம் சிறுகுவ கொள்ளற்க அல்லற்கண் ஆற்றறுப்பார் நட்பு.	798
கெடுங்காலைக் கைவிடுவார் கேண்மை அடுங்காலை உள்ளினும் உள்ளஞ் சுடும்.	799
மருவுக மாசற்றார் கேண்மையொன் நீத்தும் ஒருவுக ஒப்பிலார் நட்பு.	800

2.3.8 பழைமை

பழைமை எனப்படுவது யாதெனின் யாதும் கிழமையைக் கீழ்ந்திடா நட்பு.	801
நட்பிற் குறுப்புக் கெழுதகைமை மற்றதற்கு உப்பாதல் சான்றோர் கடன்.	802
பழகிய நட்பெவன் செய்யுங் கெழுதகைமை செய்தாங்கு அமையாக் கடை.	803
விழைதகையான் வேண்டி இருப்பர் கெழுதகையாற் கேளாது நட்டார் செயின்.	804
பேதைமை ஒன்றோ பெருங்கிழமை என்றுணர்க நோதக்க நட்டார் செயின்.	805
எல்லைக்கண் நின்றார் துறவார் தொலைவிடத்தும் தொல்லைக்கண் நின்றார் தொடர்பு.	806
அழிவந்த செய்யினும் அன்பறார் அன்பின் வழிவந்த கேண்மை யவர்.	807
கேளிழுக்கம் கேளாக் கெழுதகைமை வல்லார்க்கு நாளிழுக்கம் நட்டார் செயின்.	808
கெடாஅ வழிவந்த கேண்மையார் கேண்மை விடாஅர் விழையும் உலகு.	809
விழையார் விழையப் படுப பழையார்கண் பண்பின் தலைப்பிரியா தார்.	810

2.3.9 தீ நட்பு

பருகுவார் போலினும் பண்பிலார் கேண்மை பெருகலிற் குன்றல் இனிது.	811
உறின்நட்டு அறின்ஙருஉம் ஒப்பிலார் கேண்மை பெறினும் இழப்பினும் என்?	812
உறுவது சீர்தூக்கும் நட்பும் பெறுவது கொள்வாரும் கள்வரும் நேர்.	813
அமரகத்து ஆற்றறுக்கும் கல்லாமா அன்னார் தமரின் தனிமை தலை.	814
செய்தேமஞ் சாராச் சிறியவர் புன்கேண்மை எய்தலின் எய்தாமை நன்று.	815
பேதை பெருங்கெழீஇ நட்பின் அறிவுடையார் ஏதின்மை கோடி உறும்.	816
நகைவகைய ராகிய நட்பின் பகைவரால் பத்தடுத்த கோடி உறும்.	817
ஒல்லும் கருமம் உடற்று பவர்கேண்மை சொல்லாடார் சோர விடல்.	818
கனவினும் இன்னாது மன்னோ வினைவேறு சொல்வேறு பட்டார் தொடர்பு.	819
எனைத்தும் குறுகுதல் ஓம்பல் மனைக்கெழீஇ மன்றில் பழிப்பார் தொடர்பு.	820

2.3.10 கூடாநட்பு

சீரிடம் காணின் எறிதற்குப் பட்டடை நேரா நிரந்தவர் நட்பு.	821
இனம்போன்று இனமல்லார் கேண்மை மகளிர் மனம்போல வேறு படும்.	822
பலநல்ல கற்றக் கடைத்து மனநல்லர் ஆகுதல் மாணார்க் கரிது.	823
முகத்தின் இனிய நகாஅ அகத்தின்னா வஞ்சரை அஞ்சப் படும்.	824
மனத்தின் அமையா தவரை எனைத்தொன்றும் சொல்லினால் தேற்றப்பாற்று அன்று.	825
நட்டார்போல் நல்லவை சொல்லினும் ஒட்டார்சொல் ஒல்லை உணரப் படும்.	826
சொல்வணக்கம் ஒன்னார்கண் கொள்ளற்க வில்வணக்கம் தீங்கு குறித்தமை யான்.	827
தொழுதகை யுள்ளும் படையொடுங்கும் ஒன்னார் அழுதகண் ணீரும் அனைத்து.	828
மிகச்செய்து தம்மெள்ளு வாரை நகச்செய்து நட்பினுள் சாப்புல்லற் பாற்று.	829
பகைநட்பாம் காலம் வருங்கால் முகநட்டு அகநட்பு ஒரீஇ விடல்.	830

2.3.11 பேதைமை

பேதைமை என்பதொன்று யாதெனின் ஏதங்கொண்டு
ஊதியம் போக விடல்.   831
பேதைமையுள் எல்லாம் பேதைமை காதன்மை
கையல்ல தன்கட் செயல்.   832
நாணாமை நாடாமை நாரின்மை யாதொன்றும்
பேணாமை பேதை தொழில்   833
ஓதி உணர்ந்தும் பிறர் க்குரைத்தும் தானடங்காப்
பேதையின் பேதையார் இல்.   834
ஒருமைச் செயலாற்றும் பேதை எழுமையும்
தான்புக் கழுந்தும் அளறு.   835
பொய்படும் ஒன்றோ புனைபூணும் கையறியாப்
பேதை வினைமேற் கொளின்.   836
ஏதிலார் ஆரத் தமர்பசிப்பர் பேதை
பெருஞ்செல்வம் உற்றக் கடை.   837
மையல் ஒருவன் களித்தற்றால் பேதைதன்
கையொன்று உடைமை பெறின்.   838
பெரிதினிது பேதையார் கேண்மை பிரிவின்கண்
பீழை தருவதொன் றில்.   839
கழாஅக்கால் பள்ளியுள் வைத்தற்றால் சான்றோர்
குழாஅத்துப் பேதை புகல்.   840

2.3.12 புல்லறிவாண்மை

அறிவின்மை இன்மையுள் இன்மை பிறிதின்மை
இன்மையா வையா துலகு.   841
அறிவிலான் நெஞ்சுவந்து ஈதல் பிறிதியாதும்
இல்லை பெறுவான் தவம்.   842
அறிவிலார் தாந்தம்மைப் பீழிக்கும் பீழை
செறுவார்க்கும் செய்தல் அரிது.   843
வெண்மை எனப்படுவ தியாதெனின் ஒண்மை
உடையம்யாம் என்னும் செருக்கு.   844
கல்லாத மேற்கொண் டொழுகல் கசடற
வல்லதூஉம் ஐயம் தரும்.   845
அற்றம் மறைத்தலோ புல்லறிவு தம்வயின்
குற்றம் மறையா வழி.   846
அருமறை சோரும் அறிவிலான் செய்யும்
பெருமிறை தானே தனக்கு.   847
ஏவும் செய்கலான் தான்தேறான் அவ்வுயிர்
போஒம் அளவுமோர் நோய்.   848
காணாதான் காட்டுவான் தான்காணான் காணாதான்
கண்டானாம் தான்கண்ட வாறு.   849
உலகத்தார் உண்டென்பது இல்லென்பான் வையத்து
அலகையா வைக்கப் படும்.   850

2.3.13 இகல்

இகலென்ப எல்லா உயிர்க்கும் பகலென்னும் பண்பின்மை பாரேக்கும் நோய்.	851
பகல்கருதிப் பற்றா செயினும் இகல்கருதி இன்னாசெய் யாமை தலை.	852
இகலென்னும் எவ்வநோய் நீக்கின் தவலில்லாத் தாவில் விளக்கம் தரும்.	853
இன்பத்துள் இன்பம் பயக்கும் இகலென்னும் துன்பத்துள் துன்பங் கெடின்.	854
இகலெதிர் சாய்ந்தொழுக வல்லாரை யாரே மிக்லூாக்கும் தன்மை யவர்.	855
இகலின் மிகலினிது என்பவன் வாழ்க்கை தவலும் கெடலும் நணித்து.	856
மிகல்மேவல் மெய்ப்பொருள் காணார் இகல்மேவல் இன்னா அறிவி னவர்.	857
இகலிற்கு எதிர்சாய்தல் ஆக்கம் அதனை மிக்லூாக்கின் ஊக்குமாம் கேடு.	858
இகல்காணான் ஆக்கம் வருங்கால் அதனை மிகல்காணும் கேடு தரற்கு.	859
இகலானாம் இன்னாத எல்லாம் நகலானாம் நன்னயம் என்னும் செருக்கு.	860

2.3.14 பகைமாட்சி

வலியார்க்கு மாறேற்றல் ஓம்புக ஓம்பா மெலியார்மேல் மேக பகை.	861
அன்பிலன் ஆன்ற துணையிலன் தான்துவ்வான் என்பரியும் ஏதிலான் துப்பு.	862
அஞ்சும் அறியான் அமைவிலன் ஈகலான் தஞ்சம் எளியன் பகைக்கு.	863
நீங்கான் வெகுளி நிறையிலன் எஞ்ஞான்றும் யாங்கணும் யார்க்கும் எளிது.	864
வழிநோக்கான் வாய்ப்பன செய்யான் பழிநோக்கான் பண்பிலன் பற்றார்க்கு இனிது.	865
காணாச் சினத்தான் கழிபெருங் காமத்தான் பேணாமை பேணப் படும்.	866
கொடுத்தும் கொளல்வேண்டும் மன்ற அடுத்திருந்து மாணாத செய்வான் பகை.	867
குணனிலனாய்க் குற்றம் பலவாயின் மாற்றார்க்கு இனிலனாம் ஏமாப் புடைத்து.	868
செறுவார்க்குச் சேணிகவா இன்பம் அறிவிலா அஞ்சும் பகைவர்ப் பெறின்.	869
கல்லான் வெகுளும் சிறுபொருள் எஞ்ஞான்றும் ஒல்லானை ஒல்லா தொளி.	870

2.3.15 பகைத்திறந்தெரிதல்

பகையென்னும் பண்பி லதனை ஒருவன்	
நகையேயும் வேண்டற்பாற்று அன்று.	871
வில்லேர் உழவர் பகைகொளினும் கொள்ளற்க	
சொல்லேர் உழவர் பகை.	872
ஏமுற் றவரினும் ஏழை தமியனாய்ப்	
பல்லார் பகைகொள் பவன்.	873
பகைநட்பாக் கொண்டொழுகும் பண்புடை யாளன்	
தகைமைக்கண் தங்கிற்று உலகு.	874
தன்துணை இன்றால் பகையிரண்டால் தான்ஒருவன்	
இன்துணையாக் கொள்கவற்றின் ஒன்று.	875
தேறினும் தேறா விடினும் அழிவின்கண்	
தேறான் பகாஅன் விடல்.	876
நோவற்க நொந்தது அறியார்க்கு மேவற்க	
மென்மை பகைவர் அகத்து.	877
வகையறிந்து தற்செய்து தற்காப்ப மாயும்	
பகைவர்கண் பட்ட செருக்கு.	878
இளைதாக முள்மரம் கொல்க களையுநர்	
கைகொல்லும் காழ்த்த இடத்து.	879
உயிர்ப்ப உளரல்லர் மன்ற செயிர்ப்பவர்	
செம்மல் சிதைக்கலா தார்.	880

2.3.16 உட்பகை

நிழல்நீரும் இன்னாத இன்னா தமர்நீரும்	
இன்னாவாம் இன்னா செயின்.	881
வாள்போல பகைவரை அஞ்சற்க அஞ்சுக	
கேள்போல் பகைவர் தொடர்பு.	882
உட்பகை அஞ்சித்தற் காக்க உலைவிடத்து	
மட்பகையின் மாணத் தெறும்.	883
மனமாணா உட்பகை தோன்றின் இனமாணா	
ஏதம் பலவும் தரும்.	884
உறல்முறையான் உட்பகை தோன்றின் இறல்முறையான்	
ஏதம் பலவும் தரும்.	885
ஒன்றாமை ஒன்றியார் கட்படின் எஞ்ஞான்றும்	
பொன்றாமை ஒன்றல் அரிது.	886
செப்பின் புணர்ச்சிபோல் கூடினும் கூடாதே	
உட்பகை உற்ற குடி.	887
அரம்பொருத பொன்போலத் தேயும் உரம்பொருது	
உட்பகை உற்ற குடி.	888
எட்பக வன்ன சிறுமைத்தே ஆயினும்	
உட்பகை உள்ளதாங் கேடு.	889
உடம்பாடு இலாதவர் வாழ்க்கை குடங்கருள்	
பாம்போடு உடனுறைந் தற்று.	890

2.3.17 பெரியாரைப் பிழையாமை

ஆற்றுவார் ஆற்றல் இகழாமை போற்றுவார் போற்றலுள் எல்லாம் தலை.	891
பெரியாரைப் பேணாது ஒழுகிற் பெரியாரால் பேரா இடும்பை தரும்.	892
கெடல்வேண்டின் கேளாது செய்க அடல்வேண்டின் ஆற்று பவர்கண் இழுக்கு.	893
கூற்றத்தைக் கையால் விளித்தற்றால் ஆற்றுவார்க்கு ஆற்றாதார் இன்னா செயல்.	894
யாண்டுச் சென்று யாண்டும் உளராகார் வெந்துப்பின் வேந்து செறப்பட் டவர்.	895
எரியால் சுடப்படினும் உய்வுண்டாம் உய்யார் பெரியார்ப் பிழைத்தொழுகு வார்.	896
வகைமாண்ட வாழ்க்கையும் வான்பொருளும் என்னாம் தகைமாண்ட தக்கார் செறின்.	897
குன்றன்னார் குன்ற மதிப்பின் குடியொடு நின்றன்னார் மாய்வர் நிலத்து.	898
ஏந்திய கொள்கையார் சீரின் இடைமுரிந்து வேந்தனும் வேந்து கெடும்.	899
இறந்தமைந்த சார்புடையர் ஆயினும் உய்யார் சிறந்தமைந்த சீரார் செறின்.	900

2.3.18 பெண்வழிச்சேரல்

மனைவிழைவார் மாண்பயன் எய்தார் வினைவிழையார் வேண்டாப் பொருளும் அது.	901
பேணாது பெண்விழைவான் ஆக்கம் பெரியதோர் நாணாக நாணுத் தரும்.	902
இல்லாள்கண் தாழ்ந்த இயல்பின்மை எஞ்ஞான்றும் நல்லாருள் நாணுத் தரும்.	903
மனையாளை அஞ்சும் மறுமையி லாளன் வினையாண்மை வீறெய்த லின்று.	904
இல்லாளை அஞ்சுவான் அஞ்சுமற் றெஞ்ஞான்றும் நல்லார்க்கு நல்ல செயல்.	905
இமையாரின் வாழினும் பாடிலரே இல்லாள் அமையார்தோள் அஞ்சு பவர்.	906
பெண்ணேவல் செய்தொழுகும் ஆண்மையின் நாணுடைப் பெண்ணே பெருமை உடைத்து.	907
நட்டார் குறைமுடியார் நன்றாற்றார் நன்னுதலாள் பெட் டாங்கு ஒழுகு பவர்.	908
அறவினையும் ஆன்ற பொருளும் பிறவினையும் பெண்ஏவல் செய்வார்கண் இல்.	909
எண்சேர்ந்த நெஞ்சத் திடனுடையார்க்கு எஞ்ஞான்றும் பெண்சேர்ந்தாம் பேதைமை இல்.	910

2.3.19 வரைவின்மகளிர்

அன்பின் விழையார் பொருள்விழையும் ஆய்தொடியார்	
இன்சொல் இழுக்குத் தரும்.	911
பயன்தூக்கிப் பண்புரைக்கும் பண்பின் மகளிர்	
நயன்தூக்கி நள்ளா விடல்.	912
பொருட்பெண்டிர் பொய்ம்மை முயக்கம் இருட்டறையில்	
ஏதலே பிணந்தழீஇ அற்று.	913
பொருட்பொருளார் புன்னலந் தோயார் அருட்பொருள்	
ஆயும் அறிவி னவர்.	914
பொதுநலத்தார் புன்னலம் தோயார் மதிநலத்தின்	
மாண்ட அறிவி னவர்.	915
தந்நலம் பாரேப்பார் தோயார் தகைசெருக்கிப்	
புன்னலம் பாரிப்பார் தோள்.	916
நிறைநெஞ்சம் இல்லவர் தோய்வார் பிறநெஞ்சிற்	
பேணிப் புணர்பவர் தோள்.	917
ஆயும் அறிவினர் அல்லார்க்கு அணங்கென்ப	
மாய மகளிர் முயக்கு.	918
வரைவிலா மாணிழையார் மென்தோள் புரையிலாப்	
பூரியர்கள் ஆழும் அளறு.	919
இருமனப் பெண்டிரும் கள்ளும் கவறும்	
திருநீக்கப் பட்டார் தொடர்பு.	920

2.3.20 கள்ளுண்ணாமை

உட்கப் படாஅர் ஒளியிழப்பர் எஞ்ஞான்றும்	
கட்காதல் கொண்டொழுகு வார்.	921
உண்ணற்க கள்ளை உணில்உண்க சான்றோரான்	
எண்ணப் படவேண்டா தார்.	922
ஈன்றாள் முகத்தேயும் இன்னாதால் என்மற்றுச்	
சான்றோர் முகத்துக் களி.	923
நாண்என்னும் நல்லாள் புறங்கொடுக்கும் கள்ளென்னும்	
பேணாப் பெருங்குற்றத் தார்க்கு.	924
கையறி யாமை உடைத்தே பொருள்கொடுத்து	
மெய்யறி யாமை கொளல்.	925
துஞ்சினார் செத்தாரின் வேறல்லர் எஞ்ஞான்றும்	
நஞ்சுண்பார் கள்ளுண் பவர்.	926
உள்ளொற்றி உள்ளூர் நகப்படுவர் எஞ்ஞான்றும்	
கள்ளொற்றிக் கண்சாய் பவர்3	927
களித்தறியேன் என்பது கைவிடுக நெஞ்சத்து	
ஒளித்ததூஉம் ஆங்கே மிகும்.	928
களித்தானைக் காரணம் காட்டுதல் கீழ்நீர்க்	
குளித்தானைத் தீத்துரீஇ அற்று.	929
கள்ளுண்ணாப் போழ்திற் களித்தானைக் காணுங்கால்	
உள்ளான்கொல் உண்டதன் சோர்வு.	930

2.3.21 சூது

வேண்டற்க வென்றிடினும் சூதினை வென்றதூஉம்
தூண்டிற்பொன் மீன்விழுங்கி அற்று. 931

ஒன்றெய்தி நூறிழக்கும் சூதர்க்கும் உண்டாங்கொல்
நன்றெய்தி வாழ்வதோர் ஆறு. 932

உருளாயம் ஓவாது கூறின் பொருளாயம்
போஒய்ப் புறமே படும். 933

சிறுமை பலசெய்து சீரழிக்கும் சூதின்
வறுமை தருவதொன்று இல். 934

கவறும் கழகமும் கையும் தருக்கி
இவறியார் இல்லாகி யார். 935

அகடாரார் அல்லல் உழப்பர்சூ தென்னும்
முகடியான் மூடப்பட் டார். 936

பழகிய செல்வமும் பண்பும் கெடுக்கும்
கழகத்துக் காலை புகின். 937

பொருள் கெடுத்துப் பொய்மேற் கொளீஇ அருள்கெடுத்து
அல்லல் உழப்பிக்கும் சூது. 938

உடைசெல்வம் ஊண்ஒளி கல்விஎன்று ஐந்தும்
அடையாவாம் ஆயங் கொளின். 939

இழத்தொறூஉம் காதலிக்கும் சூதேபோல் துன்பம்
உழத்தொறூஉம் காதற்று உயிர். 940

2.3.22 மருந்து

மிகினும் குறையினும் நோய்செய்யும் நூலோர்
வளிமுதலா எண்ணிய மூன்று. 941

மருந்தென வேண்டாவாம் யாக்கைக்கு அருந்தியது
அற்றது போற்றி உணின். 942

அற்றால் அறவறிந்து உண்க அஃதுடம்பு
பெற்றான் நெடிதுய்க்கும் ஆறு. 943

அற்றது அறிந்து கடைப்பிடித்து மாறல்ல
துய்க்க துவரப் பசித்து. 944

மாறுபாடு இல்லாத உண்டி மறுத்துண்ணின்
ஊறுபாடு இல்லை உயிர்க்கு. 945

இழிவறிந்து உண்பான்கண் இன்பம்போல் நிற்கும்
கழிபேர் இரையான்கண் நோய். 946

தீயள வன்றித் தெரியான் பெரிதுண்ணின்
நோயள வின்றிப் படும். 947

நோய்நாடி நோய்முதல் நாடி அதுதணிக்கும்
வாய்நாடி வாய்ப்பச் செயல். 948

உற்றான் அளவும் பிணியளவும் காலமும்
கற்றான் கருதிச் செயல். 949

உற்றவன் தீர்ப்பான் மருந்துழைச் செல்வானென்று
அப்பால் நாற் கூற்றே மருந்து. 950

2.4 ஒழிபியல்

2.4.1 குடிமை

இற்பிறந்தார் கண்அல்லது இல்லை இயல்பாகச்	
செப்பமும் நாணும் ஒருங்கு.	951
ஒழுக்கமும் வாய்மையும் நாணும் இம் மூன்றும்	
இழுக்கார் குடிப்பிறந் தார்.	952
நகைஈகை இன்சொல் இகழாமை நான்கும்	
வகையென்ப வாய்மைக் குடிக்கு.	953
அடுக்கிய கோடி பெறினும் குடிப்பிறந்தார்	
குன்றுவ செய்தல் இலர்.	954
வழங்குவ துள்வீழ்ந்தக் கண்ணும் பழங்குடி	
பண்பில் தலைப்பிரிதல் இன்று.	955
சலம்பற்றிச் சால்பில செய்யார்மா சற்ற	
குலம்பற்றி வாழ்தும் என் பார்.	956
குடிப்பிறந்தார் கண்விளங்கும் குற்றம் விசும்பின்	
மதேக்கண் மறுப்போல் உயர்ந்து.	957
நலத்தின்கண் நாரின்மை தோன்றின் அவனைக்	
குலத்தின்கண் ஐயப் படும்.	958
நிலத்தில் கிடந்தமை கால்காட்டும் காட்டும்	
குலத்தில் பிறந்தார்வாய்ச் சொல்.	959
நலம்வேண்டின் நாணுடைமை வேண்டும் குலம் வேண்டின்	
வேண்டுக யார்க்கும் பணிவு.	960

2.4.2 மானம்

இன்றி அமையாச் சிறப்பின ஆயினும்	
குன்ற வருப விடல்.	961
சீரினும் சீரல்ல செய்யாரே சீரொடு	
பேராண்மை வேண்டு பவர்.	962
பெருக்கத்து வேண்டும் பணிதல் சிறிய	
சுருக்கத்து வேண்டும் உயர்வு.	963
தலையின் இழிந்த மயிரனையர் மாந்தர்	
நிலையின் இழிந்தக் கடை.	964
குன்றின் அனையாரும் குன்றுவர் குன்றுவ	
குன்றி அனைய செயின்.	965
புகழ்இன்றால் புத்தேள்நாட்டு உய்யாதால் என்மற்று	
இகழ்வார்பின் சென்று நிலை.	966
ஒட் டார்பின் சென்றொருவன் வாழ்தலேன் அந்நிலையே	
கெட்டான் எனப்படுதல் நன்று.	967
மருந்தோமற்று ஊன்ஓம்பும் வாழ்க்கை பெருந்தகைமை	
பீடழிய வந்த இடத்து.	968
மயிர்நீப்பின் வாழாக் கவரிமா அன்னார்	
உயிர்நீப்பர் மானம் வரின்.	969
இளிவரின் வாழாத மானம் உடையார்	
ஒளிதொழுது ஏத்தும் உலகு.	970

2.4.3 பெருமை

ஒளிஒருவற்கு உள்ள வெறுக்கை இளிஒருவற்கு அஃதிறந்து வாழ்தும் எனல்.	971
பிறப்பொக்கும் எல்லா உயிர்க்கும் சிறப்பொவ்வா செய்தொழில் வேற்றுமை யான்.	972
மேலிருந்தும் மேல்லார் மேலல்லர் கீழிருந்தும் கீழல்லார் கீழல் லவர்.	973
ஒருமை மகளிரே போலப் பெருமையும் தன்னைத்தான் கொண்டொழுகின் உண்டு.	974
பெருமை யுடையவர் ஆற்றுவார் ஆற்றின் அருமை உடைய செயல்.	975
சிறியார் உணர்ச்சியுள் இல்லை பெரியாரைப் பேணிக் கொள் வேம் என்னும் நோக்கு.	976
இறப்பே புரிந்த தொழிற்றாம் சிறப்புந்தான் சீரல் லவர்கண் படின்.	977
பணியுமாம் என்றும் பெருமை சிறுமை அணியுமாம் தன்னை வியந்து.	978
பெருமை பெருமிதம் இன்மை சிறுமை பெருமிதம் ஊர்ந்து விடல்.	979
அற்றம் மறைக்கும் பெருமை சிறுமைதான் குற்றமே கூறி விடும்.	980

2.4.4 சான்றாண்மை

கடன்என்ப நல்லவை எல்லாம் கடன்அறிந்து சான்றாண்மை மேற்கொள் பவர்க்கு.	981
குணநலம் சான்றோர் நலனே பிறநலம் எந்நலத்து உள்ளதூஉம் அன்று.	982
அன்புநாண் ஒப்புரவு கண்ணோட்டம் வாய்மையொடு ஐந்துசால் ஊன்றிய தூண்.	983
கொல்லா நலத்தது நோன்மை பிறர்தீமை சொல்லா நலத்தது சால்பு.	984
ஆற்றுவார் ஆற்றல் பணிதல் அதுசான்றோர் மாற்றாரை மாற்றும் படை.	985
சால்பிற்குக் கட்டளை யாதெனின் தோல்வி துலையல்லார் கண்ணும் கொளல்.	986
இன்னாசெய் தார்க்கும் இனியவே செய்யாக்கால் என்ன பயத்ததோ சால்பு.	987
இன்மை ஒருவற்கு இளிவன்று சால்பென்னும் திண்மை உண் டாகப் பெறின்.	988
ஊழி பெயரினும் தாம்பெயரார் சான்றாண்மைக்கு ஆழி எனப்படு வார்.	989
சான்றவர் சான்றாண்மை குன்றின் இருநிலந்தான் தாங்காது மன்னோ பொறை.	990

2.4.5 பண்புடைமை

எண்பதத்தால் எய்தல் எளிதென்ப யார்மாட்டும் பண்புடைமை என்னும் வழக்கு.	991
அன்புடைமை ஆன்ற குடிப்பிறத்தல் இவ்விரண்டும் பண்புடைமை என்னும் வழக்கு.	992
உறுப்பொத்தல் மக்களொப்பு அன்றால் வெறுத்தக்க பண்பொத்தல் ஒப்பதாம் ஒப்பு.	993
யனொடு நன்றி புரிந்த பயனுடையார் பண்புபா ராட்டும் உலகு.	994
நகையுள்ளும் இன்னா திகழ்ச்சி பகையுள்ளும் பண்புள பாடறிவார் மாட்டு.	995
பண்புடையார்ப் பட்டுண்டு உலகம் அதுஇன்றேல் மண்புக்கு மாய்வது மன்.	996
அரம்போலும் கூர்மை ரேனும் மரம்போல்வர் மக்கட்பண்பு இல்லா தவர்.	997
நண்பாற்றார் ஆகி நயமில செய்வார்க்கும் பண்பாற்றார் ஆதல் கடை.	998
நகல்வல்லர் அல்லார்க்கு மாயிரு ஞாலம் பகலும்பாற் பட்டன்று இருள்.	999
ண்பிலான் பெற்ற பெருஞ்செல்வம் நன்பால் கலந்தீமை யால்திரிந் தற்று.	1000

2.4.6 நன்றியில்செல்வம்

வைத்தான்வாய் சான்ற பெரும்பொருள் அஃதுண்ணான் செத்தான் செயக்கிடந்தது இல்.	1001
பொருளானாம் எல்லாமென்று ஈயாது இவறும் மருளானாம் மாணாப் பிறப்பு	1002
ஈட்டம் இவறி இசைவேண்டா ஆடவர் தோற்றம் நிலக்குப் பொறை.	1003
எச்சமென்று என்எண்ணுங் கொல்லோ ஒருவரால் நச்சப் படாஅ தவன்.	1004
கொடுப்பதூஉம் துய்ப்பதூஉம் இல்லார்க்கு அடுக்கிய கோடியுண் டாயினும் இல்.	1005
ஏதம் பெருஞ்செல்வம் தான்துய்வான் தக்கார்க்கொன்று ஈதல் இயல்பிலா தான்.	1006
அற்றார்க்கொன்று ஆற்றாதான் செல்வம் மிகநலம் பெற்றாள் தமியள்மூத் தற்று.	1007
நச்சப் படாதவன் செல்வம் நடுவூருள் நச்சு மரம்பழுத் தற்று.	1008
அன்பொரீஇத் தற்செற்று அறநோக்காது ஈட்டிய ஒண்பொருள் கொள்வார் பிறர்.	1009
சீருடைச் செல்வர் சிறுதுனி மாரே வறங்கூர்ந் தனையது உடைத்து.	1010

2.4.7 நாணுடைமை

கருமத்தால் நாணுதல் நாணுந் திருநுதல்	
நல்லவர் நாணுப் பிற.	1011
ஊணுடை எச்சம் உயிர்க்கெல்லாம் வேறல்ல	
நாணுடைமை மாந்தர் சிறப்பு.	1012
ஊனைக் குறித்த உயிரெல்லாம் நாணென்னும்	
நன்மை குறித்தது சால்பு.	1013
அணியன்றோ நாணுடைமை சான்றோர்க்கு அஃதின்றேல்	
பிணியன்றோ பீடு நடை.	1014
பிறர்பழியும் தம்பழியும் நாணுவார் நாணுக்கு	
உறைபதி என்னும் உலகு.	1015
நாண்வேலி கொள்ளாது மன்னோ வியன்ஞாலம்	
பேணலர் மேலா யவர்.	1016
நாணால் உயிரைத் துறப்பர் உயிர்ப்பொருட்டால்	
நாண்துறவார் நாணாள் பவர்.	1017
பிறர்நாணத் தக்கது தான்நாணா நாயின்	
அறம்நாணத் தக்கது உடைத்து.	1018
குலஞ்சுடும் கொள்கை பிழைப்பின் நலஞ்சுடும்	
நாணின்மை நின்றக் கடை.	1019
நாண்அகத் தில்லார் இயக்கம் மரப்பாவை	
நாணால் உயிர்மருட்டி அற்று.	1020

2.4.8 குடிசெயல்வகை

கருமம் செயஒருவன் கைதூவேன் என்னும்	
பெருமையின் பீடுடையது இல்.	1021
ஆள்வினையும் ஆன்ற அறிவும் எனஇரண்டின்	
நீள்வினையால் நீளும் குடி.	1022
குடிசெயவல் என்னும் ஒருவற்குத் தெய்வம்	
மடிதற்றுத் தான்முன் துறும்.	1023
சூழாமல் தானே முடிவெய்தும் தம்குடியைத்	
தாழாது உஞற்று பவர்க்கு.	1024
குற்றம் இலனாய்க் குடிசெய்து வாழ்வானைச்	
சுற்றமாச் சுற்றும் உலகு.	1025
நல்லாண்மை என்பது ஒருவற்குத் தான்பிறந்த	
இல்லாண்மை ஆக்கிக் கொளல்.	1026
அமரகத்து வன்கண்ணர் போலத் தமரகத்தும்	
ஆற்றுவார் மேற்றே பொறை.	1027
குடிசெய்வார்க் கில்லை பருவம் மடிசெய்து	
மானங் கருதக் கெடும்.	1028
இடும்பைக்கே கொள்கலம் கொல்லோ குடும்பத்தைக்	
குற்ற மறைப்பான் உடம்பு.	1029
இடுக்கண்கால் கொன்றிட வீழும் அடுத்தூன்றும்	
நல்லாள் இலாத குடி.	1030

2.4.9 உழவு

சுழன்றும்ஏர்ப் பின்னது உலகம் அதனால் உழந்தும் உழவே தலை.	1031
உழுவார் உலகத்தார்க்கு ஆணிஅஃ தாற்றாது எழுவாரை எல்லாம் பொறுத்து.	1032
உழுதுண்டு வாழ்வாரே வாழ்வார்மற் றெல்லாம் தொழுதுண்டு பின்செல் பவர்.	1033
பலகுடை நீழலும் தங்குடைக்கீழ்க் காண்பர் அலகுடை நீழ லவர்.	1034
இரவார் இரப்பார்க்கொன்று ஈவர் கரவாது கைசெய்தூண் மாலை யவர்.	1035
உழவினார் கைம்மடங்கின் இல்லை விழைவதூஉம் விட்டேமென் பார்க்கும் நிலை.	1036
தொடிப்புழுதி கஃசா உணக்கின் பிடித்தெருவும் வேண்டாது சாலப் படும்.	1037
ஏரினும் நன்றால் எருவிடுதல் கட்டபின் நீரினும் நன்றதன் காப்பு.	1038
செல்லான் கிழவன் இருப்பின் நிலம்புலந்து இல்லாளின் ஊடி விடும்.	1039
இலமென்று அசைஇ இருப்பாரைக் காணின் நிலமென்னும் நல்லாள் நகும்.	1040

2.4.10 நல்குரவு

இன்மையின் இன்னாதது யாதெனின் இன்மையின் இன்மையே இன்னா தது.	1041
இன்மை எனவொரு பாவி மறுமையும் இம்மையும் இன்றி வரும்.	1042
தொல்வரவும் தோலும் கெடுக்கும் தொகையாக நல்குரவு என்னும் நசை.	1043
இற்பிறந்தார் கண்ணேயும் இன்மை இளிவந்த சொற்பிறக்கும் சோர்வு தரும்.	1044
நல்குரவு என்னும் இடும்பையுள் பல்குரைத் துன்பங்கள் சென்று படும்.	1045
நற்பொருள் நன்குணர்ந்து சொல்லினும் நல்கூர்ந்தார் சொற்பொருள் சோர்வு படும்.	1046
அறஞ்சாரா நல்குரவு ஈன்றதா யானும் பிறன்போல நோக்கப் படும்.	1047
இன்றும் வருவது கொல்லோ நெருநலும் கொன்றது போலும் நிரப்பு.	1048
நெருப்பினுள் துஞ்சலும் ஆகும் நிரப்பினுள் யாதொன்றும் கண்பாடு அரிது.	1049
துப்புர வில்லார் துவரத் துறவாமை உப்பிற்கும் காடிக்கும் கூற்று.	1050

2.4.11 இரவு

இரக்க இரத்தக்கார்க் காணின் கரப்பின் அவர்பழி தம்பழி அன்று.	1051
இன்பம் ஒருவற்கு இரத்தல் இரந்தவை துன்பம் உறாஅ வரின்.	1052
கரப்பிலா நெஞ்சின் கடனறிவார் முன்நின்று இரப்புமோ ரேஎர் உடைத்து.	1053
இரத்தலும் ஈதலே போலும் கரத்தல் கனவிலும் தேற்றாதார் மாட்டு.	1054
கரப்பிலார் வையகத்து உண்மையால் கண்ணின்று இரப்பவர் மேற்கொள் வது.	1055
கரப்பிடும்பை யில்லாரைக் காணின் நிரப்பிடும்பை எல்லாம் ஒருங்கு கெடும்.	1056
இகழ்ந்தெள்ளாது ஈவாரைக் காணின் மகிழ்ந்துள்ளம் உள்ளுள் உவப்பது உடைத்து.	1057
இரப்பாரை இல்லாயின் ஈர்ங்கண்மா ஞாலம் மரப்பாவை சென்றுவந் தற்று.	1058
ஈவார்கண் என்னுண்டாம் தோற்றம் இரந்துகோள் மேவார் இலாஅக் கடை.	1059
இரப்பான் வெகுளாமை வேண்டும் நிரப்பிடும்பை தானேயும் சாலும் கரி.	1060

2.4.12 இரவச்சம்

கரவாது உவந்தீயும் கண்ணன்னார் கண்ணும் இரவாமை கோடி உறும்.	1061
இரந்தும் உயிர்வாழ்தல் வேண்டின் பரந்து கெடுக உலகியற்றி யான்.	1062
இன்மை இடும்பை இரந்துதீர் வாமென்னும் வன்மையின் வன்பாட்ட தில்.	1063
இடமெல்லாம் கொள்ளாத் தகைத்தே இடமில்லாக் காலும் இரவொல்லாச் சால்பு.	1064
தெண்ணீர் அடுபுற்கை ஆயினும் தாள்தந்தது உண்ணலின் ஊங்கினிய தில்.	1065
ஆவிற்கு நீரென்று இரப்பினும் நாவிற்கு இரவின் இளிவந்த தில்.	1066
இரப்பன் இரப்பாரை எல்லாம் இரப்பின் கரப்பார் இரவன்மின் என்று.	1067
இரவென்னும் ஏமாப்பில் தோணி கரவென்னும் பார்தாக்கப் பக்கு விடும்.	1068
இரவுள்ள உள்ளம் உருகும் கரவுள்ள உள்ளதூஉம் இன்றிக் கெடும்.	1069
கரப்பவர்க்கு யாங்கொளிக்கும் கொல்லோ இரப்பவர் சொல்லாடப் போஓம் உயிர்.	1070

2.4.13 கயமை

மக்களே போல்வர் கயவர் அவரன்ன ஒப்பாரி யாங்கண்ட தில்.	1071
நன்றறி வாரிற் கயவர் திருவுடையர் நெஞ்சத்து அவலம் இலர்.	1072
தேவர் அனையர் கயவர் அவருந்தாம் மேவன செய்தொழுக லான்.	1073
அகப்பட்டி ஆவாரைக் காணின் அவரென் மிகப்பட்டுச் செம்மாக்கும் கீழ்.	1074
அச்சமே கீழ்களது ஆசாரம் எச்சம் அவாவுண்டேல் உண்டாம் சிறிது.	1075
அறைபறை அன்னர் கயவர்தாம் கேட்ட மறைபிறர்க்கு உய்த்துரைக்க லான்.	1076
ஈர்ங்கை விதிரார் கயவர் கொடிறுடைக்கும் கூன்கையர் அல்லா தவர்க்கு.	1077
சொல்லப் பயன்படுவர் சான்றோர் கரும்புபோல் கொல்லப் பயன்படும் கீழ்.	1078
உடுப்பதூஉம் உண்பதூஉம் காணின் பிறர்மேல் வடுக்காண வற்றாகும் கீழ்.	1079
எற்றிற் குரியர் கயவரொன்று உற்றக்கால் விற்றற்கு உரியர் விரைந்து.	1080

ஒழிபியல் முற்றிற்று

பொருட்பால் முற்றிற்று

3. காமத்துப்பால்

3.1 களவியல்

3.1.1 தகையணங்குறுத்தல்

அணங்குகொல் ஆய்மயில் கொல்லோ கனங்குழை மாதர்கொல் மாலும் என் நெஞ்சு.	1081
நோக்கினாள் நோக்கெதிர் நோக்குதல் தாக்கணங்கு தானைக்கொன் டன்ன துடைத்து.	1082
பண்டறியேன் கூற்றென் பதனை இனியறிந்தேன் பெண்டகையால் பேரமர்க் கட்டு.	1083
கண்டார் உயிருண்ணும் தோற்றத்தால் பெண்டகைப் பேதைக்கு அமர்த்தன கண்.	1084
கூற்றமோ கண்ணோ பிணையோ மடவரல் நோக்கமிம் மூன்றும் உடைத்து.	1085
கொடும்புருவம் கோடா மறைப்பின் நடுங்கஞர் செய்யல மன்இவள் கண்.	1086
கடாஅக் களிற்றின்மேற் கட்படாம் மாதர் படாஅ முலைமேல் துகில்.	1087
ஒண்ணுதற் கோடு உடைந்ததே ஞாட்பினுள் நண்ணாரும் உட்குமென் பீடு.	1088

பிணையேர் மடநோக்கும் நாணும் உடையாட்கு
அணியெவனோ ஏதில தந்து.   1089
உண்டார்கண் அல்லது அடுநறாக் காமம்போல்
கண்டார் மகிழ்செய்தல் இன்று.   1090

3.1.2   குறிப்பறிதல்

இருநோக்கு இவளுண்கண் உள்ளது ஒருநோக்கு
நோய்நோக்கொன் றந்நோய் மருந்து.   1091
கண்களவு கொள்ளும் சிறுநோக்கம் காமத்தில்
செம்பாகம் அன்று பெரிது.   1092
நோக்கினாள் நோக்கி இறைஞ்சினாள் அஃதவள்
யாப்பினுள் அட்டிய நீர்.   1093
யான்நோக்கும் காலை நிலன்நோக்கும் நோக்காக்கால்
தான்நோக்கி மெல்ல நகும்.   1094
குறிக்கொண்டு நோக்காமை அல்லால் ஒருகண்
சிறக்கணித்தாள் போல நகும்   1095
உறாஅ தவர்போல் சொலினும் செறாஅர்சொல்
ஒல்லை உணரப் படும்.   1096
செறாஅச் சிறுசொல்லும் செற்றார்போல் நோக்கும்
உறாஅர்போன்று உற்றார் குறிப்பு.   1097
அசையியற்கு உண்டாண்டோர் ஏர்யான் நோக்கப்
பசையினள் பைய நகும்.   1098
ஏதிலார் போலப் பொதுநோக்கு நோக்குதல்
காதலார் கண்ணே உள.   1099
கண்ணொடு கண்இணை நோக்கொக்கின் வாய்ச்சொற்கள்
என்ன பயனும் இல.   1100

3.1.3   புணர்ச்சி மகிழ்தல்

கண்டுகேட்டு உண்டுயிர்த்து உற்றறியும் ஐம்புலனும்
ஒண்தொடி கண்ணே உள.   1101
பிணிக்கு மருந்து பிறமன் அணியிழை
தன்நோய்க்குத் தானே மருந்து.   1102
தாம்வீழ்வார் மென்றோள் துயிலின் இனிதுகொல்
தாமரைக் கண்ணான் உலகு.   1103
நீங்கின் தெறூஉம் குறுகுங்கால் தண்ணென்னும்
தீயாண்டுப் பெற்றாள் இவள்?   1104
வேட்ட பொழுதின் அவையவை போலுமே
தோட்டார் கதுப்பினாள் தோள்.   1105
உறுதோறு உயிர்தளிர்ப்பத் தீண்டலால் பேதைக்கு
அமிழ்தின் இயன்றன தோள்.   1106
தம்மில் இருந்து தமதுபாத்து உண்டற்றால்
அம்மா அரிவை முயக்கு.   1107
வீழும் இருவர்க்கு இனிதே வளியிடை
போழப் படாஅ முயக்கு.   1108
ஊடல் உணர்தல் புணர்தல் இவைகாமம்
கூடியார் பெற்ற பயன்.   1109

அறிதோறு அறியாமை கண்டற்றால் காமம்
செறிதோறும் சேயிழை மாட்டு. 1110

3.1.4 நலம்புனைந்துரைத்தல்

நன்னீரை வாழி அனிச்சமே நின்னினும்
மென்னீரள் யாம்வீழ் பவள். 1111
மலர்காணின் மையாத்தி நெஞ்சே இவள்கண்
பலர்காணும் பூவொக்கும் என்று. 1112
முறிமேனி முத்தம் முறுவல் வெறிநாற்றம்
வேலுண்கண் வேய்த்தோ எவட்கு. 1113
காணின் குவளை கவிழ்ந்து நிலநோக்கும்
மாணிழை கண்ணொவ்வேம் என்று. 1114
அனிச்சப்பூக் கால்களையாள் பெய்தாள் நுகப்பிற்கு
நல்ல படாஅ பறை. 1115
மதியும் மடந்தை முகனும் அறியா
பதியின் கலங்கிய மீன். 1116
அறுவாய் நிறைந்த அவிர்மதேக்குப் போல
மறுவுண்டோ மாதர் முகத்து. 1117
மாதர் முகம்போல் ஒளிவிட வல்லையேல்
காதலை வாழி மதே. 1118
மலரன்ன கண்ணாள் முகமொத்தி யாயின்
பலர்காணத் தோன்றல் மதி. 1119
அனிச்சமும் அன்னத்தின் தூவியும் மாதர்
அடிக்கு நெருஞ்சிப் பழம். 1120

3.1.5 காதற்சிறப்புரைத்தல்

பாலொடு தேன்கலந் தற்றே பணிமொழி
வாலெயிறு ஊறிய நீர். 1121
உடம்பொடு உயிரிடை என்னமற் றன்ன
மடந்தையொடு எம்மிடை நட்பு. 1122
கருமணியிற் பாவாய்நீ போதாயாம் வீழும்
திருநுதற்கு இல்லை இடம். 1123
வாழ்தல் உயிர்க்கன்னள் ஆயிழை சாதல்
அதற்கன்னள் நீங்கும் இடத்து. 1124
உள்ளுவன் மன்யான் மறப்பின் மறப்பறியேன்
ஒள்ளமர்க் கண்ணாள் குணம். 1125
கண்ணுள்ளின் போகார் இமைப்பின் பருகுவரா
நுண்ணியர்எம் காத லவர். 1126
கண்ணுள்ளார் காத லவராகக் கண்ணும்
எழுதேம் கரப்பாக்கு அறிந்து. 1127
நெஞ்சத்தார் காத லவராக வெய்துண்டல்
அஞ்சுதும் வேபாக் கறிந்து. 1128
இமைப்பின் கரப்பாக்கு அறிவல் அனைத்திற்கே
ஏதிலர் என்னும் இவ் ஊர். 1129
உவந்துறைவர் உள்ளத்துள் என்றும் இகந்துறைவர்
ஏதிலர் என்னும் இவ் ஊர். 1130

3.1.6 நாணுத்துறவுரைத்தல்

காமம் உழந்து வருந்தினார்க்கு ஏமம்
மடலல்லது இல்லை வலி. 1131
நோனா உடம்பும் உயிரும் மடலேறும்
நாணினை நீக்கி நிறுத்து. 1132
நாணொடு நல்லாண்மை பண்டுடையேன் இன்றுடையேன்
காமுற்றார் ஏறும் மடல். 1133
காமக் கடும்புனல் உய்க்கும் நாணொடு
நல்லாண்மை என்னும் புணை. 1134
தொடலைக் குறுந்தொடி தந்தாள் மடலொடு
மாலை உழக்கும் துயர். 1135
மடலூர்தல் யாமத்தும் உள்ளுவேன் மன்ற
படல்ஒல்லா பேதைக்கென் கண். 1136
கடலன்ன காமம் உழந்தும் மடலேறாப்
பெண்ணின் பெருந்தக்க தில். 1137
நிறையரியர் மன்அளியர் என்னாது காமம்
மறையிறந்து மன்று படும். 1138
அறிகிலார் எல்லாரும் என்றேன் காமம்
மறுகின் மறுகும் மருண்டு. 1139
யாம்கண்ணின் காண நகுப அறிவில்லார்
யாம்பட்ட தாம்படா ஆறு. 1140

3.1.7 அலரறிவுறுத்தல்

அலரெழ ஆருயிர் நிற்கும் அதனைப்
பலரறியார் பாக்கியத் தால். 1141
மலரன்ன கண்ணாள் அருமை அறியாது
அலரெமக்கு ஈந்ததிவ் வூர். 1142
உறாஅதோ ஊரறிந்த கௌவை அதனைப்
பெறாஅது பெற்றன்ன நீர்த்து. 1143
கவ்வையால் கவ்விது காமம் அதுவின்றேல்
தவ்வென்னும் தன்மை இழந்து. 1144
களித்தொறும் கள்ளுண்டல் வேட்டற்றால் காமம்
வெளிப்படுந் தோறும் இனிது. 1145
கண்டது மன்னும் ஒருநாள் அலர்மன்னும்
திங்களைப் பாம்புகொண் டற்று. 1146
ஊரவர் கௌவை எருவாக அன்னைசொல்
நீராக நீளும்இந் நோய். 1147
நெய்யால் எரிநுதுப்பேம் என்றற்றால் கௌவையால்
காமம் நுதுப்பேம் எனல். 1148
அலர்நாண ஒல்வதோ அஞ்சலோம்பு என்றார்
பலர்நாண நீத்தக் கடை. 1149
தாம்வேண்டின் நல்குவர் காதலர் யாம்வேண்டும்
கௌவை எடுக்கும்இவ் வூர். 1150

களவியல் முற்றிற்று

3.2 கற்பியல்

செல்லாமை உண்டேல் எனக்குரை மற்றுநின் வல்வரவு வாழ்வார்க் குரை.	1151
இன்கண் உடைத்தவர் பார்வல் பிரிவஞ்சும் புன்கண் உடைத்தால் புணர்வு.	1152
அரிதரோ தேற்றம் அறிவுடையார் கண்ணும் பிரிவோ ரிடத்துண்மை யான்.	1153
அளித்தஞ்சல் என்றவர் நீப்பின் தெளித்தசொல் தேறியார்க்கு உண்டோ தவறு.	1154
ஓம்பின் அமைந்தார் பிரிவோம்பல் மற்றவர் நீங்கின் அரிதால் புணர்வு.	1155
பிரிவுரைக்கும் வன்கண்ணர் ஆயின் அரிதவர் நல்குவர் என்னும் நசை.	1156
துறைவன் துறந்தமை தூற்றாகொல் முன்கை இறைஇறவா நின்ற வளை.	1157
இன்னாது இனன்இல்ஊர் வாழ்தல் அதனினும் இன்னாது இனியார்ப் பிரிவு.	1158
தொடிற்சுடின் அல்லது காமநோய் போல விடிற்சுடல் ஆற்றுமோ தீ.	1159
அரிதாற்றி அல்லல்நோய் நீக்கிப் பிரிவாற்றிப் பின்இருந்து வாழ்வார் பலர்.	1160

3.2.2 படர்மெலிந்திரங்கல்

மறைப்பேன்மன் யானிஃதோ நோயை இறைப்பவர்க்கு ஊற்றுநீர் போல மிகும்.	1161
கரத்தலும் ஆற்றேன்இந் நோயைநோய் செய்தார்க்கு உரைத்தலும் நாணுத் தரும்.	1162
காமமும் நாணும் உயிர்காவாத் தூங்கும்என் நோனா உடம்பின் அகத்து.	1163
காமக் கடல்மன்னும் உண்டே அதுநீந்தும் ஏமப் புணைமன்னும் இல்.	1164
துப்பின் எவனாவர் மன்கொல் துயர்வரவு நட்பினுள் ஆற்று பவர்.	1165
இன்பம் கடல்மற்றுக் காமம் அஃதடுங்கால் துன்பம் அதனிற் பெரிது.	1166
காமக் கடும்புனல் நீந்திக் கரைகாணேன் யாமத்தும் யானே உளேன்.	1167
மன்னுயிர் எல்லாம் துயிற்றி அளித்திரா என்னல்லது இல்லை துணை.	1168
> கொடியார் கொடுமையின் தாம்கொடிய இந்நாள் நெடிய கழியும் இரா.	1169
உள்ளம்போன்று உள்வழிச் செல்கிற்பின் வெள்ளநீர் நீந்தல மன்னோஎன் கண்.	1170

3.2.3 கண்விதுப்பழிதல்

கண்தாம் கலுழ்வ தெவன்கொலோ தண்டாநோய் தாம்காட்ட யாம்கண் டது.	1171
தெரிந்துணரா நோக்கிய உண்கண் பரிந்துணராப் பைதல் உழப்பது எவன்?	1172
கதுமெனத் தாநோக்கித் தாமே கலுழும் இதுநகத் தக்க துடைத்து.	1173
பெயலாற்றா நீருலந்த உண்கண் உயலாற்றா உய்வில்நோய் என்கண் நிறுத்து.	1174
படலாற்றா பைதல் உழக்கும் கடலாற்றாக் காமநோய் செய்தளன் கண்.	1175
ஓஒ இனிதே எமக்கிந்நோய் செய்தகண் தாஅம் இதற்பட் டது.	1176
உழந்துழந் துள்நீர் அறுக விழைந்திழைந்து வேண்டி அவர்க்கண்ட கண்.	1177
பேணாது பெட்டார் உளர்மன்னோ மற்றவர்க் காணாது அமைவில கண்.	1178
வாராக்கால் துஞ்சா வரின்துஞ்சா ஆயிடை ஆரஞர் உற்றன கண்.	1179
மறைபெறல் ஊரார்க்கு அரிதன்றால் எம்போல் அறைபறை கண்ணார் அகத்து.	1180

3.2.4 பசப்புறுபருவரல்

நயந்தவர்க்கு நல்காமை நேர்ந்தேன் பசந்தவென் பண்பியார்க்கு உரைக்கோ பிற.	1181
அவர்தந்தார் என்னும் தகையால் இவர்தந்தென் மேனிமேல் ஊரும் பசப்பு.	1182
சாயலும் நாணும் அவர்கொண்டார் கைம்மாறா நோயும் பசலையும் தந்து.	1183
உள்ளுவன் மன்யான் உரைப்பது அவர்திறமால் கள்ளம் பிறவோ பசப்பு.	1184
உவக்காண்எம் காதலர் செல்வார் இவக்காண்என் மேனி பசப்பூர் வது.	1185
விளக்கற்றம் பார்க்கும் இருளேபோல் கொண்கன் முயக்கற்றம் பார்க்கும் பசப்பு.	1186
புல்லிக் கிடந்தேன் புடைபெயர்ந்தேன் அவ்வளவில் அள்ளிக்கொள் வற்றே பசப்பு.	1187
பசந்தாள் இவள்என்பது அல்லால் இவளைத் துறந்தார் அவர்என்பார் இல்.	1188
பசக்கமன் பட்டாங்கென் மேனி நயப்பித்தார் நன்னிலையர் ஆவர் எனின்.	1189
பசப்பெனப் பேர்பெறுதல் நன்றே நயப்பித்தார் நல்காமை தூற்றார் எனின்.	1190

3.2.5 தனிப்படர்மிகுதி

தாம்வீழ்வார் தம்வீழப் பெற்றவர் பெற்றாரே காமத்துக் காழில் கனி.	1191
வாழ்வார்க்கு வானம் பயந்தற்றால் வீழ்வார்க்கு வீழ்வார் அளேக்கும் அளி.	1192
வீழுநர் வீழப் படுவார்க்கு அமையுமே வாழுநம் என்னும் செருக்கு.	1193
வீழப் படுவார் கெழீஇயிலர் தாம்வீழ்வார் வீழப் படாஅர் எனின்.	1194
நாம்காதல் கொண்டார் நமக்கெவன் செய்பவோ தாம்காதல் கொள்ளாக் கடை.	1195
ஒருதலையான் இன்னாது காமங்காப் போல இருதலை யானும் இனிது.	1196
பருவரலும் பைதலும் காணான்கொல் காமன் ஒருவர்கண் நின்றொழுகு வான்.	1197
வீழ்வாரின் இன்சொல் பெறாஅது உலகத்து வாழ்வாரின் வன்கணார் இல்.	1198
நசைஇயார் நல்கார் எனினும் அவர்மாட்டு இசையும் இனிய செவிக்கு.	1199
உறாஅர்க்கு உறுநோய் உரைப்பாய் கடலைச் செறாஅஅய் வாழிய நெஞ்சு.	1200

3.2.6 நினைந்தவர்புலம்பல்

உள்ளினும் தீராப் பெருமகிழ் செய்தலால் கள்ளினும் காமம் இனிது.	1201
எனைத்தொனறு ஏனிதேகாண் காமந்தாம் வீழ்வார் நினைப்ப வருவதொன்று ஏல்.	1202
நினைப்பவர் போன்று நினையார்கொல் தும்மல் சினைப்பது போன்று கெடும்.	1203
யாழும் உளேங்கொல் அவர்நெஞ்சத்து எந்நெஞ்சத்து ஓஓ உளரே அவர்.	1204
தம்நெஞ்சத்து எம்மைக் கடிகொண்டார் நாணார்கொல் எம்நெஞ்சத்து ஓவா வரல்.	1205
மற்றியான் என்னுளேன் மன்னோ அவரொடி யான் உற்றநாள் உள்ள உளேன்.	1206
மறப்பின் எவனாவன் மற்கொல் மறப்பறியேன் உள்ளினும் உள்ளம் சுடும்.	1207
எனைத்து நினைப்பினும் காயார் அனைத்தன்றோ காதலர் செய்யும் சிறப்பு.	1208
விளியுமென் இன்னுயிர் வேறல்லம் என்பார் அளியின்மை ஆற்ற நினைந்து.	1209
விடாஅது சென்றாரைக் கண்ணினால் காணப் படாஅதி வாழி மதி.	1210

3.2.7 கனவு நிலையுரைத்தல்

காதலர் தூதொடு வந்த கனவினுக்கு யாதுசெய் வேன்கொல் விருந்து.	1211
கயலுண்கண் யானிரப்பத் துஞ்சிற் கலந்தார்க்கு உயலுண்மை சாற்றுவேன் மன்.	1212
நனவினால் நல்கா தவரைக் கனவினால் காண்டலின் உண்டென் உயிர்.	1213
கனவினான் உண்டாகும் காமம் நனவினான் நல்காரை நாடித் தரற்கு.	1214
நனவினால் கண்டதூஉம் ஆங்கே கனவுந்தான் கண்ட பொழுதே இனிது.	1215
நனவென ஒன்றில்லை ஆயின் கனவினால் காதலர் நீங்கலர் மன்.	1216
நனவினால் நல்காக் கொடியார் கனவனால் என்எம்மைப் பீழிப் பது.	1217
துஞ்சுங்கால் தோள்மேலர் ஆகி விழிக்குங்கால் நெஞ்சத்தர் ஆவர் விரைந்து.	1218
நனவினால் நல்காரை நோவர் கனவினால் காதலர்க் காணா தவர்.	1219
நனவினால் நம்நீத்தார் என்பர் கனவினால் காணார்கொல் இவ்வூ ரவர்.	1220

3.2.8 பொழுது கண்டிரங்கல்

மாலையோ அல்லை மணந்தார் உயிருண்ணும் வேலைநீ வாழி பொழுது.	1221
புன்கண்ணை வாழி மருள்மாலை எம்கேள்போல் வன்கண்ண தோநின் துணை.	1222
பனிஅரும்பிப் பைதல்கொள் மாலை துனிஅரும்பித் துன்பம் வளர வரும்.	1223
காதலர் இல்வழி மாலை கொலைக்களத்து ஏதிலர் போல வரும்.	1224
காலைக்குச் செய்தநன்று என்கொல் எவன்கொல்யான் மாலைக்குச் செய்த பகை?	1225
மாலைநோய் செய்தல் மணந்தார் அகலாத காலை அறிந்த திலேன்.	1226
காலை அரும்பிப் பகலெல்லாம் போதாகி மாலை மலரும்இந் நோய்.	1227
அழல்போலும் மாலைக்குத் தூதாகி ஆயன் குழல்போலும் கொல்லும் படை.	1228
பதிமருண்டு பைதல் உழக்கும் மதிமருண்டு மாலை படர்தரும் போழ்து.	1229
பொருள்மாலை யாளரை உள்ளி மருள்மாலை மாயும்என் மாயா உயிர்.	1230

3.2.9 உறுப்பு நலனழிதல்

சிறுமை நமக்கொழியச் சேட்சென்றார் உள்ளி நறுமலர் நாணின கண்.	1231
நயந்தவர் நல்காமை சொல்லுவ போலும் பசந்து பனிவாரும் கண்.	1232
தணந்தமை சால அறிவிப்ப போலும் மணந்தநாள் வீங்கிய தோள்.	1233
பணைநீங்கிப் பைந்தொடி சோரும் துணைநீங்கித் தொல்கவின் வாடிய தோள்.	1234
கொடியார் கொடுமை உரைக்கும் தொடியொடு தொல்கவின் வாடிய தோள்.	1235
தொடியொடு தோள்நெகிழ நோவல் அவரைக் கொடியர் எனக்கூறல் நொந்து.	1236
பாடுபெறுதியோ நெஞ்சே கொடியார்க்கென் வாடுதோட் பூசல் உரைத்து.	1237
முயங்கிய கைகளை ஊக்கப் பசந்தது பைந்தொடிப் பேதை நுதல்.	1238
முயக்கிடைத் தண்வளி போழப் பசப்புற்ற பேதை பெருமழைக் கண்.	1239
கண்ணின் பசப்போ பருவரல் எய்தின்றே ஒண்ணுதல் செய்தது கண்டு.	1240

3.2.10 நெஞ்சொடுகிளத்தல்

நினைத்தொன்று சொல்லாயோ நெஞ்சே எனைத்தொன்றும் எவ்வநோய் தீர்க்கும் மருந்து.	1241
காதல் அவரிலர் ஆகநீ நோவது பேதைமை வாழியென் நெஞ்சு.	1242
இருந்துள்ளி என்பரிதல் நெஞ்சே பரிந்துள்ளல் பைதல்நோய் செய்தார்கண் இல்.	1243
கண்ணும் கொளச்சேறி நெஞ்சே இவையென்னைத் தின்னும் அவர்க்காணல் உற்று.	1244
செற்றார் எனக்கை விடல்உண்டோ நெஞ்சேயாம் உற்றால் உறாஅ தவர்.	1245
கலந்துணர்த்தும் காதலர்க் கண்டாற் புலந்துணராய் பொய்க்காய்வு காய்தின் நெஞ்சு.	1246
காமம் விடுஒன்றோ நாண்விடே நன்னெஞ்சே யானோ பொறேன்இவ் விரண்டு.	1247
பரிந்தவர் நல்காரென்று ஏங்கிப் பிரிந்தவர் பின்செல்வாய் பேதைஎன் நெஞ்சு.	1248
உள்ளத்தார் காத லவரால் உள்ளிநீ யாருழைச் சேறியென் நெஞ்சு.	1249
துன்னாத் துறந்தாரை நெஞ்சத்து உடையேமா இன்னும் இழத்தும் கவின்.	1250

3.2.11 நிறையழிதல்

காமக் கணிச்சி உடைக்கும் நிறையென்னும் நாணுத்தாழ் வீழ்த்த கதவு.	1251
காமம் எனவொன்றோ கண்ணின்றென் நெஞ்சத்தை யாமத்தும் ஆளும் தொழில்.	1252
மறைப்பேன்மன் காமத்தை யானோ குறிப்பின்றித் தும்மல்போல் தோன்றி விடும்.	1253
நிறையுடையேன் என்பேன்மன் யானோஎன் காமம் மறையிறந்து மன்று படும்.	1254
செற்றார்பின் செல்லாப் பெருந்தகைமை காமநோய் உற்றார் அறிவதொன்று அன்று.	1255
செற்றவர் பின்சேரல் வேண்டி அளித்தரோ எற்றென்னை உற்ற துயர்.	1256
நாணென ஒன்றோ அறியலம் காமத்தால் பேணியார் பெட்ப செயின்.	1257
பன்மாயக் கள்வன் பணிமொழி அன்றோநம் பெண்மை உடைக்கும் படை.	1258
புலப்பல் எனச்சென்றேன் புல்லினேன் நெஞ்சம் கலத்தல் உறுவது கண்டு.	1259
நினந்தீயில் இட்டன்ன நெஞ்சினார்க்கு உண்டோ புணர்ந்தூடி நிற்பேம் எனல்.	1260

3.2.12 அவர்வயின்விதும்பல்

வாளற்றுப் புற்கென்ற கண்ணும் அவர்சென்ற நாளொற்றித் தேய்ந்த விரல்.	1261
இலங்கிழாய் இன்று மறப்பின்என் தோள்மேல் கலங்கழியும் காரிகை நீத்து.	1262
உரன்நசைஇ உள்ளம் துணையாகச் சென்றார் வரல்நசைஇ இன்னும் உளேன்.	1263
கூடிய காமம் பிரிந்தார் வரவுள்ளிக் கோடுகொ டேறுமென் நெஞ்சு.	1264
காண்கமன் கொண்கனைக் கண்ணாரக் கண்டபின் நீங்கும்என் மென்தோள் பசப்பு.	1265
வருகமன் கொண்கன் ஒருநாள் பருகுவன் பைதல்நோய் எல்லாம் கெட.	1266
புலப்பேன்கொல் புல்லுவேன் கொல்லோ கலப்பேன்கொல் கண்அன் கேளிர் விரன்.	1267
வினைகலந்து வென்றீக வேந்தன் மனைகலந்து மாலை அயர்கம் விருந்து.	1268
ஒருநாள் எழுநாள்போல் செல்லும்சேண் சென்றார் வருநாள்வைத்து ஏங்கு பவர்க்கு.	1269
பெறின்என்னாம் பெற்றக்கால் என்னாம் உறின்என்னாம் உள்ளம் உடைந்துக்கக் கால்.	1270

3.2.13 குறிப்பறிவுறுத்தல்

கரப்பினுங் கையிகந் தொல்லாநின் உண்கண் உரைக்கல் உறுவதொன் றுண்டு.	1271
கண்ணிறைந்த காரிகைக் காம்பேர்தோட் பேதைக்குப் பெண்ணிறைந்த நீர்மை பெரிது.	1272
மணியில் திகழ்தரு நூல்போல் மடந்தை அணியில் திகழ்வதொன்று உண்டு.	1273
முகைமொக்குள் உள்ளது நாற்றம்போல் பேதை நகைமொக்குள் உள்ளதொன் றுண்டு.	1274
செறிதொடி செய்திறந்த கள்ளம் உறுதுயர் தீர்க்கும் மருந்தொன்று உடைத்து.	1275
பெரிதாற்றிப் பெட்பக் கலத்தல் அரிதாற்றி அன்பின்மை சூழ்வ துடைத்து.	1276
தண்ணந் துறைவன் தணந்தமை நம்மினும் முன்னம் உணர்ந்த வளை.	1277
நெருநற்றுச் சென்றார்எம் காதலர் யாமும் எழுநாளேம் மேனி பசந்து.	1278
தொடிநோக்கி மென்தோளும் நோக்கி அடிநோக்கி அஃதாண் டவள்செய் தது.	1279
பெண்ணினால் பெண்மை உடைத்தென்ப கண்ணினால் காமநோய் சொல்லி இரவு.	1280

3.2.14 புணர்ச்சிவிதும்பல்

உள்ளக் களித்தலும் காண மகிழ்தலும் கள்ளுக்கில் காமத்திற் குண்டு.	1281
தினைத்துணையும் ஊடாமை வேண்டும் பனைத் துணையும் காமம் நிறைய வரின்.	1282
பேணாது பெட்பவே செய்யினும் கொண்கனைக் காணா தமையல கண்.	1283
ஊடற்கண் சென்றேன்மன் தோழி அதுமறந்து கூடற்கண் சென்றது என் நெஞ்சு.	1284
எழுதுங்கால் கோல்காணாக் கண்ணேபோல் கொண்கன் பழிகாணேன் கண்ட இடத்து.	1285
காணுங்கால் காணேன் தவறாய காணாக்கால் காணேன் தவறல லவை.	1286
உய்த்தல் அறிந்து புனல்பாய் பவரேபோல் பொய்த்தல் அறிந்தென் புலந்து.	1287
இளித்தக்க இன்னா செயினும் களித்தார்க்குக் கள்ளற்றே கள்வநின் மார்பு.	1288
மலரினும் மெல்லிது காமம் சிலர்அதன் செவ்வே தலைப்படு வார்.	1289
கண்ணென் துனித்தே கலங்கினாள் புல்லுதல் என்னினும் தான்விதுப் புற்று.	1290

3.2.15 நெஞ்சொடுபுலத்தல்

அவர்நெஞ்சு அவர்க்காதல் கண்டும் எவன்நெஞ்சே நீமெமக்கு ஆகா தது.	1291
உறாஅ தவர்க்கண்ட கண்ணும் அவரைச் செறாஅரெனச் சேறியென் நெஞ்சு.	1292
கெட்டார்க்கு நட்டார்இல் என்பதோ நெஞ்சேநீ பெட்டாங்கு அவர்பின் செலல்.	12983
இனிஅன்ன நின்னொடு சூழ்வார்யார் நெஞ்சே துனிசெய்து துவ்வாய்காண் மற்று.	1294
பெறாஅமை அஞ்சும் பெறின்பிரிவு அஞ்சும் அறாஅ இடும்பைத்தென் நெஞ்சு.	1295
தனியே இருந்து நினைத்தக்கால் என்னைத் தினிய இருந்தெதென் நெஞ்சு.	1296
நாணும் மறந்தேன் அவர்மறக் கல்லாஎன் மாணா மடநெஞ்சிற் பட்டு.	1297
எள்ளின் இளிவாம்என்று எண்ணி அவர்திறம் உள்ளும் உயிர்க்காதல் நெஞ்சு.	1298
துன்பத்திற்கு யாரே துணையாவார் தாமுடைய நெஞ்சந் துணையல் வழி.	1299
தஞ்சம் தமரல்லர் ஏதிலார் தாமுடைய நெஞ்சம் தமரல் வழி.	1300

3.2.16 புலவி

புல்லா திராஅப் புலத்தை அவர் உறும் அல்லல்நோய் காண்கம் சிறிது.	1301
உப்பமைந் தற்றால் புலவி அதுசிறிது மிக்கற்றால் நீள விடல்.	1302
அலந்தாரை அல்லல்நோய் செய்தற்றால் தம்மைப் புலந்தாரைப் புல்லா விடல்.	1303
ஊடி யவரை உணராமை வாடிய வள்ளி முதலரிந் தற்று.	1304
நலத்தகை நல்லவர்க்கு ஏஎர் புலத்தகை பூஅன்ன கண்ணார் அகத்து.	1305
துனியும் புலவியும் இல்லாயின் காமம் கனியும் கருக்காயும் அற்று.	1306
ஊடலின் உண்டாங்கோர் துன்பம் புணர்வது நீடுவ தன்று கொல் என்று.	1307
நோதல் எவன்மற்று நொந்தாரென்று அஃதறியும் காதலர் இல்லா வழி.	1308
நீரும் நிழலது இனிதே புலவியும் வீழுநர் கண்ணே இனிது.	1309
ஊடல் உணங்க விடுவாரோடு என்நெஞ்சம் கூடுவேம் என்பது அவா.	1310

3.2.17 புலவி நுணுக்கம்

பெண்ணியலார் எல்லாரும் கண்ணின் பொதுஉண்பர் நண்ணேன் பரத்தநின் மார்பு.	1311
ஊடி இருந்தேமாத் தும்மினார் யாம்தம்மை நீடுவாழ் கென்பாக் கறிந்து.	1312
கோட்டுப் பூச் சூடினும் காயும் ஒருத்தியைக் காட்டிய சூடினீர் என்று.	1313
யாரினும் காதலம் என்றேனா ஊடினாள் யாரினும் யாரினும் என்று.	1314
இம்மைப் பிறப்பில் பிரியலம் என்றேனாக் கண்நிறை நீர்கொன் டனள்.	1315
உள்ளினேன் என்றேன்மற் றென்மறந்தீர் என்றென்னைப் புல்லாள் புலத்தக் கனள்.	1316
வழுத்தினாள் தும்மினேன் ஆக அழித்தழுதாள் யாருள்ளித் தும்மினீர் என்று.	1317
தும்முச் செறுப்ப அழுதாள் நுமர்உள்ளல் எம்மை மறைத்திரோ என்று.	1318
தன்னை உணர்த்தினும் காயும் பிறர்க்கும்நீர் இந்நீரர் ஆகுதிர் என்று.	1319
நினைத்திருந்து நோக்கினும் காயும் அனைத்துநீர் யாருள்ளி நோக்கினீர் என்று.	1320

3.2.18 ஊடலுவகை

இல்லை தவறவர்க்கு ஆயினும் ஊடுதல் வல்லது அவர்அளிக்கு மாறு.	1321
ஊடலின் தோன்றும் சிறுதுனி நல்லளி வாடினும் பாடு பெறும்.	1322
புலத்தலின் புத்தேள்நாடு உண்டோ நிலத்தொடு நீரியைந் தன்னார் அகத்து.	1323
புல்லி விடாஅப் புலவியுள் தோன்றுமென் உள்ளம் உடைக்கும் படை.	1324
தவறிலர் ஆயினும் தாம்வீழ்வார் மென்றோள் அகறலின் ஆங்கொன் றுடைத்து.	1325
உணலினும் உண்டது அரல்இனிது காமம் புணர்தலின் ஊடல் இனிது.	1326
ஊடலில் தோற்றவர் வென்றார் அதுமன்னும் கூடலிற் காணப் படும்.	1327
ஊடிப் பெறுகுவம் கொல்லோ நுதல்வெயர்ப்பக் கூடலில் தோன்றிய உப்பு.	1328
ஊடுக மன்னோ ஒளியிழை யாமிரப்ப நீடுக மன்னோ இரா.	1329
ஊடல் காமத்திற்கு இன்பம் அதற்கின்பம் கூடி முயங்கப் பெறின்.	1330

கற்பியல் முற்றிற்று
காமத்துப்பால் முற்றிற்று
திருக்குறள் முற்றிற்று

CPSIA information can be obtained
at www.ICGtesting.com
Printed in the USA
LVHW040409280720
661654LV00008B/1569

9 781466 378216